Kingdom's Quest
The series

First Edition

Published by

Sense Of Think Books

All rights reserved.

Sense Of Think

Published by Sense Of Think.

Hoboken. New Jersey. USA

Copyright © 2019 C. J. P i o t r o w s k i

First published in Great Britain 2019

ISBN **978 109785 157 7**

The Journey
Vol. I
part I
by
C. J. Piotrowski

Imagine...
John Lennon

A note from the Author:

Greetings dear reader!

The novel which you are about to read was originally written in Polish language. At the beginning I thought that the whole story shall be locked in four books. Yet, soon I have realized that my creative head had written enough material to fill up around seven books. My story will be that long, epic, full of emotions (those good or bad, we need them all anyway to fully understand the world in which we are living.)

The story kick-started on one ordinary day when I saw a movie trailer to the upcoming movie: Arthur and the Invisibles from the author and director Luc Besson. My first attempt of writing was not good at all. So I started reading more books from the genre: Joe Abercombie, George Martin, J.R.R. Tolkien, I watched a lot of old school fantasy movies: "Conan, Red Sonia, The Never-ending Story, Krull, Willow, Labyrinth, The Princes Bride", and many more that have forever tangled in my brain.

Not to mention, of course, computer games: "Diablo, Baldur's Gate, Gothic, Morrowind, Skyrim" and a lot of other titles that were recorded in the players' annals as cult. An important role was also played by several sessions from the "Warhamer" series where we use to alternated tell episodes and quests, playing dice, biting snacks and sipping cold drinks.

The final product was a creation of a bunch of people to whom I am extremely grateful. First of all I would like to mention Dr Colin Hancock who noticed a great potential in my story. Delving into the pages of the manuscript, he let himself be carried away by imagination and intuition. He had contacted me with Mr David Bentley, who materialized my dream, and who brought it to life.

Of course nothing of that would ever happen if not the efforts of my beloved wife Kay (Khadija), my first reader who simply fell in love with the characters and the story. Thanks to her I managed to reach my goal, to fulfil my dream and publish a book which you are holding in your hand.

Enjoy the story and don't miss your stop (I did it many times sinking completely in the pages of a book, what a blessed feeling).

C.J.P 17.03.19

~ Contents ~

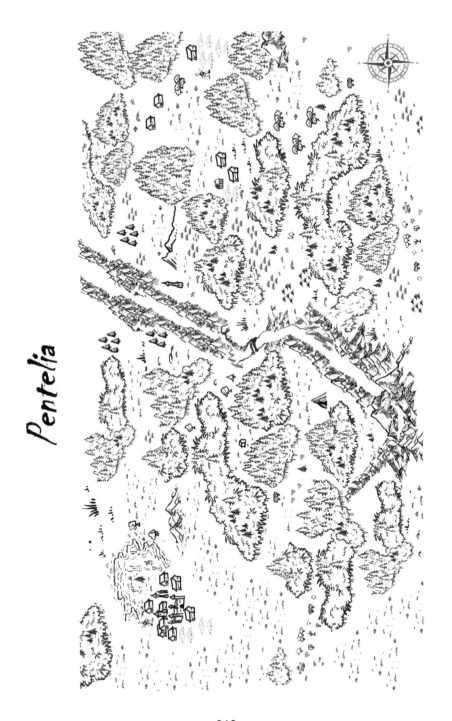

Pentelia

~ Chapter .1. The escape. ~

Each one of us has that strange feeling, a mysterious hunch making us believe that we are someone else, or we came from somewhere else. Chiefly it happens to me when I close my eyes, imagining all those strange and splendid dreams about many adventures, distant travels, large cities and unconquered mountains. Unfortunately, the sweet taste of freedom was still unknown to me, and there were no signs of changing this state of affairs.

It was a beautiful morning, the sun was streaming into my room through the wide-open window, while the clear skies reminded me of my dream, which seemed just as real.

"Aron! Are you still sleeping?" I heard a shout from behind the door. It was my uncle, the man with whom I lived, if you call the endless duties and responsibilities which I had to carry out a living.

"I'm already up, Uncle." The door creaked open and there he was standing, adjusting the nightcap on his head and looking at me in a repulsive and critical way, his little piggy eyes were drilling through me.

"Get up you lazybones!" This was my morning greeting every day. "You have many tasks today." He took out a small key from his pocket and unfastened the fetters attached to my leg. Every night he kept me like a slave so that I could not go anywhere. My uncle always said that sooner or later he would knock all these fanciful ideas out of my head and try to raise me like a real farmer, who would be grateful to him until death.

Why such a fate? I wanted to be an adventurer rather than a peasant. I would prefer to hold the sword and the torch instead of the hoe and the bucket. So many times I had dreamed about all those mysterious places of the Land: immense forests, unexplored caves, vast deserts and deep mines full of treasures and skeletons, oh, those dreams were endless.

Dream on you foolish boy, I thought to myself. *Sooner the king will become a servant, before your uncle will allow you to go anywhere without permission, you will stay here on the farm working as a simple man.*

Following my uncle downstairs, I looked in the mirror hanging between the door and the large wardrobe. Uncle gave it to me as a gift; he bought himself a better one with a decorative oak wood frame.

My face had not changed at all, perhaps with the exception of the facial hair. Where the twenty-one years had gone, it was not easy to recollect.

Fate is unfair, I thought again, and sighing heavily looked at my reflection. The same as usual: black hair, slightly sloping forehead. I slicked my hair up with my hand.

I would never become an adventurer. It was not the first time such a thought harassed me. Looking into those dark eyes it was not difficult to notice a spark of rage, a desire for freedom, a rebellious feeling caused by a laborious life, not forgetting the anger that had accumulated over so many years, all thanks to Uncle, of course.

Through the open window, I could smell the manure and straightaway I knew what my uncle had prepared for me. It was the worst of all the tasks. The sacks bought by Uncle in the city market were so cheap that they tore easily, making the contents scatter everywhere. Try to guess, who else but me, would become a dung collector? Instead of lost treasure I was gathering piles of shit.

Spending my whole life with a stick in my hand and chasing goats was not what I expected from life, my ambitions were much higher than my uncle's. In his eyes I had always been a weak and rebellious nephew, barely performing his entrusted duties, a typical rustic farmhand.

Every day I passed the same corridor where nothing changed at all. On the wall hung the same image, the same web still in the corner of its battered frame; no one bothered to clean it. The painting was a self-portrait of Uncle's mama. She looked terrible, but actually she was a kind woman, looks can be deceptive, can't they?

I remember when she visited us, a long time ago, just for one night. I laughed at the thought of my cousin Molten carting her huge trunk through the field of potatoes. Granny was an older person from a good house; she did not like her son or grandson, and considered them sluggards and gluttons. She constantly complained that neither of them was any good.

When Granny looked at me her heart bled; in her eyes I was a hardworking little boy. She wanted to take me with her and send me to the royal barracks so that I could become a squire and, if fortune allowed it, even a knight.

When she announced her idea to my uncle during supper, he almost choked on a crust of bread. Molten had to pat him on the back several times, while his red face and tearful eyes said only one word.

"No."

The mother looked at her son as severely as she could; she did not like it when someone opposed her. She left the next day and I lost all trace of her, but I always remember her with great affection.

There were a couple of occasions when I tried to persuade my uncle to let me go, but he was stubborn, nothing would convince him, and any such conversation ended with a blow to my head. He refused to get rid of me, his only servant, an extra pair of hands that always helped him; in fact, they were the only working hands. Uncle always said that he would teach me discipline so I would conform like his son. He was so proud of Molten and often praised him portraying his firstborn to all our guests as a good farmer, with a sharp business mind and a strong will.

"Molten will make something of his life."

I have heard it hundreds of times. You know what, one day I will become the ruler of the Land, and this fantasy created about Molten by his father will disappear. The truth is the only things my cousin could do were make it to the kitchen during mealtimes, go to bed to sleep and to the latrine behind the old oak tree.

There he was, sitting at the table and finishing his meal, if you could call fifteen scrambled eggs and fifteen sausages a meal. My cousin devoured it all and if he had his way, he would have gobbled the dishes up. Molten relished the food like a young hog; his chubby hands greedily putting massive amounts of food into his constantly chewing mouth. He could almost rest his potbelly on the table, his shirt barely fitted him, and the leather suspenders were stretched to the limit.

My cousin had already finished the meal, his small blue pig eyes were following my every step. Letting out a long belch as a greeting, he began to massage his fat belly, giving me a toothy grin. Such a view would strip you of your appetite, I assure you. He always did it, gorging at breakfast, later explaining that he could not work and taking a nap in the shade. Luckily the glutton did not eat everything.

"Here's your list of tasks for today, boy." Uncle showed me the yellowed piece of paper on which twenty-one tasks were written in a line, some of them belonging to my fat cousin.

Make this. Clean that up. Carry this here. Move it there. It would take me till sunset, I had never had so many tasks in one day.

"When you finish the first six tasks, I want you to transport the manure." Uncle pointed to task number seven, chewing a crust of bread. "Just don't tear these new bags which I bought a week ago, will you?" Uncle threatened me with a finger, while I ate my scrambled eggs, remembering how two weeks ago I had to carry manure from the eastern to the western barn. Having torn all the bags, my uncle went mad. That was a nightmare.

"Then feed the animals, today is your turn." He turned around and went upstairs to dress for breakfast. He was always wearing a yellowed ruff, which was tightly fitted around his wide neck. On one of the ruffles, I noticed some dried egg; Uncle always made a mess when he ate.

Another drab day, which I had to spend working on hard, endless tasks, always something to do, every day. Such a miserable fate, why me, why in such a boring place? Buttering a slice of bread, I read the list. Molten belched again and left the table without a word. I asked him only once for his help, he snorted like a pig and walked away.

Going down the stairs Uncle tripped on a dirty cloth and slid down the last four steps onto his bum, cursing everything. Helping him, I plucked up the courage to ask the one question which had been playing on my mind for a long time.

"Uncle, do you know who my father was?"
My uncle's face turned a furious red, and he gave me a dull slap that could have been heard outdoors.

"How dare you, you ungrateful scoundrel!" He growled like a bulldog. "How many times have I told you that your father's dead, he was the same as you, head full of dreams about travels and riches. Get on with your work otherwise you won't get dinner." He chuckled foolishly while I rubbed my head. Every question that wasn't related to ploughing always ended with a strike on me.
Uncle had never told me about my parents, where they came from or their profession, the question on my mind always remained unanswered. My only family was Uncle and his son, what a shame. I was about to leave the house, when I heard a call.

"If you learn to work as a young man, you'll be grateful to me later."

"But I don't want to—" Uncle was already approaching me with his raised fist, so I quickly opened the door and left.

The farm was bathed in the morning sun, the day promised to be great, if not the prospect of twenty-one assignments, which would certainly take up all my time. I looked at the big pile of shit and decided to get to work on the tasks from my list.

And so, my endless labour had begun. Trying to organize my tasks, one after the other, each seemed to be completed. The sun moved further across the sky and, as noon approached, I moved towards the large barrel of water where I quenched my thirst and then rinsed my face; the gentle breeze was pleasantly cooling.

That short moment was enough to awaken my wild imagination.

The visions of my last dream were so realistic and splendid. Oh, what a price I would have paid just to be there. If my uncle had heard that, he would soon lose his temper; the only thing that mattered to him was hard work. Molten already knew everything, thus all the "pleasure" was left for me.

While I was splitting my guts, Molten was skiving under an oak tree. So many times he had mentioned a great and wonderful farm, with plenty of servants, including me of course, his father was so proud. The truth was that berk could not even hammer a nail; he was merely trying to impress his father.

Never! I would never become a servant of this bulky hog, even if I had to escape and live in poverty. There, I said it and stopped dead in my tracks, I had never thought about escaping from here, I was too accustomed to this monotonous life.

I imagined breaking the chains and escaping into the surrounding forest; Uncle and Molten's faces would look stupefied at the news that I had managed to run away.

Yes, I made up my mind to run away that night and leave it all behind, let them work alone. A gentle sting appeared at the back of my head, usually when someone was looking at me. Even this time my sense was right, in the corner of my eye I noticed my uncle attentively observing all my movements. In the life of an adventurer it is a useful skill to be able to explore guarded places unseen and steal unnoticeably. I knew one more thing: how to use a sword, maybe not as well as a knight, but I coped fine.

I remembered when the messengers from the city came seeking young men to join the royal army. From a distance emissaries paraded in outlandish costumes, armour of feathers, and silver claymore swords. Uncle unwillingly agreed to send us both for the trial, so Molten and I got armour and weapons. Neither of us had seen chainmail that close and in order to try it we needed help.

Standing on bare ground looking into each other's eyes, we were trying to make the greatest impression; Molten and I had been waiting for this moment, he had the opportunity to beat me to a pulp and prevent my chance for the trip, I just wanted to get out of there.

At the signal, we set out to attack. The sword was comfortable in my hand and, for a split second, I wondered how many brave young men had wielded it. The armour was not as light as it seemed, I was much thinner than my bulky cousin but on the other hand his movements were sluggish and predictable.

My uncle shouted and cheered his son telling him what he should do to strike me. Molten awkwardly wielded his sword, and waved it in all directions trying to impress his father. I could smell in his sweat that desire to strike me. The whole time I avoided his attacks that were only hitting the air. Unfortunately, I could not get close enough to hit my opponent. Molten was sweeping his sword like a farmer with his scythe on the field. To defeat my foe I needed a ruse. Through the visor I noticed a wooden picket in the middle of the field, stuck into the ground.

I provoked him and threw insults at him. My cousin did not expect anything like that; he rushed at me like a raging bull. I walked back, turned around and headed in the right direction. Molten waded behind me; he waved his sword trying to hit me even if only a slight scratch. I turned my head quickly, "All right, almost there".

"Well son! Forward, show him how to fight." Uncle was cheering, while the royal emissaries watched us in amazement. I was focused on the fight, parrying every blow that reached me, leading my foe to the wooden picket, standing one foot behind me.

Molten grabbed the sword with both hands and aimed with full force, at the same time I leaned back, he missed the target, whisked over my head and buried the sword deep into the pole. The splinters flew everywhere as the blade stuck in it, probably for good.

Oh, what a marvellous view, my cousin was trying to wrest his weapon in vain, standing on one leg, the other one resting on the pole, pulling the handle with all his strength. I could see his terrified eyes through the visor as he tried to retrieve the blade. I knocked him down with one strike and a dull thud that caused my uncle to stop cheering his son, his jaw dropped in amazement, while I put my sword to Molten's head making my cousin weep.

"Magnificent, bravo!" said the greatly impressed delegates.

"This young man will certainly be suitable." One of them approached and patted me on the shoulder. Although I felt a little tired, it made me feel satisfied.

"Pack your things, boy, you're going with us to Pentelia and soon you will see His Majesty and the army." I put my helmet straight, smiling confidently to my uncle, but already I knew something was wrong.

"No!" roared Uncle. "He's not going anywhere with you." He crossed his arms, his face upset and angry; I had beaten his son and had not let him win the fight.

"But why not?" The tallest man asked kindly, scratching his

forehead and looking at the others delegates.

"He knows how to use a sword, he's resourceful and clever, we need such young men in the army," argued the second delegate, but my uncle was adamant, stubborn as usual.

"His place is here, he'll work on the farm."

"But—" the delegates continued.

"Get out of here! I've decided that this boy won't go, no matter how efficient he is, my answer is no."

The guests packed their equipment, thanked everyone and headed to the other farms nearby, leaving me at the mercy of Uncle and his anger. It was a terrible punishment for conquering Molten.

My only chance was ruined, if it had not been for my uncle, within a few days I would have met the bravest knights of the entire Land and trained under their watchful eye, helping them as a squire and then, who knows.

It seemed that the only way out of this place, the way to my freedom, to the realization of my dreams, would be to escape. A spasm of pleasure and excitement went through my body when I started to prepare a plan in my mind. Countless times I wondered where my uncle kept the key from my shackles. I suspected that it had to be somewhere in his room and the only time I could search was during his absence, for example tonight, when he would be checking my work.

While washing my hardworking hands, a second thought popped into my mind: how to leave the house? My uncle did not seem to be an overly cautious person, but he always locked all the doors in the house for the night. He would rather play safe than be robbed by anybody. The truth was a thief would not have too much to carry out of this house, I've never heard about anyone interested in cabbages, which the pantry was full of.

The chimney could be the only way, I thought to myself, remembering how last month I had to clean it, so the layout was not a mystery to me. After that there was only half an acre of rye field to pass and finally the forest, from where no force could make me turn back.

Having made my decision, I was so excited that could not wait for nightfall. All the work was done, all twenty-one tasks completed, my last ones on the farm. The sun slowly went down, giving way to night sky and the moon.

Tired but happy I went for a meal and, as expected, everything was ready on the table. Closing the door, I noticed Uncle pouring the mulled wine for himself and Molten, my cup was already full. I sat down at the table, while Uncle was staring at me angrily.

"Have you done everything that I told you?"

"Yes, Uncle," I replied, slowly cutting my food.

Again, that feeling that no one could see me. Out of the corner of my eye I glanced at the opposite side of the table; indeed, Molten was talking about his stupid ideas again with his father, who was very pleased as usual.

I was sick and tired of their conversations. Every night they discussed how to make our great farm even more prosperous, should we buy a new milk cow from the neighbour, how much should we charge for goat milk, and on and on.

Through the window in my room I observed Uncle with a torch entering the barn. While trying to sneak down to the hall I stumbled on Molten coming up the stairs. He looked ridiculous, barely raising his feet; his long limp hands were hitting his side with every step. The folds of fat surged under his shirt and the buttons were stretched to the limit.

"Where are you going?" he asked sleepily.

"I'm going to help your father, you fatty." Molten shrugged his shoulders, yawned protractedly and disappeared into his room.

Now or never, I sneaked into Uncle's chamber, nothing special, a big bed in the middle, a wardrobe, table and chairs. On the small shelf next to the empty potty was a familiar book bound in red leather *About Planting and Ploughing*. How I desired to tear this so-called "work" to shreds.

Prowling around quietly looking for anything that might be useful for my escape, I heard a terrible noise behind the wall. It was my cousin snoring like a giant, something clicked inside me, I did not need a key at all.

First I searched the bed trying to leave everything just as it was, the pillows and a blanket. The handcrafted piece on the wall caught my attention; it was not hung straight. Uncle must have hung it hastily, before somebody could discover his small hiding place.

I looked behind the crafted art piece; a small recess, which looked like a shelf where one could keep small items. Instead of the key I found a purse and without thinking what was inside, I took it, leaving the wall piece in the same position. I made appropriate arrangements in my room, now the only thing I had to do was to hide and wait until Uncle fell asleep.

He went into the house and locked all the doors. Blowing the candles out, he hurriedly rushed into my room.

"You little prat. You haven't done anything properly. Again, every bag with the manure is slit. Tomorrow you'll get up earlier and clean it up, otherwise you'll not get breakfast!" After a minute of shouting Uncle realized I was sleeping. Rolling up the blanket, he locked the piece of cold metal to the leg and walked out laughing, slamming the door behind.

I could hear everything that was going on around the house, every sense of mine was sharpened. I could hear my uncle shifting the art piece on the other side of the wall. Then he yelled, "Son, have you seen, by any chance, a leather purse? I was keeping all our savings in it." There was no answer, Molten was sleeping like a dead man, so Uncle swore and slammed the door. After a few moments, the bed creaked and father, just like his son, began to play "the snore symphony", absolutely wonderful chords emanating from the depths of their throats.

I thought it would be worthwhile to take some food with me, so I went downstairs on tiptoes and started looking in the wooden cabinets, choosing the best of all. Somewhere upstairs across the hall a buzzing insect was mercilessly teasing the silence.

Something creaked upstairs, the sound made me freeze. It sounded like my uncle shaking in bed; I knew how sensitive he was about insects, especially the noisy ones. When I was about to leave the pantry and scramble into the chimney, the door slammed; I think I lost a heartbeat or two, in a split second I dashed under the kitchen table waiting in complete silence.

My uncle was standing in the bedroom doorway, wearing a night robe and holding a slipper and lighted candle in his hand, I could tell that he was tired and nervous, the buzzing sound intensified considerably.

He went to the end of the hall, creeping like a cat, I could hear his every move. After a while... Bang! He missed. My uncle tried to hunt some insect, he swung couple of times and finally, he smashed the slipper on his forehead.

"Bloody flies will not let me sleep..."Mumbled the half-asleep man, and returned to bed while I was breathing heavily and counting the seconds,which were escaping like sand from my fist.

I came out from under the table. Slowly and steadily, I began to climb the rocks on the inner side of the chimney, carefully and quietly,pulling up with my hands and balancing my body with the knapsack, The chimney was tight, but it was clean. I'd had to wash it twice because Molten found it too dirty; I managed to reach halfway.

Now I was deadly silent, hardly breathing, while drops of sweat were covering my face. The slightest murmur would probably wake the sleeping ones. Trying to climb up, unfortunately, I trod on a loose brick. This treacherous piece of rock would alert them. It felt like it had fallen down, and I closed my eyes in horror.

I waited patiently for the stone to hit the bottom of the fireplace. I imagined my uncle jumping out of bed and checking who or what had made such a noise, fortunately nothing like that happened. I could still hear him snoring, so I got up into the attic and out from there.

The evening sky looked beautiful; the brisk and lively air hit my nostrils, while the stars were blinking at me illuminating the way, thousands of tiny dots flashing brightly in the sky participating in my enjoyment of freedom. A light breeze came down making me feel the crispness of the rising dawn, when the sun was slowly preparing itself to change the guard with the moon.

Walking to the edge and holding tightly onto the protruding logs, I jumped down on the haystack, which I had prepared earlier. Freedom at last, farewell hard work and torment, welcome adventure and unknown fate, I had been waiting for this moment for twenty-one years.

Clambering out from the hay I started to run like the wind, I knew that nothing and nobody could stop me. No one could ever guess how this moment of happiness captured me, leaving my uncle's farm without regret, that monotonous life, full of torture from Uncle and Molten. That was the end of my escape from Uncle's farm and the beginning of my journey, my greatest adventure.

***

The new day had begun. Aron's uncle immediately opened his eyes, pleased that his nephew would have to get up earlier than usual to clean up the spilled manure. He sat on the edge of the bed, stretching and began to scratch his head. The dead body of the hunted fly dropped from his face and fell onto the floor. Despite the overnight clash with an insect, he was rested.

The first thing that came to his mind was the purse. Wanting to ask Aron about it, he got up, opened the door and barged into the next room, the sun was rushing through the window. The uncle looked at his farm.

"Get up! You have to clean up manure before breakfast!" A dull sound of snoring answered him.

"Sluggard, stand up!" He roared and threw the blanket onto the floor. What he saw flabbergasted him; it was Molten shackled in chains and sucking his thumb like a baby.

~ Chapter .2. Chieftain and his gang. ~

With tears in my eyes, knapsack on my back and heart beating like a drum, I was running as fast as I could, rushing like never before. The fresh forest air released inside me an indomitable joy, while the inner voice in my head was telling me not to stop, to run away as far as my feet could carry me. For the first time in my life, I tasted freedom.

With each step, the forest turned thicker, the trees were higher and the vegetation more luxuriant. Trees were showing off their impressive height, many of them were over fifty metres, with high, wide branches soaring majestically towards the sky, their spiral needles gently pointing downward, shimmering brightly like natural torches in the last gleam of the moon and stars.

I ran down from the small sandy slope dotted in some places with lichens and accidently stepped on something; the sound of crunching scared some kind of animal roaming nearby. The cones were lying everywhere and there was no way to get around them. Broad branches and lush leaves did not let the light through. The darkness was completely dominated by ferns and other kinds of horsetails, rising proudly developing strong, healthy sprouts.

After a while, having slowed down my pace, the knapsack was feeling heavier. I pulled out a dagger stolen from the pantry and set it behind the belt. It was the only weapon I possessed. Looking around, I tried to pass silently to not attract any attention, at the same time convincing myself not to be distracted by anything that might make me want to turn back.

It was a perfect time to have a little snack. My first meal as a free man was simple and modest but it made me feel excited, my hands were trembling while I started to peel the carrot, not because of the temperature, but because of the adrenaline buzzing in my veins. A sip of water from the leather goatskin made me feel a lot better.

I knew exactly which direction to choose. Once, my uncle had shown us a map of the Land and the spot where our homestead was located; it had made a great impression on me. Till that moment I had no idea we were living in such a vast kingdom. One look at it and I wanted to be an adventurer; the desire to explore every corner of the Land was increasing my curiosity.

The world belongs to the brave and let God's will be done! I told myself, hoping not to meet anybody such as neighbours from the other farms and manors, who sometimes came to pay a visit, to barter, drink or to gossip about some news. That would mean being caught in a stupid way, which could lead me back shackled by my uncle and then taken straight to the barn. Just the thought of returning to the farm was giving me jitters, so, trying not to think about it, I continued on my journey.

The road had now become denser and even more overgrown, broad leaves were giving a great cover, all the ferns, hazels, blackberries, clubmosses and horsetails were dominating both sides of the trade route, forming a natural curtain which the human eye was unable to penetrate. If someone walked or drove by I would not be visible at all, on both sides stood misty silence. The crisp freshness of the forest was twirling in my nostrils lending me strength and courage.

I walked with steady steps, admiring everything around me, turning my head to capture as much of the view as possible, and to catch any danger. It was my first expedition into the deep forest. The fact that I could not see the end of the road did not scare me at all. My uncle, together with Molten, used to ride that way to get all sorts of goods, usually they bought anything that was missing or necessary.

One thing was certain, going along this track I would surely get to any of the towns. It did not matter to me which one, but I would prefer to enter Pentelia, the capital city of the Land, it was one of the largest dots on the map shown by my uncle. There would be many possibilities to purchase some decent clothes, weapons and equipment. Thinking about all those merchants and shops, I smiled widely. And I could look for some comrades with whom I could make the perilous journey, while plundering the vaults, mines and other places to lay our hands on the long lost booty.

The cool breeze fondled my face and the gold weighed pleasantly in my purse, resting in the bottom of my knapsack. Putting my foot on the smooth forest floor, I walked into the unknown and was about to take the next step, when I heard the crack of a twig. My heart started pounding.

Looking around frantically trying to sense out where the sound came from, I did not notice the figure that silently crept over me, I was not used to looking up at the upper parts of the forest.

I closed my eyes for a moment and stopped under a large oak tree to take a breath and sip of water, I looked around slowly, trying to track down the slightest movement. I brushed my hair, partially covering my forehead and, grinning to myself, wondered if Uncle had managed to force Molten to collect the dung, or if he would do that part of the work himself. I would love to have seen his face when he found out who was in my bed chained with the fetters.

Out of nowhere the sound of a speeding carriage reached my ears. I heard it approaching; the person riding it was certainly driving at breakneck speed. The sound of the hoof beats became clear and an idea popped up into my mind. What if it was my uncle holding the reins? I quickly moved away from its track, to make sure that no one would spot me and looked behind to check if I had left any significant traces.

With a steady step, I moved two hundred metres away but now the sound of galloping was coming from all directions and it was not just a carriage, I heard many horses. I hid myself among the bushes trying to grasp the sight of the battue.

They surrounded me. It brought a thousand pictures in my mind, as if all farms had joined together to hunt me, with Uncle at the forefront. Hemmed in and scared, I started to run as far away as I could.

After some time, the sound of the hoof beats disappeared, which was a relief. With each successive step, the forest began to thin, which could mean one thing: a farm was near. Hoping to avoid any surprises, my head started calculating if somehow I could have turned back towards my uncle's farm. *It cannot be...* I did not want to go back to that hell from which I had escaped.

At the end of the forest line, I noticed a small clearing with patches of bushes and trees, and right behind them stretched a massive ravine, which looked like someone had sketched the earth had marked it with a great blunt tool. I remembered the point on the map, which was a boundary separating different parts of the Land. To arrive at the capital and use its facilities, I had to pass to the other side.

A pleasant view appeared, it was the bridge about 300 metres away. On the other side, it would definitely be impossible for my uncle and the rest of the battue to get hold of me. I moved ahead slowly, getting closer to my target. Imagining Pentelia with its numerous dwellings, busy streets, merchants and stalls, I had not sensed the figure that followed directly behind me, keeping its distance, and still moving quietly among the trees.

Slowly I approached the bridge that, merged with the cliffs, looked like a solid finished work from both ends. With every step, the bridge became bigger making it even more impressive, especially when standing in the middle and looking down. A few metres in front of the columns supporting the entire structure grew tall clumps of bushes.

I thought it might be the perfect hideout for thieves and bandits robbing the merchants. I had not taken a step, when my body felt a paralyzing jolt. Why was it always me who never had any good luck?

In front of me appeared a small band of men, ten if I counted correctly, still it was a bit too many, even for me. They were all armed and seemed to be dangerous, standing in a row, from the largest to the smallest, with scruffy clothes, numerous scars and marks, dirty and unkempt, but who cared, I had no desire to smell those cronies. They glanced defiantly, in those eyes glowed anger with a hint of madness. Their ringleader came out to greet me.

"Hello stranger, what brings you here into the middle of nowhere?" A note of malicious courtesy ordered me to choose my words carefully. He was the only one from the whole gang who did not emanate hostility.

"None of your business!" I wanted to finish this conversation as soon as possible and move on. However, the chieftain continued. His black vest was buckled with two silver buttons gently shimmering in the morning sun, his sharp eyes bored into me from head to toe.

You can tell us, maybe we can do business together?" He asked sharply, looking at his own gang and grinning.

"My uncle told me to not to talk to strangers."

"Did he now? In that case, pay us for crossing to the other side, then we'll let you go," he said.

I patted my empty pockets. "I have no money." My reply amused them; I was not the first one who gave them such an answer.

"So we'll take all the other things that you're carrying!" said the small robber standing at the end of the row; he had much more desire to fight than the others, or maybe he just wanted to show off in front of his chief.

Slowly the gang started approaching me, brandishing their swords, sticks and clubs. Their eyes were like sparks, black teeth clenched almost painfully, and frothing from their mouths like a pack of furious mongrels.

Without any idea of how to get out of this situation, instinctively I took out a dagger, securing my knapsack with my other hand. The chieftain looked into my eyes and then, paying attention to the handle of my weapon, smiled for a moment and turned towards his gang.

"Tut, tut, we have the first brave one today. Lads, teach this yokel how a real man uses his weapon!" The smallest robber with a black leather eyepatch covering his right eye began to run in my direction. It was difficult to guess the intention of the half-blind midget holding a short curved sword. I took a side position, ready to repel the attack or to dodge. The foe was about to attack, when I stepped away from his path while tripping him badly. He lost his balance, flew further, tumbling to the ground and hit his head on a nearby stone. The wound on his head slowly began to trickle with blood; he closed his eye and passed out.

Everyone was amazed, apparently realizing that they were not dealing with just a greenhorn. The chieftain looked at me, making a face as if he understood something and snapped his fingers.

The tallest of the band, a big bald lout in a skin-tight shirt with torn sleeves withdrew from the row, his big toe was sticking out of his left boot. The boor swung vigorously with his long sword slightly curved at the end, while I ducked; fortunately the blade only cut the air a few inches from my ear. My opponent turned around and attacked again, this time slashing even harder; it was obvious that I was annoying him with my ability and speed.

The churl rushed at my back, I rebounded. With the knapsack the fight was definitely uncomfortable, but I could not take it off because of the hidden gold.

"Jerch, stop playing around and knock him down!" shouted the leader of the gang, while the others cheered their companion fiercely; the giant began to show off with his sword, brandishing it in all directions, shifting the hilt from one hand to the other. He waved like a man possessed losing his strength, reminding me of my cousin Molten, but with the exception of his attitude he fought far better than that fat pig.

I wanted in some way to distract this ruffian, having realized I could not repel all attacks with this small dagger. Judging the situation, surprise and escape was my only solution. I looked down on the ground, focusing on a clump of grass, staring at it persistently, praying inwardly that the others would look there as well.

The giant, like the rest, did not know what I was up to and looked, trying to understand what was so interesting. All of them stood with puzzled faces staring blankly at the ground; this was my chance. I grabbed the dagger with both hands and took a swing, hitting my opponent above the wrist.

A strong impact caused the blade to easily pierce the leather glove and Jerch's hand; it struck completely and emerged on the other side. The drops of blood started dripping, Jerch groaned and dropped his weapon, clutching his injured hand; the rest of the band was dumbfounded.

"Aaaa!" He screamed while the rest stared in disbelief. Having managed to escape, there was no time to retrieve my weapon from Jerch's bloody hand, after a moment, everyone headed in my direction.

Hearing the sinister shouts behind, I ran across the bridge, conquering two beams at a time, praying that they would withstand my weight along with the knapsack. The bridge looked solid, but you never know, excessive use of it by merchants could have caused deterioration of the boards.

Clenching my teeth and running further, I thought about the fall from that bridge, it was not that small at first glance. The wild river below was rapid and sharp, picking up all that was on its way, all the time undermining the sandy shores of the overgrown and inaccessible slope. Whoever jumped from the bridge would end up dead, engulfed by the blue snake wiggling at the bottom.

Around the middle of the bridge, I heard a whistle then an arrow flew over my head and dug into the bark of the nearest tree on the other side. Surprised that there were no more shots, I could not believe my luck. But not for long. After a moment two rogues appeared from behind the tree marked by an arrow, they had been waiting for a signal from the opposite side.

It was an excellent way to beset the fleeing traders with their commodities; a frightened coward caught in the middle of the bridge would be robbed of everything, including their own lives. Merchants had been thrown into the river, so it looked like an accident; there were never any witnesses.

I found myself trapped, without a weapon there was no chance of getting through to the other side, I had no idea how to get out. Jerch walked at the head of this battue, lugging the same slightly curved sword. Trying not to look at the bloody hand with a dagger pierced into it, without a moment's thought I took a purse from side pocket of my knapsack and turned around towards the ringleader, who with one gesture stopped his men. They all grinned out of spite throwing curses in my direction; Jerch was like a mad dog waiting for permission from his master.

"Is this what you want? Catch this!" I threw the purse in their direction, rapidly it flew between them and fell into the bushes on the slope, and several frightened birds flew up into the blue sky.

"Who's got it? Where is it?"

The diverted attention saved me some precious seconds, so I

crossed to the other side of the rope barriers holding back the bridge, now my only escape seemed the river. The purse, however, did not attract everyone; Jerch quickened his pace, he did not care about his share, for him it only meant lost honour.

"Hold your horses, boy!" shouted the ringleader, hiding his sword in its scabbard and smiling broadly. "You won't survive the jump, and even if you do, the river will finish you off."

Bending my knees I jumped, while at the same time Jerch struck me on my scalp with the handle of his weapon. Stars appeared in front of my head swirling and splashing. Falling into the abyss the blurred picture of the bridge disappeared.

I hit the surface of the cold water, landing on my back, fortunately my knapsack cushioned the fall keeping me on the surface like a life raft. My unconscious body was swept by the wild river; I felt nothing, surrounded by water and darkness.

***

Jerch carefully removed the blade from his hand, clenching his teeth in pain. His wound was bleeding profusely so he applied a makeshift bandage and some medicinal leaves to it and bit off the piece of the strap, looking at the bloody blade of the dagger. He was about to throw it into the river, which had absorbed the owner as well, when the chieftain grabbed his wrist.

"Leave it, this lad's alive. I'll bet my whole share if you want that we'll meet this pilgrim again."

"How do you know he's not dead, chief?" asked Rekel, scratching his bushy moustache.

"People of his kind don't give up so easily."

"Chief, I've found that purse!" One of the thugs climbed the rope, walked over and passed it to the ringleader. He weighed the bundle in his hand and smiled broadly.

He undid the strap and poured the contents into his hand. They had been expecting gold and got some small rocks instead.

The chieftain gritted his teeth, threw everything into the water and slammed his fist on the wooden stake, frowning.

"I'll get you, young pilgrim!"

***

Drifting into the unknown, my knapsack was keeping me on the surface. I could feel the surrounding nature breathing and whispering about death.

I had wandered into a tunnel and the smell of putrefaction hit my nostrils. Looking around, I began to walk in an unknown direction, every step was dully echoing from the walls and ceiling. I had the distinct feeling that someone was watching me; it almost drove me crazy. Right behind the wall came a strange noise; I paused for a moment trying to catch even the slightest sound.

A flash of light cut through the darkness and I noticed a terrible sight: the floor was sticky with dried blood, strewn with human bones, rats crowding among them. I heard the screech of a heavy gate. Something was standing on the other side and it certainly wasn't a man.

A nasty, hairy creature stood in the doorway, sniffing the whole tunnel, its huge nostrils sensitive to any foreign smell were sucking the air, trying to feel any presence. The massive creature jerked and rushed through the tunnel like a wild boar, which had seen its hunter. It was about seven feet tall on its long limbs, chattering ominously with its mandibles, its body covered with hair matted with dried blood. Its red deadly eyes were fixed on me.

This tunnel was built especially for it. Released from time to time, it was hunting for everything and everyone who ventured into its kingdom. The terrifying screech was unbearable; I had never run so fast before, desperately passing the tunnel, searching for shelter, with a cry of horror in my mouth. *Run for your life.* I tried to hide somewhere, but there was no space, not a single curve or niche.

Running headlong I almost hit my head against a stone wall, which suddenly appeared in front of me. Slamming it with both fists did not help, I could hear the muffled squeal of the running creature.

I'm screwed. I began to look around for a lever or stick, anything that could open the damn gate, but there was nothing except the skulls of wretches like me trying to escape. The beast stopped in front of me. It opened its jaws and revealed its ugly grey tongue, sharpened at the end. I screamed in horror, while the monster brutally stuck it in my head.

Waking up on the shore, I felt dizzy, shivering and bedraggled. I looked around; the ravine had disappeared a long time ago.

The darkness, about which I had dreamed, covered the whole forest like a blanket. I was soaked through, with a wet knapsack, without any weapon or food and with a bunch of thugs behind, ready to disembowel me just for their pleasure. I had no idea where to go now.

The ringleader would not overlook the trick I played on him. Those stones certainly did not meet his expectation; perhaps I should have put some hornfels or mica in the purse instead.

The coolness pierced my body in a split second, and the pain in my head pulsated with every heartbeat. *If I meet Jerch again, I'll make sure he won't have his limb to wipe his ass,* I promised myself, guessing that he would never forgive me.

When I was standing on the bridge, I had noticed a sign marked on the road, but now, having deviated from the path, I looked around for a place to stay the night.

Straining my ears to hear the quietest murmur, even the buzzing of the insects, somewhere above me I heard an owl. It was considered a bad omen in my peasant life, so I knew something bad would happen. I didn't hear the figure moving gingerly and silently overcoming the distance separating us. It did not even occur to me that someone could sneak up. The slightest gust of wind was giving me the creeps, and fatigue made moving more difficult.

It was a frigid night, as if the summer season had slowly given way to autumn. The leaves from time to time were playing obediently, moved by an invisible hand. Skirting the shrubs and other smaller trees growing near the river, even my sneeze scared some birds that flew away from their nest right above my head.

Lighting a campfire seemed to me a priority; my uncle had once shown me what to do when you are out of flints. I took off my knapsack and felt my aching back. I praised God that I was wearing it at the time of the fall otherwise it would have been a serious problem.

I picked some twigs and branches, and collected a piece of dry bark and a dead branch, which ideally would make a fire. I put some flat bark on the ground and with a rounded stick I began to drill down trying to warm it.

Rubbing and rubbing, grinding and grinding, nothing happened, did I remember what to do or was my memory playing tricks on me? I had the flat board and the round stick for rubbing, tut, tut, I'd forgotten about the kindle. Dry grass perfectly fulfilled its task and this time the result was much better, first smoke appeared and then some red sparks.

While I was blowing gently, the grass began to fume abundantly, at last a fire so now the night would not be that cold. Hiding the gold with a knapsack, I lay down comfortably by the orange flames, which blazed merrily. The sparks were shooting up high in the sky, the smell of burning wood, like the fireplace in my previous home, calmed me, and made me feel sleepy. My eyes closed for a moment, and when they opened I found myself in unpleasant company.

Above me were standing the chieftain with Jerch, looking at me with surprise and satisfaction at the same time. I jumped up; with one hand Jerch grabbed my throat. I wanted to break free, but his grip was too strong, pinning me to a tree and looking with disgust and anger, our noses were only a few centimetres away from each other, the stench from his mouth was unbearable.

"Now I got you, you son of a whore!" He lisped and snorted with anger, I felt drops of his spit on my face. "Look what you did!" He showed me his hand wrapped in a leaf, it was swollen and not healing properly. "Now it's my turn to cut something." He smiled at the ringleader, who was scouring the area looking for my stuff. After a moment, our eyes met, the fire was reflected in his pupils, he clenched his teeth shaking in anger, as if he could he would breathe fire. Strange enough, I knew why he was upset and what he would ask me.

"Where did you hide the knapsack?" He was trying to control his nerves, tightening his fists.

"Lost it in the river," I replied hastily. "How did you find me here?" I was trying to change the subject and turn their attention away from the gold.

"Wiseacre, you had a lot of luck in the river." He pointed at the campfire.

"Your fire is visible from a large distance, unfortunately for you." He exchanged a glance with Jerch and they both started laughing. The lout was squeezing me tighter and harder, I could barely catch a breath, while tears flowed down my face.

"The knapsack is there." I choked and Jerch immediately loosened his grip. The chieftain brushed nearby bushes where the backpack was hidden. He emptied the contents on the ground, a spare pair of clothes, packed food, soggy and definitely not suitable for eating, and a few sacks. He knelt down immediately and frantically searched all of it.

The first one was empty, he tossed it aside swearing under his breath, in the second one were some herbs, with the third one he had some problems untying the knot. He gave me a quick glance, smiling, it was probably the one he wanted. Removing my dagger from his belt, he cut the strap and found inside a handful of sand and a little lump of gold, which he hid in his pocket.

"Tell me where the rest is." He was smiling. "I know you have much more."

I was silent. Jerch again clenched his hand on my throat. Leaving me with no choice, I grabbed his wounded hand and squeezed it with all my strength. Tearing off the leaf from his wound, I had broken the scab at the point where my dagger pierced his skin. The blood splashed directly on Jerch's face, he let go of me and grabbed his own hand. Just as I was about to run away, the chieftain appeared in front of me.

"At last! Now let's see what kind of roots you're coming from and how strong they are!" He was armed with my dagger in one hand and his sword in the other ready for any attack.

Jerch with a double-wounded hand was not aware what was going on. I picked up a nearby stick and took a swing, trying to hit my opponent, but in vain as he defended himself without any problems, in addition, my stick had shrunk considerably.

The chieftain laughed and began to cut my stick, every time he hit it with his sword a piece was winging away. But it didn't distract my attention. I stared at the branch of a nearby tree, where someone or something was rustling twigs.

"Fool, surely you're not thinking I'll be taken in by your trick twice?"

But it was not a trick. A figure jumped out from behind, the chieftain had no time to turn around and received a powerful strike on the head with a stick. He stumbled and fell down. It happened so fast that I did not realize my rescuer had grabbed my hand and was leading me in the opposite direction.

This time Jerch stood in our way, with his bleeding wound. His splattered face and two fires glowing in his eyes made him look scary. Only one hand was able, dangling ominously with his sword. Fortunately the giant was feeble and had lost a lot of blood. I heard the voice of my saviour, gentle and firm at the same time, certainly belonging to a girl.

"Out of the way you one-handed bandit!" She let go of my hand, grabbed her stick with both hands and bashed him with great force in the crotch. I heard a quiet, short groan. Jerch dropped his sword and a moment later, holding his family jewels, he fell to the ground.

"The coast is clear, come on," she said and as we were about to start fleeing, I recalled something and turned back.

"What are you waiting for?"

"Just give me a second, will you?" Turning back quickly and

grabbing my knapsack, I started collecting my clothes and the rest, not forgetting the hollow in the tree, where the largest purse full of my wealth was sitting. Having hidden the gold at the bottom of my knapsack, I realized there was one more treasure that I cherished, the old dagger from the buttery, which had actually drawn the attention of the ringleader, I wondered why.

"Well, how long do I have to wait for you?" I heard a voice behind.

"I'm coming." There was no sign of the dagger so I turned back, which was the biggest mistake I made that day. The chieftain stood up and I felt a strong hit in the exact spot where earlier Jerch had struck me. My body slumped limply to the ground. Why is it always me?

I fell into the dark again, having restless thoughts. My uncle and Molten were maligning me at every step, my escape from the hell-farm, a frenzied run and a blow to the head from the ringleader. The images swirled in my head, everything was blurred; I was not able to recognize any shape, and now all of these images flashed in slow motion: the tunnel with the creature, the meeting by the campfire and finally the mysterious figure following me from the beginning of my journey. I opened my eyes, praying in secret that I would not meet the chieftain and his lubbers.

The afternoon sun warmed me and my clothes were drying on the racks, it took some time before my eyes sharpened. I found myself in a cottage, where everything was made of wood, the interior decoration was simple and modest, a mat of leaves, a small table and chair and a wardrobe. Something was missing. Where was my knapsack and the gold?

I jumped up, all drenched in sweat, somebody's warm hand, nice to the touch, would not let me get up. It was delicate, but at the same time familiar with work and struggle. I looked straight in the eyes of its owner; she pushed me gently on my back placing a pillow under my head.

The most charming person I had ever met was kneeling over me, long, light brown hair, pointed nose slightly turned up. Natural beauty accentuated her almond-shaped eyes, large, passionate, brown, and full of care and affection, they were shining so wonderfully in the rays of the glimmering sun. You are probably wondering why I am saying this, but for my whole life I had to look at the greasy snouts of my uncle and Molten, although we were regularly visited by a neighbour who had a daughter not even worthy of a second look, and he was visiting us for one reason - to pair her with Molten. Once I caught them frolicking in the hay behind the barn.

As the girl lifted a wooden bowl with some leaves, her ears were exposed. She was an elf, and probably knew exactly how the concoction worked. When the medicine was ready she put it on my head, the ache returned, but it was not as strong as in the beginning. I hissed in pain, shaking and kicking restlessly like my body was covered with ants, my guardian was teasing me, pressing the poultice harder.

"Stop fidgeting, it's for your own good!"
She was right, after a short time the pain had almost disappeared. It was the first time someone was taking care of me. Usually, when I was sick on the farm, I would get a kick from my uncle, and told to continue my routine.

"What's your name?" I was intrigued to know who my saviour was. The elfgirl smiled at me. "My name is Melea." I noticed that she blushed slightly and, trying to hide it, she asked curiously, "And you? Who are you stranger, and what are you doing in this part of the forest?"

I was trying to collect my thoughts. "You can call me Aron, yesterday I ran away from my uncle's farm."
She looked at me in disbelief. While sipping my nourishing forest stew, I started to narrate my story.

"You can't imagine how horribly I was being treated, getting told all the time that I'm a useless parasite." As I told Melea my story she listened patiently, while changing my compresses. She was shocked when I mentioned the safety measures, which my uncle was using in case I wanted to get away. At the end of this sad story, I closed my eyes.

"I'll never go back there." She nodded gently and checked the temperature on my forehead.

"Where are we? How did I get here?"

"We're in my cottage, once it was the cabin of the local hermit. I tailed you, almost from dawn. I saw the whole incident with Warend's gang, it was impressive, stabbing that lout, then jumping into the river. Not many survive such encounter with the current of the flow in the Great Gorge."

"I've heard that before. Where's my coat and the rest of my stuff? I had something hidden in the knap—"

"Your backpack is there." She showed it standing in the corner, leaning against the wall all dry. I gave a sigh of relief.

"I changed you into dry clothes, the rest are drying." I suddenly felt wet and cold pants under the blanket, Melea probably noticed that.

"Oh, I didn't change your trousers; we don't know each other that well."
I smiled to myself, the gold was laying safely at the bottom, and not

everything was lost, last night was a great adventure on its own.

I got up and sat down on the mattress, rubbing the back of my head.

"Where you think you're going? You must rest."

"I'm truly grateful that you're looking after me," I sighed heavily, "but I have to move on, if those bandits find me they'll probably kill me."

"You won't move off in this state."

She was right, having tried to get up my whole body felt as if thousands of needles were stabbing it.

"As soon as you get better, we'll hit the road." She sprinkled some leaves in a wooden bowl of hot water. How did she know I was going on a long journey?

"Did I say something wrong?"

I looked at her for a moment catching her reaction. "No, it just amazed me why you said "we" will go."

"You were murmuring all about it during your sleep, treasures and fights, fame and wealth. You also mentioned plundering tombs and mines. I'd like to go with you. Perhaps you don't know, but we're much alike. I was also a prisoner in my home, where my parents didn't want me to wander alone around the city and surrounding forests. All the time they tried to convince me that my place was with them." She took a sip from a wooden mug. "You have no idea how much I suffered because of that. Being aware that my dreams may not come true made me choose this life of exile."

One glance was enough to notice that beauty was not her only advantage; a gallant attitude and combative movements with the stick explained a lot. She told me how her father discovered some weapons in her room, which she had purchased at the market investing all her savings on them. She smuggled them into her home, and practised warcraft for a long time. Spending quite a lot of time with her nose in books, flipping through the pages for knights, travellers, and adventurers, her father went berserk. He told her that he had not brought her up to be killed by thugs, or another equally cowardly way. She was thrown out of the house and disowned by her family.

I listened to that sad story, and could not believe that there was someone else in this miserable world who was suffering for the same reason that I was: the inability to spread one's wings and set off into the unknown. Not wanting to let such skills go wasted, I decided that Melea should accompany me on my epic adventure.

"Does this…Warend… know where we are? How do you know

him?"

"No, he won't find us here. Any self-respecting traveller, thief or robber, has heard of him and his gang in this part of the Land. They charge the merchants a fee, that's what they call it."

I closed my eyes for a moment. "I guess you saved my ass. How can I thank you?"

"Don't worry, I shall demand repayment at an appropriate place and time. Now you need to rest, I'll check on you tomorrow morning."

I woke up the next morning while Melea was training outside with a sword. Her form was impressive and polished, no wonder she practised daily, her feet moved superbly, left, right, left, right and strike. It was a pleasure to watch her fighting imaginary enemies. I leaned against the wall of the cabin and admired her jumps and strikes, which were unusual: slim curves allowing for all kinds of attacks by cutting fast, brandishing her weapon and inflicting blows. After some time, she realized that I was watching her.

"You already got up? Eat breakfast and get to work."

"For what?"

"For training. We need to improve your form."

"But—"

"No but! Take that sword."

I reached for the blade leaning against the nearest tree and I took it out of its sheath. It was light, well balanced and well kept, as if it had been assembled just for me.

Melea stood alongside, making an angry expression and attacked me without warning.

I fought as best as I could, avoiding her strikes, trying to attack my opponent.

"Nothing like practising in the early hours of dawn to make one perfect." She was trying to out-voice the sound of striking metal.

"I agree—"

She did not let me finish, just ran and raised her sword, striking with great force, my weapon fell to the ground flatly. Quickly I tried to pick it up, jumping back and leaning over. I reached for the handle, while her blade was an inch from my nose. I looked first at the edge and then at her, the pleasure of reward was shining on her face. She had beaten me.

"See what I mean? We need to help each other, you can teach me, and I can teach you." I looked at her with undisguised satisfaction and admiration.

"Fine, as you wish."

She kneeled and picked up the blade lying on the ground, with a sarcastic smile. "Don't show me this attitude, only your ego was hurt. This is for you, keep it." Melea handed me my new sword. "I'm not really happy with this blade and you're pretty proficient with it."

"Now that's a fine blade. Where did you get it?"

"I bought it for my friend, but our paths diverged." There was a short awkward silence. We had just met and I had to ask for something that she did not want to talk about. Blimey.

"In a few days, we should be ready to go. The city is full of supplies and from there we'll begin our journey." She smiled at the thought of adventure, with a glint in her eye.

Holding my new sword firmly, and admiring the shiny blade, I looked forward to this journey with a companion like her!

~ Chapter .3. The body and soul training. ~

For the first time in my life, I could sleep enough, and was able to get up and walk around my room whenever I wanted, no fetters were holding back my legs, and there was no uncle, who from morning to evening would only shout instructions or insults. Instead there was Melea's humming, and mysterious smells coming from the other chamber. It would be a lie to say that my uncle's pork was not tasty, but on the other hand, my nostrils had never smelled such a different aroma in my life.

I got up and out of habit made my bed, Uncle told me to do this every day directly after he unfastened my chain. I opened the door and the smell became even more intense. Melea was standing over the stone stove and tossing something in the iron pan. Wanting to surprise her I began to sneak up, as quietly as possible, holding my breath. The thin wooden floor was challenging, the boards could be really tricky, and the creaking noise was loud enough to be heard outside the cottage, it would have been easy to find out if anyone was bustling around inside.

Standing a step behind Melea, I wanted to scare her, just for fun. Violently I grabbed her side and with the other hand held her throat. Frightened, she did not know who it was and raised her leg and struck me with her foot on my right toe. I jumped up in pain, held my toe and started rubbing it. She turned around with the hot iron pan ready to strike.

"What the hell do you think you're doing? I could've smashed you with this pan." Her arms were shaking with anger and fright.

"I think you would not spoil such a nice breakfast."
She shook her head and returned to the cooking. "I didn't hear you sneaking up on me. It's almost impossible to do that to an elf, you know. Can you teach me?" She gave me a warm smile, which I felt was an apology for the blue toe.

"At least one person appreciated it. Once I played a similar joke on Molten. He was so scared, he wet his pants and ran away crying to his father, and because of that, I wasn't given supper that night." I helped to set the table and Melea handed me the breakfast.

"I won't let such a talent go to waste, sit down and tuck in."

The aroma of fried mushrooms was scintillating, and the taste just delectable, as was the smooth herb bread. Melea knew the ins and outs of the forest kitchen like no one else; simple ingredients and suitable spices could really do wonders. The next day I would prepare a meal, and already knew what it was going to be.

All the time we were talking to each other, speaking about what we intended to do in the following days. Melea was a good listener and she knew a lot about Pentelia and places where we could get a map, suitable weapons, decent equipment and of course some ideas about how to reach our goal. We planned to plunder the infamous and forgotten grottos, tombs or dolmens, wherever it was possible, to get some treasure, all the booty would be divided in half. Chewing hot mushrooms in gravy, I knew that she would be a splendid supporter.

As soon as we finished the meal, Melea smiled. "Ready for morning training?" She tried to make me lose my balance, walking a few steps, and pulling out her practice sword. "Show me what you've got!"

I took out my wooden weapon, determined not to let her beat me like last time. Having attacked first by cutting and striking, she rebounded to my left and slashed from one side to the other, our tempo was equal and worthy of admiration.

I managed to turn and block her strike, at the same time Melea attacked swinging herself onto the other side; she was much faster than me.

"What's the matter, sleepyhead? Stop pretending and fight!" She deflected when I finished my attack; Melea knew exactly what my weak points were.

I grabbed my sword with both hands and started to rush my opponent. At the last moment she got out of the way, almost tripping me at the end.

Now it was her turn to attack. Breathing heavily and seeking my vulnerabilities, she aimed at my heart and my neck. I barely managed to fend off two quick thrusts and catch my breath. Melea jumped and almost stabbed the right side of my chest, thanks to the technique more than her strength; her attacks were well performed and sophisticated. She was focused on the anticipation of the ideal moment to attack an opponent.

I can't fight back. Thinking about her strikes, too frequent to be honest, I often had to leap to the side and back.

I did notice one thing: while she was attacking, her reversing hand was taking her too long to cover her body. That could be my chance in the next close encounter. I started to back away three steps, Melea followed me brandishing her blade, and waving it in front of my chest. When she attacked again, I dodged and stood directly in front of her unprotected chest. I raised my sword lightly and pointed it at the target. My opponent did not manage to withdraw her hand to protect herself; Melea dropped the weapon as a sign of surrender. Satisfied with winning, I wanted to whisper something into her ear, but she took my gesture in a totally different way.

"Hey, we're just partners, so no such things, all right?" She stopped my head with her finger.

"What things?" I did not get what she meant but I noticed that she was pleased with my progress. Such everyday skirmishes show our mistakes so we can learn to correct them.

We sat down in the shade of the trees enjoying cool refreshing water with mint leaves; the wind was pushing its way between the branches, bending them slightly. The smell of the forest, the gentle warm sun, and the pleasant blue sky filled me with peace and joy; the silence was interrupted by a nearby stream and birds tweeting, the time was passing so quickly.

The green grass sprinkled with morning dew smelled lush and soothing. I opened my right eye and glanced at Melea, lying beside me, grateful that fate or destiny had brought us together.

Melea got up and nudged me with her foot. "Get up lazy bones! Time to get more active." We began to run at a steady pace between the trees and hills, the rays piercing through the leaves and branches fell onto the ground, making the serene sun look magnificent.

"We'll practice every day," she said. "First the fight, and then other exercises like stamina, sneaking, climbing and archery. Have you ever shot a bow?"

"Hmm... no, Uncle only showed me how to fish."

"Splendid, you will be my first apprentice." She smiled and suddenly changed direction. I had to jump over a small ditch to keep up with her pace.

Melea had a perfect sense of orientation, based on the surrounding vegetation she knew in which part of the forest she was. She explained a number of simple rules and I listened intently; her knowledge about living in the forest was tremendous.

Just like she promised, Melea taught me how to use a bow, the result was not good, but at least I could hit near the target. Unlike me, Melea could shoot a moving object with her eyes closed. While I was throwing the shield up in the air, she would pull her arrow and hit it every time.

Maybe I was exaggerating a little, but I had an excellent teacher for throwing light weapons. I looked in disbelief as she hit the target from improbable distances, right in the middle, and from different positions, hanging from a tree with her legs hooked over the branch, or while jumping from one tree to another. She took well-aimed shots; accuracy was her greatest advantage. We did not walk away too far from the hut to avoid attention, especially from merchants travelling on the nearby trade road. News travels fast around the Land.

In the afternoon we had hazelnut salad and fresh berries. Melea wanted to practice some sneaking, she did not cope well but she learned quickly though, and for the ground exercises we used the cottage with its creaking floor. I placed an object in the middle of the kitchen and sat down next to it blindfolded. Melea had to sneak in without making any sound at all.

"Stiffen your legs and relax your breathing." I repeated, and finally she got it. By the fourth time, she performed the task deftly and silently setting her knife to my neck, she managed quite well. I took off my blindfold and tried to get up, but she did not let me, pressing the blade to my neck.

"I want to do it faster, please stay here one last time."

"Sure, this time, try to replace my sword with something else."

My partner was ambitious, and I covered my eyes once again listening carefully. In less than three minutes, Melea began to laugh. She had replaced my sword with a wooden cup filled with water taken from a cupboard, all of this without the least little murmur, she was pleased with her progress.

The sneaking training was finished, and our journey, the adventure full of treasures and dangers, was soon about to begin. With Melea's help, after two days I did not feel the effects of my fall into a rushing river; her herbal concoctions and potions quickly restored me to full strength.

While we sat down to our meal, Melea told me how every time she tried to go around and snatch a knife, her initial failures were related to her attitude, she wanted to do it too fast. Sneaking around trees requires great skill and speed, but not on the ground, where calm and composure is needed.

The sun had already gone behind the horizon; the last bright orange glow disappeared, giving way to the night. Inside the house I felt safe and cosy, a fire in the chimney was crackling cheerfully, scented with cones and resin, while darkness embraced the entire forest, all night animals were peeking out from their nests and hideouts.

"Good night." I disappeared into my room, and closed the door, pleased with how the recent days had gone. Lying on the mattress with my hands under my head, I stared at the ceiling unable to sleep, thinking about the past few days.

What should I do? During this short time so many things had happened. Melea had become special to me. I thought about her intriguing looks and wondered how her lips would taste; I tried to imagine her standing naked.

Stupid, we're only partners, we share half and half. Why everything is so complicated? I closed my eyes, thinking about her smile and almond-shaped eyes.

I got up and walked silently to her room, Melea had fallen asleep a long time ago, but she was fidgeting from side to side, having a restless dream. I thought she murmured, "Tibbach". Kneeling beside her, I held her hand, stroking it to calm down the rough waves of her nightmare.

"I'm he..."

She grabbed me tight, and clung to my hand, she did not want to let go. I had to lie down on the floor beside her, maybe it was not too comfortable, but I had to sleep to gather my strength and rest. I stayed in that position, holding Melea's hand and dreaming about her, I could tell you this dream but, honestly, nothing exciting happened.

It is difficult to survive in the forest at night; it is only superficially calm. If you were a small forest creature leaving its burrow as soon as night falls, the slightest sound would make your hair stand up and your jaws begin to tremble. Cold air piercing into your lungs, and the glow of the moon lighting you wherever you hid, thousands of eyes staring at you, changing their shape and size, protruding from every dark recess, patrolling each space between trees and roots. If you think, you are safe, better think twice, the bloody pursuits, yelping of injured animals and hastily attacking predators. Now imagine the circumstances in which I had to get up in the morning and start preparing a surprise for Melea.

A wolf howled at the moon, which was dismissed slowly, giving birth to the new day. I woke up silently, observing the dawn. The silence was interrupted by a woodpecker tapping in the nearby tree, lazy rays of the sun were obliquely illuminating the cottage, and the first of them fell on the thatched roof.

Having freed myself from Melea's gentle clutches, I stopped in the doorway, looking at my sleeping companion, breathing steadily and quietly, the small knife was hidden under her pillow, she looked so innocent and dangerous at the same time.

I walked out of her room, closing the door softly, and began to bustle around the kitchen, preparing the necessary ingredients.

The rabbit stew should satisfy her palate. I remembered the easy recipe from Uncle's cookbook. When I used to look at page after page in that stout book bound in brown leather, I found many interesting notes. Uncle, of course, most valued country food; he despised the gifts of the forest, as he ate only animals.

I lit a fire under the stone stove, and prepared the ingredients such as herbs and spices along with essential mushrooms and roots, after a while the little animal itself was the only thing missing.

Silently I took a bow and arrows which were on the table in the corner, and two carrots as bait, only two chances to track down my prey. I left the house with a commitment to come back with a hunted animal. It would be excellent archery practice, and at the same time a delicious meal for breakfast.

Thanks to Melea, I was well informed about the forest, and paid attention to the things that seemed trivial to most people. Yesterday, when we ran together in the nearby area, I had discovered by accident the burrow-hole close to a small pile of stones behind a large oak tree next to the pine forest.

The arrows were resting in the quiver and the bow was slung over my shoulder, I did not put on my boots, most of the trappers did so, while hunting for small prey. Following a forest path, carefully looking around, I was examining the litter in search of clues. Melea taught me how to recognize them both, animals and human.

The hike to the rabbit hole passed fairly quickly, I tried not to make any noise because animals such as small rabbits have excellent hearing, the slightest crack of twigs may frighten them, it was the best way to prove one's skill.

While living with my uncle, he and Molten sometimes hunted venison in the nearby forest, so I knew that the hunter chose the ground for their game, not the other way round.

From my point of view the trench that was cutting through the forest deceptively resembled a miniature moat and the entrance to the burrow was dug in the middle of that small ditch, the whole glade was surrounded by small trees and shrubs. Smiling to myself at the sight of rabbit tracks, I stuck a carrot in the ground in the middle and at the end of the rabbit path.

Well rested and fully awake, I lurked on the higher ground ready for the game, the fresh forest air stimulated me with my every breath, and the chirping birds were soothing me in mysterious ways. Waiting motionless behind the bushes with all my muscles prepared and all my senses focused, the arrows were ready to go.

I imagined our breakfast. Melea would be full of joy when she stood up and smelled the rabbit stew, a smile on her face and a twinkle in her eye. Lost in that vision, I missed the moment when two rabbits dashed out of the hole.

Dammit! I set an arrow to the bow and tried to aim; small animals were running like mad, it was hard to spot them in the ditch. I pulled the string tighter and released the feathers. An arrow flew after a little hare, which jumped aside and stopped right in front of the shot driven into the wood stump.

Missed! Without thinking I reached for a second arrow and set it on a string, this time aiming on other prey, which had already approached the carrot. I had to lean right for a better view; the hare grabbed the bait in its mouth and jumped out of the ditch. I released an arrow when the animal was about to put his nimble feet outside, the arrowhead pierced it through, nailing it to the ground. I noticed another rabbit, which did not look back, only raced for its life.

Bull's-eye! I quickly ran to the game in fear that somehow it would be able to stand and escape, there was no trace of the other one. I broke the animal's neck so it did not suffer anymore.

The sound of the cracking bones was like whiplash, which awakened the birds sleeping on a nearby tree. Raising my head I saw a huge swarm of whitters flying over the treetops into the crystal clear blue sky.

***

A dozen or so furlongs from the spot of the hunting, on a small mountain dominating the surroundings, somebody was observing the forest. It was Zelur, one of Warend's subordinates, the smallest pilferer, an eagle-eyed man. When he was a young boy, he had a nasty accident in the mountains where he lost his eye in a skirmish with an eagle. A sudden movement in the sky made him notice the birds frightened by the hunter.

"Hey!" The observer began to yell. "Hey, chaps!"

Rekel walked towards him and punched him in the mouth.

"Idiot! Do you want someone to hear us? After the silver coffin incident chieftain is in disrepute these days, and we don't want to make it worse. We have to wait until he comes back with Jerch. Then everyone'll get their booty from this youngster's knapsack. What's so important?"

"I noticed some birds which flew into the air in the north-west part of the forest, fearful about something."

"Is that it?" Rekel snorted indignantly. "That's all you have to say, yelling like a street vendor at the bazaar?" He was about to punch him one more time when he stopped, his eyes began to scan the horizon.

"North-west part you said?"

"Yep. It's a secluded area, not inhabited by anyone."

Rekel walked away, thinking frantically. "Are you sure about the direction?"

"I swear by my only eye," he affirmed with a hint of madness.

***

Melea greeted me with an undisguised smile on her face, and then took two plates from the cabinet.

"Good morning, how was the hunting?"

"How did you know?"

"The smell says it all." She smiled, sitting at the table.

I served her the juicy rabbit with vegetables on a wooden dish; she relished my cooking.

"So, what did you use for bait? Carrots from the pantry?"

I wondered how she knew. Had she guessed that I had spent all night in her room, with my hand under her cheek? While Melea was eating the stew, I mentioned to her about the hunt, and the practice with a bow, looking at her eyes I could tell she was impressed.

After the meal, it was time for morning training. These were the last days, so the sword fight was different to the previous one. We each had a long wooden sword and a wooden dagger in the other hand. We stood with our backs to each other in the middle of the field, bathed with the rays of the sun; the blowing wind was cooling our bodies.

"Are you ready?" Melea, adjusted the grip of her dagger. "This time it shall be a duel to death. Agree?"

"A duel to death? With a wooden weapon? We're not children."

"Whoever strikes first will be the winner."

"What will the award be for the winner, then?" Melea rolled her eyes guessing my intention, while I stood grinning.

"Let the winner take it all!" Melea jumped back exactly when I did, she turned left and tried to stab me in the back. Dodging to the right, I blocked the attack, we both crossed our weapons again at the same time; she stepped on my foot and tried to push me, I had to knock her down myself.

We whirled on the ground. I lost my sword and landed on Melea, pinning her with my body. She crossed her sword with a dagger and blocked my attack, holding both the weapons. My eyes fixed on my lost weapon. That second was enough to throw me off, flipping rapidly I grabbed my sword firmly preparing to parry my opponent.

Another attack, Melea stroked with the right side, aiming at my ribs while her left hand armed with dagger tried to stab my heart. Willing to improve the cut, she immediately jumped to the side attacking with the push.

Circling and choosing the right moment, Melea jumped with her sword outstretched and was about to stab me, I dodged grabbing her wrist and twisting her hand behind her back. I was just about to stab her with the dagger, when she knocked me again, this time landing on top, her knees were pinning my hand with the sword.

With all her strength she tried to reach her dagger lying a foot from my head, she leaned and grabbed it. I did the only thing I could: I kissed her.

For a moment, I had a feeling that she might kiss me back, but the impression burst into thousands of pieces, when I felt a light kick in my balls. Literally in that second I noticed desire, fear, curiosity, anger and something else in her eyes.

"What was that?" She asked lying next to me.

"That was a sweet taste of victory." I smiled, rubbing my injured part; I knew that she was only pretending to be angry.

"What victory? None of us has been stabbed."
With great surprise I put the wooden weapon to her heart.

"Now you have." She looked at me in disbelief and shock. "You cheat, how could you?"

"I'm sorry, I was just curious."

"You've been curious if I'll open the door and let you in?" She made a funny move with her eyes.

"No! It's not that! I have wondered how your lips taste." I looked deep into her eyes, perhaps too deep for that situation.

"Well, how do they taste?"

"Like the morning dew on a ripe, sweet strawberry." I noticed out of the corner of my eye how she smiled, and slid her tongue over her lips.

"Enough dreaming you foolish boy, time for some tree jumping."

"Oh no, not again!" I moaned and, dusting my clothes, followed her. She taught me how to move quickly through the trees.

"You have to maintain balance at all times, and look where you put your feet..."

"Or else a small mistake could end with a fall." I finished the sentence for her.

When I climbed the chestnut tree holding myself with two splitting branches, Melea was already on the next tree waving to me.

"Choose stiff branches and make your decisions quickly." She was repeating over and over again. Taking her advice, I jumped onto the next branch, which cracked with my weight, but at the last moment I saved my skin by holding onto a tougher one.

"And if you've already used the soft ones, try to hold onto the branches above." Melea was only a short distance from me.

"I was thinking, we can easily get a proper climbing set in one of the shops in Pentelia, don't you think?" I asked her, coming down the tree.

"We'll purchase the necessary equipment, and the next day we'll set off, is that all right?"

"Sure, but may I ask why you wish to stay overnight?"

"Being your first time in town you never know, you could witness an occasion to attend. Let's see what Pentelia has to offer us. Have you ever been there?"

"Unfortunately, my uncle never took me there." I answered a little confused and embarrassed. Melea must have noticed because she quickly added, "No need to worry, except for Pentelia and my own town, I haven't been anywhere."

While we sat together on the porch, Melea entered the cottage for a moment, and after a while she came out with a yellowed piece of paper, it was a map of this part of the Land. She spread it on the table and pointed somewhere in the middle.

"We're here, tomorrow we'll arrive in Pentelia, the capital city of the Land."

I looked at the distance between our current position and the black dot, on the map it looked like about five fingers which was almost one day's journey, it would be much faster using horses and travelling on the side roads of course.

"Behind the city gates there are many possibilities, all kinds of shops and services, smiths and war-craftsman, armourers and wise wizards. Just ask around a bit and you'll get some leads on abandoned mines and other places filled with valuable ore." Melea's eyes sparkled as she mentioned it; the adventure was stimulating us in such a magical way.

I did not want to admit the thought that once the adventure was over, there would not be any caves to plunder, vaults to rob or enemies to massacre, we had all the time in the world, no one was chasing us, except maybe Warend and his gang. The Land was so extensive I was glad I did not have to explore it alone, having the greatest companion; two adventurers are surely better than one.

It was getting dark so we went back to the cottage and Melea cooked supper. I set the table and we both ate with an appetite. She speared a fried yellow chanterelle with her fork.

"Can I see it?" She swallowed a morsel.

"See what?" I was not sure what she meant by that.

"The gold of course, what else did you think?"

The bag full of shiny ore lying on the table looked like a small fortune, but for us it was just an investment, a key to success.

"Let's divide the contents into two parts, it'll be much safer to carry." While I started to share the amount, Melea grabbed one piece carefully tracing its glossy surface as if reading the future with this piece of rock, which aroused such passion in people.

"With this, we can buy excellent equipment." She hid the purse carefully at the bottom of her knapsack, and yawned widely covering her mouth with her hand.

"Get some sleep, tomorrow will be a great day." I went to my room, where all I dreamed about was the comfortable mattress.

~ Chapter .4. The great preparations. ~

Meanwhile, a dozen or so furlongs north-west of the cottage, in the great city of Pentelia, preparations were underway for the wedding. The king's daughter Sara, the only heiress to the throne, was getting married to Count De Marge.

From morning to late at night there was a great uproar, everyone helped as they could, cleaning the streets, the main ones were even embellished with intricate ornaments and flowers. On each city gate there was a big poster representing the celebrations that were about to happen in the coming days. The city could not remember such a celebration since the king was crowned.

There was enough work in the palace for everyone, even for the king himself who was trying to keep an eye on every detail, from the guests' accommodation to the taste of the food. Three days before the ceremony he ordered the rooms to be prepared for far-off guests, the elite people who always attend such events. After several visits, they think of the palace like a second home. If the king is paying, why not? The cream of society are like leeches, waiting for any occasion to get drunk, stuff their bellies and mock the poor and oppressed, having fun at their expense.

The guest list was announced including Baroness Virgil, a moaning and whinging close aunt of Sara. She was one of those who had a permanent place in the palace. Baroness Virgil always wished to be seated at the side to be able to observe the dresses of other elite women from different manors and to comment loudly on what their husbands were eating and drinking. Just like last time, she was occupying a room on the fourth floor.

The baroness's chamber was versatile and sophisticated, indeed, this was a room designed for the elderly and demanding woman: soft carpet, embroidered curtains and bedding along with a canopy. A small bookshelf and a couple of pieces of wooden furniture surrounded the stone chimney, all decked in blue which was calming for the baroness. As a result, she felt almost at home and did not have such strong headaches as she did when staying in the other rooms.

Beside Baroness Virgil many other splendid guests with all sorts of titles would soon be arriving in Pentelia to please the King with the news, ideas, or speak about raising tolls, duties, taxes and customs. All respected people have to somehow support their families and mansions.

Unfortunately it was a difficult time for the Land. People complained about rising taxes, incompetent politicians, corrupted judges and dignitaries fulfilling their duties lazily and charging fees for any small thing, just to fill their private vaults and send a small part of it to the royal palace.

The magnates, lords and other noblemen and landowners had been deliberating every month, quarrelling incessantly. The meetings sometimes lasted for a long time and some of them ended in chaos. Each congregation discussed the problems of slavery, harlotry and differences in wealth and racial hierarchy. It was all written down and switched to the statutes, regulations and ordinances, which every citizen had to respect and obey.

Widespread pestilence and famine were just a few problems that faced the king, however, today the royal's mind was focusing only on the wedding.

The man entered the Great Room dressed in a red cape with white fur, his greying head solemnly held a golden crown with gems. It was Horen, ruler and conqueror of the wild tribes who were plaguing the central part of the Land, an obliging man, very righteous, gracious and beloved by all.

Surveying the arrangements, his eyes focused on the long tables with white tablecloths and floral decorations offering scent and colour. He was pleased with what had been done so far. Large mirrors were on the walls, above them white and red curtains, and huge chandeliers with elegant pearl candles hung from the ceiling. All silver dishes and cutlery were bespoke especially for the ceremony; each vessel contained the royal emblem and initials of the bride and groom.

The Great Room was decorated in honour of the bride symbolizing a meadow full of flowers, lots of them; the aroma filled the entire palace, and the green carpet under the tables only intensified the feeling that everything was fresh and delicious. Flowers could be found everywhere, in bowls, in every corner of the room and along the walls, even in pots on each table.

Sara truly had green fingers and everything was blooming in her garden, she had more than two hundred species of plants, multi-coloured, small and large, fragrant and inodorous, everything one's heart would desire to have. It was difficult to maintain the garden so there were twenty gardeners responsible for decorating, planting and sowing.

The king sat on his throne satisfied, imagining that day when his daughter would finally be married, when they all would have supper in honour of the royal couple.

Horen began to think about his future son-in-law, he had not heard much about the wooer of his beloved daughter as they had met only once at the ball. He did not have a chance to talk with the Count face to face.

The king's advisors assured him that De Marge was from a noble family well known in the entire Land as winemakers and the young Count was a perfect candidate for a future ruler of the Land. The king received as an engagement gift a barrel of noble and exquisite wine, which was still lying intact in the basement.

But there was another thought disturbing the royal's mind; De Marge was coming from the manor adjacent to the Southern Wasteland, where Horen's evil and treacherous brother Serner lived. The king shivered at the thought of his brother.

It was a story that everyone knew, the father of two brothers wondered whom he could pass the sceptre of authority to when the time came. As a final solution, he chose a duel. "The one who kills the other will become the new king."

The brothers stood facing each other and began to fight for the Land, a duel to the death. Serner was attacking viciously, hitting everywhere to hurt his competitor, to kill his foe. Horen defended himself bravely, in contrast to Serner he had learned his lesson from the royal court of warfare. One smooth movement of the sword robbed his brother of his weapon,

Serner looked at the enemy with bitterness. "What are you waiting for? Kill me!"

The winner spared his brother's life and cradled his crying sibling to his chest. The king had no doubt to whom he should leave the throne. Since then, Horen was named "Gracious"; he saved his opponent's life, knowing that Serner, who was an unscrupulous man, would have killed him.

After the death of king, the defeated prince moved away from Pentelia and settled somewhere on the far side of the Land, across the southern belt. He never invited Horen to visit and the king did not want Serner at the wedding of his daughter, knowing the real nature of his brother.

While Horen was deep in thought, suddenly he smelled burning; he jumped up and walked towards the kitchen. All known dishes from over the kingdom were being prepared by not only municipal and court cooks, but also chefs invited from distant recesses.

Hundreds of piglets, calves and lambs were being slaughtered for the ceremonial feast, in two days the palace would have many mouths to feed so the king had sent for his hunters.

"You have to bring to the kitchen several of every sort of bird that inhabits our forests. The Laird of Scarborough Fair will be one of our guests, he is well known for his refined taste and likes sparrow in mint sauce or pigeon stuffed with plums." The hunters looked in disbelief at their king.

"I know it doesn't sound too appetizing, but we have to rise to the occasion. Tell the mushroom pickers and swineherds so that they can provide some truffles."

"Your Majesty, the transport with the fish has just arrived," said one of the servants.

"Just as Your Majesty ordered, fat and juicy."
The king smiled at the sight of the baskets full of seafood. "Splendid! Make sure they scrape the scales immediately."

He turned again to the hunters. "Go now, just don't forget about the fussy Laird."
The leader of the hunters winced again. *How can you eat a sparrow in mint sauce?* He shook his head and led his men to leave.

"I can bear partridges and pheasants, but pigeon stuffed with plums? Those bourgeoisie are..."

Luckily for this man, the king was not listening, he only wished to spend some time with his daughter, who has just returned from the engagement ball.

Horen briskly climbed to Sara's chamber on the fifth floor where she was preparing for bed. He knocked twice and entered the room, breaking the conversation between the princess and her nanny, who had served over the years as a babysitter, chaperone and maidservant.

"Your Highness." The older woman bowed and curtsied, lifting the hem of her dress.

"Oh, hello father. What brings you here at this time, I thought you were sleeping?"

"And let the whole preparation be unsupervised? Over my dead body," replied Horen, taking his daughter in his arms once she had finished changing into her nightwear.

"The only person who is able to organize this celebration from the beginning till the end is standing right here." He pointed proudly at his chest, grinning widely. "I only hope that you like the Great Room."

"I was just talking to nanny about the decorations, they really look marvellous. The castle in Countberg was scarcely a shadow of our splendour."

"I'm glad to hear that, my sweet daisy but, remember, lavishness and grandeur are the pride of people for whom only money has any value. Modesty is one of the greatest virtues; don't forget about it when I'm gone."

"Don't say that. You're not going anywhere, yet."

"You're right. How was the ball? Did you have a good time?" The princess yawned, covering her mouth with her hand. "I'm exhausted, let's talk about this tomorrow at breakfast."

"Scrambled eggs with bacon?"

"And two toasts. Good night, Papa, sleep well."

"Welcome home, sunshine." Horen left her chamber and closed the door.

"Where is it, has he seen it? Did you cover it properly?" Whispered Sara to nanny, turning down the bed and adjusting the pillows. The chaperone was unpacking the travelling trunk full of magnificent tunics, dresses and other items. One of them was the undergarment that she and the princess where discussing.

"It's right here. You want me to get rid of it, Princess?"

"Yes, at once." She covered her face with her palms, holding her breath for a moment.

"Remember, you promised me, don't mention it to anyone, come what may!" Sara, in disgust, observed how the woman took out the underwear stained with blood and threw it into the burning flames of the fireplace.

"There, no evidence left. I'll take this secret with me to my grave, but mark my words I'll have no respect ever for your so-called husband to be." Nanny blew out the candle, leaving the princess alone in her dark room, along with her thoughts.

~ Chapter .5. The unexpected guests. ~

Warend took Jerch's body down from the horse and looked at his gang, no one even realized that he had arrived, he roared briefly. Everyone began to bustle around, getting up from the pallets, putting on the slacks and joining the others. The majority of the group stood in a line, half of them were looking at Warend, the others were whispering about the unconscious Jerch and his hand covered with blood and rotten leaves, which only worsened the condition of his wound.

"All right ladies, listen up..."

"It looks even worse than the last time," whispered Rekel.

"Mostir told me that the dagger pierced his hand throughout." "You two, shut up!" Warend hated it when someone interrupted him.

"Chief, I know where they are," announced Zelur with a smile on his face.

"Where?" asked Warend.

"In the north-west part of the forest."

"Don't give us that bullshit!" Mostir, the same as Rekel, smacked the one-eyed man in the head. Everyone gathered laughed and Zelur fixed his hateful gaze at his companion, only the ringleader appreciated the value of this information.

"Did you mean in..." the chieftain stopped him rubbing his head.

"Aye!" Zelur nodded and Warend turned towards the rest.

"Listen up, stinkers! We're going to the north-west forest." The whole band began to ask questions.

"But Chief, how do you know that..."

"Shut up!" Warend took out the smallest lump of gold that he had found in a purse with the sand. At the sight of this small and glowing pebble, everyone moved forward gathering around and taking a better look.

"The lad surely had the whole knapsack full of it, we just have to take it away and Jerch will do the rest." While he hid the ore, the golden magic spell stopped working, even Zelur moaned softly.

"Prepare the horses! They have to be ready in an hour, the sooner we leave, the better we'll be able to track them down."

"I got it," said Rekel and, taking a few companions with him, went out to saddle the palfreys.

"Give me something to eat, I'm starving," said Warend. Combing his hair and coming across a bump, he frantically thought about the night skirmish. He had not realized that the bowl of nourishment was already in front of him.

I had him like a sparrow in the hand, yet that escapee has more luck than sense. I'll never get back the lost thieves' honour, letting him get away with it. Warend stirred the food with a spoon.

He had heard a lot of tittle-tattle about the north-west forest. Stories about a virgin forest abyss inhabited by some terrible creatures. Apparently someone had once been told how one man ventured into the green and untamed depths. No one knew what creatures or what secrets were hidden behind such dense growing trees, it was a question for travellers, merchants and cartographers.

Jerch sat down opposite Warend and received a portion of the nourishment, and tucked into his food with his right hand. The left one was lying limply on the table, and had now taken on a purple-green colour and the thug was able to move only one finger. Warend's meal cooled down while he was thinking.

He took a pebble from his pocket and began to rotate it, observing how it shone in the dancing flames of the torch. Warend fixed his gaze at the cold dish, snorted resignedly having lost his appetite and pushed the bowl to a safe distance. He got up from the table and went to the middle of the grotto, where people had almost finished their duties and stood in front of him.

"Horses are ready?"

Rekel nodded.

"Good. We'll set off to the north-west part of the forest. I know, I know, it's a strange piece of the Land which hasn't been yet penetrated, I've seen for myself a mysterious force deflecting the tree as if some troll or a giant walked that way, but it was just the wind. Get ready because we're going for the hunt.

"Our target is the lad who deprived your comrade of his hand, and his knapsack full of gold. I'm warning you, he's not alone anymore, he's accompanied by an elfgirl." He looked at those who made some comments about it, someone even whistled softly at the news. "Don't be fooled, she's the devil incarnate, she knocked me with a regular stick." After these words the satisfaction immediately disappeared from their faces.

"Take everything you need, I'd like to see an extra weapon on each one of you!" At these words Rekel looked at Jerch and grinned.

"A knapsack full of gold is about to fall into our hands. Think how you'll spend your share."

"I'll buy a pony, because of the horses my butt hurts," said one from the group.

"I'll buy a new shiny sword," said the next one.

When everyone was exchanging their ideas, Warend beckoned Jerch and Rekel and stepped with them to the side. "I'm appointing you two to be my helpers." He looked straight into their eyes, outlining the seriousness of the conversation and their new position.

"We'll split up into three smaller groups, four men each. Tell me, who do you think this youngster is?" Rekel and Jerch looked at each other, none of them had any idea what the ringleader was talking about.

"Yes, we didn't introduce each other, but think about the profession of that man."

"He's a pilgrim," retorted Rekel.

"It's... just a youngster," added Jerch dully.
Warend slapped himself on the forehead and his hand slipped down his face. *Why did fate chastise me with such imbeciles?* "You're right, Rekel but he's not a usual pilgrim. You're also right, Jerch." He patted the thug on his healthy shoulder. "He's not an ordinary youngster; he's someone much more important." He stepped away from them and turned back.

"He's a courier."

Jerch opened his mouth and began to scratch his head. This message did not make a great impression on Rekel either. Warend took the dagger from his belt and showed it to them carefully. Jerch frowned, staring at the blade. *How come it was in the possession of the ringleader?*

"Look at the handle." Both thugs were thinking frantically, such an amusing sight, indeed. Warend was losing his temper, pointing at the symbol on the handle.

For Rekel surely it would ring a bell. He was playing with his moustache, staring at the shape, an eagle with a sceptre and sword in its beak. Fate made such a symbol. He finally said, "I've seen this symbol, somewhere." Warend looked at him in disbelief. "This shape has the royal coat of armour," he finally stammered.

"Bravo!" shouted Warend. "This unusual young traveller is a courier. Look carefully, that's King Horen's seal, burned on the handle of the dagger. I used to have a similar one when I worked for a short period as one of them. Such a dagger acts like a pass, when you show it, you can move on. Does this tell you something?"

"The owner of this blade is a royal courier."

"The king has a lot of gold," said Jerch.

"Good thinking." Warend patted the giant's back again. "This knapsack is just a small part of the treasure."

At this point, he looked at Jerch. "You'll have to spare him." He sensed the sinister intention of the lout and silenced him with a single gesture. "You shall have your revenge, but first he'll show us the royal treasure. After that, you can do with the courier whatever you want."

Jerch was about to say something, but Warend jumped the gun. "They always send two couriers, one with the guards and the other on its own. The first courier, the one with the guards, bears fake gold or just a small part of it; no one realizes that the package is actually in the backpack of the second courier. That's why we were waiting here, close to the bridge."

Jerch and Rekel were listening intently, the giant was scratching his head, staring at the wall. Rekel was playing with his moustache.

"Gather a group and don't tell anyone about the courier, he has to live. With the elfgirl, do whatever you want, but honestly and honourably. I'll never forgive her for last night."

"Never say never," murmured one of the thugs. Warend threw a glance at his soldier and his face turned red.

"Chief, are you sure about appointing Jerch as the second leader?" A malicious spark flickered in Rekel's eyes. "He'll not be able to wave when he finds a clue." He snorted and began to gesticulate at Jerch. The whole group, excluding Warend, started clapping and laughing, Jerch was silent despite the numerous jokes and comments that he had to listen to all the way. Keeping silent, he was saving his words and sword for the right moment to strike.

The long hours of the strenuous journey were dragging on unmercifully; the fatigue was making everyone miserable. They rode up the hill in the north-east part of the forest and stopped close to an old oak tree growing on the top. The tired horses snorted loudly and lowered their heads to gnaw some fresh grass.

What a breathtaking view, I wonder if any artist could capture it on his canvas thought Warend, admiring the landscape. The trees were growing close to each other, creating a perfect unity like a green castle. In some places wide branches were entwined with each other, the tree trunks were the walls with the spreading crowns of the roof. From a distance, even Zelur could not see the slightest gap.

The sun was setting in the west like a golden egg falling into a nest of darkness. Warend sent four horsemen to explore the place, to see how they could get into the forest.

"Why the hell did you drag us here? We could circle the forest from the other way," shouted Rekel aggressively, while a couple of heads nodded in agreement. Jerch snorted at him, he knew exactly how to deal with such unscrupulous men.

"Better to be safe than sorry," answered Warend and smiled at the sight of the scouts, who had found the suitable place to enter.

When they managed to set foot in the forest, the gang looked around anxiously; the sun barely shone through the trees and a fearful silence surrounded them. They could hear the last murmur of the wind passing between the branches. In this unexplored territory, the smallest mistake could cost them their lives.

They marched for a couple of hours, slowly in a line, leading the horses by the bridle; Jerch was closing the cortege, urging the stragglers. The road was not easy, turning all the time and sometimes, they had to even go back, choosing a different path, encountering quicksand and swamps. They were blinded so much by the thought of all the gold that they did not know they were being watched.

When someone suggested a break they all gladly agreed, exhausted and dead tired, no one was able to fight, nor to follow the trails. They walked a few steps further, and before them stretched a glade, it was a perfect place to rest, well protected and covered from all sides. At its centre grew a pair of wind-bent pines, the bark was peeling off one of the trunks as if a raging beast had sharpened its claws right there.

The gang set the camp under the pines, where finally they could seat their aching legs on the ground and rest. They decided to take a nap for an hour.

Warend beckoned Jerch and Rekel. "I'm glad we travelled so smoothly, however, I have a feeling that the courier will leave soon." Rekel nodded and exchanged glances with Jerch.

"He'll try to get to Pentelia. Tomorrow is the king's daughter wedding, a peasant woman mentioned it when I bought eggs from her. Horen probably ordered some extra gold as a gift for his beloved Sara. Let's take a rest for an hour and then we'll move on." He buckled his coat and stretched his legs.

All of them laid down as comfortably as they could on the grass, while sleep overcame the travellers in a flash; no one noticed as the sun finished its journey in the sky, hiding behind the horizon. The forest changed its colours and began to look scary and gloomy, on the dark curtain a shiny moon appeared, surrounding the sleeping ones with a milky glow.

Warend woke up at the sound of the grasshopper that had just landed on his nose. The man sprung to his feet, frightened and looking around. He yelled at the gang, why did no one wake him up, Jerch and Rekel looked at each other, laughing stupidly.

"Come on chaps, move it!" At Warend's command, everybody got up cursing him in secret, they had slept so soundly, the wind did not bother anyone and the soft ground imitated a comfortable mattress perfectly.

The gang entered an entirely different part of the forest, where the trees merged into one mass. Walking among the spruces in the middle, the firs and larches on the sides, it was a living nightmare, the branches and twigs were occupying every last space, growing so thick it was impossible to pass them without any scratches. If someone walked away a few steps from the path, he would disappear behind that natural obstacle.

Warend was walking as the leader, and marking the path, not worrying about those who were following. After half an hour of painful walking they trudged forward trying to get out of this forest hell.

"It's thicker than a hedgehog's ass. Are you sure it's the right way?" asked one of the band, rubbing his hands, the branches could scratch the skin leaving bloody marks.

"This is the only way." Warend stared at the darkening sky, guessing the time. When they finally came out into the clearing, they could hear the stream flowing nearby, all of them went to drink and wash after a close encounter with the flora.

"Are we there yet?" asked Rekel washing his chin and avoiding a cut under his left eye.

"We're approaching our goal."

"That's what you said before we packed up to go into these damn bushes!" protested Zelur.

"And you didn't mention anything about a wedding," added the other thug.

"We could ambush the youngster from the other side, closer to the city! Perhaps you should think about changing profession, you're getting sluggish, Warend," tossed vicious Rekel.

These words annoyed the ringleader, who approached Rekel with the intention of hitting him. Warend raised his hand, but controlling himself, crushed the thug with a glare and walked past.

Relieved, Rekel went in the opposite direction towards Jerch and they began to whisper to each other. Warend recalled the rumbling words in his ears.

You are too sluggish the echo was repeating inside his mind, *maybe it's true, I should leave all this mess, get rid of this bloody hell band and settle down in some nice place.* Suddenly he heard Jerch's shout, and everyone looked in his direction.

"Say it again," threatened Jerch.

"What for? You don't understand anything you dunderhead," shouted Rekel.

"Don't you call me a dunderhead, you whiskered short-ass!" the thug drew his sword from its sheath.

"All right, from now on you're a crippled featherbrain," he mocked and pulled out his sword. "With only one hand you're worth a heap of meat. We should chop you into quarters and sell you. We'd get more gold for that."

Jerch swung his sword rapidly, just as Warend ran up and blocked the strike with his weapon, a dull metallic sound echoed around the trees. Everyone stared at them; no one dared to move, there was complete silence.

Through the centre of the glade, a delicate little zephyr blew several leaves down. They remained gently on the surface, drifting shoreward.

After the long minute, Warend lowered his weapon. Jerch did the same, pointing with unbridled animosity at Rekel's chest.

"I'll count all your bones, you squab, sooner than you think."

Rekel snorted putting his sword away. "Better count the fingers of your coloured hand," replied the whiskered thug. "Maybe you should stay in a cave making food for us, your crippled hand would replace the ladle perfectly."

All the thugs roared with laughter. If Jerch knew how to kill with his eyesight, Rekel, Warend and the rest would have fallen dead there and then.

"Shut up, both of you, that's an order!" shouted Warend, realizing that he could not control these two any longer.

To restore order he gathered the whole group; Rekel and Jerch were standing at each end of the line. The giant took his dagger and notched the skin of his inefficient hand. While the wound began to drip with some colourless pus, Jerch grabbed the flap of skin and ripped even more. Rekel shuddered with disgust, the sight terrified him, he could not take his eyes off the self-mutilating lout.

"We're so close now, a few hours and we'll find that youngster, and get ourselves a big payoff. Let's get through the next forest, I'm sure Zelur spotted those birds right there."

They gathered their belongings and decided to leave the horses. They were hungry and tired, and in the last two days they only had slept for a few hours, but, just like Warend, the treasure motivated them to march.

"Chief, let me have a look around and figure out our position." Zelur climbed to the very top of the tallest tree where he could see almost the entire area, fortunately, the smoke from Melea's cottage was not visible.

The one-eyed midget was a few feet above the ground when his left foot broke the branch; many of them laughed when he dropped on his butt directly onto the hard ground, Rekel was the loudest.

Laugh while you can you duff. Jerch looked at him, squeezing the hilt. *I'll rip that bitch's guts out and the pilgrim's too.* He grabbed a protruding branch nearby and broke it with his good arm into small pieces.

They divided into six pairs and lit the torches, the ground they moved over was tricky, often someone tripped on the roots sticking out. The silence was broken by the hooting of an owl and the hooves of other inhabitants of the forest. They were less than half a furlong from the cottage, walking side by side evenly, exploring the area and searching for some traces, when someone shouted, "I found something!"

A couple of thugs rushed to look, pushing one another over, surrounding the little ditch, where two rabbits were escaping. Warend lit the traces of dried blood, and Rekel sniffed it. Jerch observed him, hoping that it was not Aron's blood.

"It's a bunny's blood." He smelled one more time and was just about to taste it, when something flopped down on his head and splashed.

"What the…" He looked up and right after all the others gazed upwards. Whitters were sitting on the branches – white birds that looked like pigeons, they differed only in the shape and arrangement of their feathers and beak. The birds were sleeping soundly occupying all the branches of roughly half the tree.

"I saw those birds in the morning, Chief," said Zelur.

"He must be somewhere around," said Warend looking carefully

"He didn't gut the rabbit here, just took all of it. There are even some more traces there."

"Split up," announced Jerch, holding his sword in his hand.

***

I hardly slept that night, waking up now and then, watching the dark blue sky with countless numbers of stars blinking and shining so peacefully. The time dragged on, I wondered if Melea was sleeping.

Looking at her through the open door, I could see she was lying comfortably in the embrace of the blanket, with a pillow stuffed with leaves under her head. I was a little jealous; she did not have any problems falling asleep.

I went back to bed and lay down, putting my hands behind my head and staring at the ceiling, imagining the city market packed with stands and stalls, huge houses, streets full of shops, merchant booths, and everything surrounded by a thick, red brick wall. Molten had mentioned these wonders as he had made several visits to Pentelia admiring the large main roads that led to the palace or into the market where he bought his slingshot, with which I was so annoyed.

Vague thoughts bothered me, something was telling me to hit the road immediately. Should I wake up Melea, or not?

I looked at the handle of my new sword jutting out of my knapsack, I wanted to keep my mind busy and take a nap, even an hour would do me good.

***

The circle of exploration marked by the thugs was tightening with every moment; all of them were approaching its centre where the cottage stood. It was only a matter of time until they would discover how well camouflaged it was.

Jerch beckoned the four groups of companions, looking around to make sure Warend was not nearby.

"We're wasting time with Warend, we should attack our target instead of surrounding it."

"But the chief said, we have—" While Rekel started arguing, Jerch took a swing and without batting an eye, stabbed him with his sword.

"Does anybody else want to say anything about my coloured hand, or call Warend a ringleader?" Everybody was scared to death, they had never seen Jerch behave like that.

"You're coming with me, right? There are only two of them so we eight can easily handle it."

"But…" Someone wanted to say something, but Jerch gave him a black look. The thug immediately went silent, staring at Rekel's dead body. They were all frightened and obediently followed the lubber, who after a short walk led them straight to the wooden cottage.

Jerch smiled triumphantly. "Grab your weapons and don't regret it, inside sleeps one nasty elfgirl and the youngster, who took off my hand. Don't kill the pilgrim yet, Warend mentioned something about large amounts of gold; that could be our chance for a decent swag. You can take care of the elfgirl and do whatever you want, leave something for me when you're done." The robbers burst out laughing, grinning with their dark yellow teeth.

They decided to attack the cottage from different directions, one group at the back and the others from the front, Jerch kept waiting for the rest to smoke out the sleeping courier from the hut.

Crack. Melea opened her eyes and held her breath. Someone was recklessly approaching the cottage, breaking small sticks and branches. Each night she put them on the ground to make sure that no one would approach while they slept. Melea jumped quickly out of her bed and carefully unveiled the curtain in the window, there were two shapes, neither animal nor familiar ones. She grabbed her knapsack and ran to wake her companion.

The battue walked carelessly, stumbling over stones and roots approaching the first step of the stairs. The cabin in the woods looked scary, the dark interior absorbed them like the jaws of a monster. The kitchen still had the scent of supper, while their torchlight glinted menacingly on some of the surfaces, terrifying the hunters even more. Moving slowly they tried not to make too much noise, although the floor below them was creaking horribly.

They entered Melea's room and she squinted, staring at the doorway, just sitting and listening. The four rogues surrounded the mattress so that there was no possibility of escape. Lifting their arms they began to strike, stabbing the blanket, Melea closed her eyes.

A thug with a torch walked inside, they had to squint to see anything, the flames pierced the darkness, like a blade that had just stabbed the body. They watched the blood squirting from under the blanket. Now

Jerch would get the courier and they could snag the loot.

She didn't even have time to defend herself, thought one of the assassins, who wanted to see the victim they had brutally murdered while sleeping. Nobody liked the infamous assassin job, but someone had to do it. Leaning over the bed, he flung the blanket away with one swing.

"Holy cow!" They all turned pale, not knowing what to do, they ran quickly out of the room and went into the next one. This time the thug with the torch immediately pulled the blanket from the second mattress, a dead animal was lying there as well. Aron had planted these decoys together with Melea.

The villains made a huge mistake; walking into hunter's ground, they became the prey, finding themselves in an empty cottage, on a dark night, in one of the most tenacious forests in the entire Land. The horror was dominating the whole cabin was horror.

"Oh shit, now what?" Zelur looked around expecting an attack from somewhere.

"They could be anywhere. It's a trap, we have to warn Jerch." The assassins with a torchlight showed up in the threshold, as something hissed ominously.

"What are you waiting for?" murmured the closest one, as his companion did not answer. His body slammed onto the floor like a tree felled by a lumberjack.

"What's going on?" asked Zelur anxiously. An arrow was sticking out of the forehead of the body, pointing towards the ceiling; it was perfectly aimed right between the eyes. A trickle of blood flowed down the face like bloody tears.

Melea once again had proved her accuracy, aiming at the rogue's forehead from over fifty metres and in the dark. The robbers had woken her up and along with Aron they'd had time to collect their things and put dead animals into their beds. When the thugs entered the cottage, Melea had already closed the trapdoor in the floor. The remaining seven thugs started to run like headless chickens, screaming their lungs out and calling their leader.

***

Warend and Nakros stuck to the plan; they had no idea what had happened on the other side of the forest. They climbed a small hill to look for some other clues. Nakros missed his step on a rock and fell down, rolling off on the other side of the hill.

"Get up and let's move on, the pilgrim won't wait for us." Warend knelt carefully next to the broken twig, and looked around, but no one answered him. "Come on, move your ass! Where the hell..."

"Help!"

Not being sure what was going on, the ringleader went down carefully, and discovered his companion neck deep in the swamp. Nakros could not get out and every single move caused him to sink even deeper.

Warend pulled off a branch and handed it to the drowning man; only the top of his head was on the surface. Swearing under his breath he tried to pull the stick. Something was holding on to it, for a moment he thought it was his companion, yet seconds later Warend swayed and flew into the swamp, trying not to move and breathing shallowly.

***

The sky took on a dark metal colour, the clouds gathered above the forest, making it dark and chilly, the gusty wind began to blow in every direction, so hard that we had to hold on slightly, as if an invisible mouth was trying to blow us away from the branch, like a pollen from a dandelion.

"Chief, Lerg is dead! We were ambushed! Beds were empty!" All of them were shouting. Jerch hid the sword, and picked up the torch lying on the ground.

"Pilgrim, come here and face me like a man, you son of the sword," he squalled loudly, glancing around the nearby trees. Melea was about to aim an arrow, when I stopped her with one hand.

"What are you doing?" She stared puzzled, but one second was enough to understand my intentions.

"Are you sure you can handle this?" There was a concern in her voice.

"You still have doubts?" Landing softly on the litter, right next to me fell the first drop of rain. I had mixed feelings about my swift decision to approach my destiny in the form of Jerch, who was looking in my direction all the time. Stepping confidently, my heartbeat raced and the adrenaline was running through my entire body.

Heaven burst into tears, its drops were falling like sharp icicles on a winter morning. The pressure was growing with every step. Trying to master the fear and sharpen all my senses, I focused upon my foe. I wanted to end this duel as a final step towards my journey.

Grabbing my sword firmly and lifting it up, I stood in front of the giant, the rest of the thugs surrounded us keeping their distance.

"Ah, there you are," he scowled at me. "Remember this?" Barely lifting his rotten dead arm, Jerch yelled, took a swing, and threw his dying torch in my direction. Trying to dodge it, without a further word, he ran at me like a battering ram.

I flew a few metres away and landed on my back. The impact was so strong that it made me miss a heartbeat, lying on the ground and struggling to catch a breath my sword landed a couple feet away. I heard the others applauding and cheering fiercely, Jerch stepped on me almost crushing my ribs.

"Now, tell me everything about that dagger, or I'll gut you like a pig."

"Gerroff me. I don't know what you're talking about." Testing the patience of that meathead was not a good idea.

"Warend told me everything about the royal vault, and... wait a minute, where's that elf bitch?" At the same second an ominous swish came from one of his comrades, who fell dead with an arrow sticking out of the chest.

"Sharp elf, eh, have you tried her in the bed as well?" A peal of thunder hit somewhere close by, a flash of lightning illuminated my foe standing above me with his curved sword ready to chop off my hand. In the last moment I rolled over, but could not avoid the tip of the blade which pierced the skin on my chest below the shoulder, a pinching red mark which will no doubt become a scar.

"Get back here, you eunuch, I haven't finish with you."
Jerch's taunting comments made me angry, which in turn made me more ferocious. Hardly getting a chance to steady myself, I reached the sword and attacked with all my fury, striking my foe from the left, turning quick and slashing him from the right, thrusting above and cutting below. He was avoiding my strikes pretty well, thus all his movements were predictable too.

"You're stinging like a sissy, you can do better than that." His strong blow almost deprived me of my weapon, while his elbow striked my cheek, for a second my vision blurred and stars danced in front my eyes. Gritting my teeth and swallowing my hurt pride, I took a swing, and kicked that bastard straight in his balls. Nobody, especially him, expected such a jolt.

"Sissy my ass." The final cut ended the whole duel, thus a trickle of blood flowed on my blade, dripping onto the ground. Jerch stood motionless staring at the forest, as if a bolt had suddenly hit him.

Everyone froze with fear. After only a moment the coloured green and purple hand fell off from the rest of the body, blood was oozing out gently from the wound, and those who were close enough, could see the rotten wounded flesh.

I ran towards Melea, she jumped down from the tree and patted me on the shoulder with the red mark.

"I thought you might kill him." She rolled up my shirt and examined the wound, it did not look too bad.

"It'll heal up for your wedding, dear." She comforted me, and handed me my coat.

"I'll never get married."

"Don't be so sure, I have a feeling that during this journey you'll meet someone special." Tired and soaked to the skin, we collected our knapsacks, vanishing into the dark wet forest. Melea knew exactly where the gang had set up camp and left their horses. We chose the most rested animals grazing at the clearing. I helped Melea to mount the horse and handed her knapsack, then I hopped onto the saddle and together we trotted ahead.

Galloping straight onto the path leading to the exit of the forest, the earth was flowing out from under the hooves. About two hundred metres in front of us lightning struck setting fire to a tree that collapsed immediately blocking the passage. The horses sped up, bouncing off the ground and jumping over the trunk. We ran out of the woods, where the rain had lost its fury, and the clouds brightened a little.

The condition on the north road leading to the city was fine. The journey to Pentelia would only take a few hours, so we could rest for the remainder of the night at the porterhouse. I thought about the following days and smiled at the sound of the gold ringing quietly and pleasantly in my knapsack.

***

Jerch pulled himself together accepting another defeat; he wrapped his stump in a rag and picked up his chopped hand from the ground. Standing for some time in the rain, he swore to himself that one day Aron would pay.

The gang returned to the camp and immediately noticed Warend's absence. They did not know what to do, and sat in silence trying to keep warm with dying torches, no one dared to open their mouth. It was not long before someone discovered Warend fighting the swamp and crying for help, everyone climbed on the hill to watch as their former chief was clinging to a branch.

"Get me out!"

Jerch grinned and began to laugh, everyone looked at him like he was insane; Warend stared at him in disbelief.

"Rekel was right, you really are too sluggish."

"So, now you're in charge," he shouted, sinking another couple of inches.

"Now I'm giving the orders, I won't kill you like that lousy pig Rekel, I'll let you join him in a natural way." Jerch turned around to climb up the hill.

"Don't leave me here. I can still be useful. Give me your hand." The sinking man had immense will and pulled his right hand waiting for help, but he did not dare to move.

"Here, catch this." The lout threw his chopped off coloured hand at Warend's face. It sank in a second, he turned around and choking with laughter vanished from sight with the others.

Betrayed and left for dead, Warend cried aloud, so that all could hear him. "Mark my word you sons of bitches, it's not over yet!"

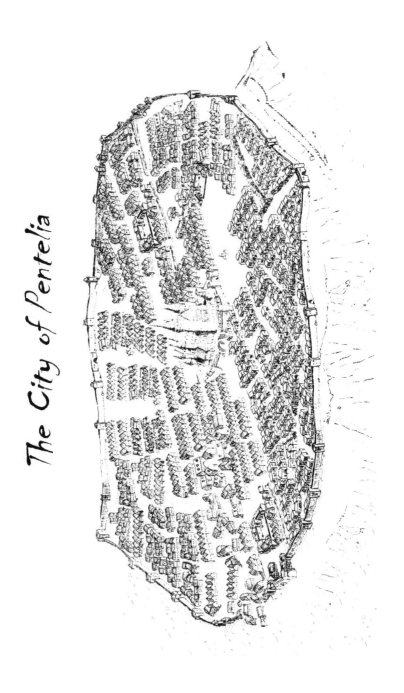

The City of Pentelia

~ Chapter .6. The porterhouse. ~

We let the horses breath a bit and slowed down their pace, at the sametimegiving my butt a bit of a rest from the constant hammering of the saddle. We turned right and slowly approached the eastern gate of the city, and the walls and all the buildings came into view, even though it was still dark, everything looked incredible.

The fortification was surrounding and protecting the contents like a giant's hands, the red brick wall was impressive, higher than the height of three men, stretching in both directions there was no end in sight. The last drops of overnight rain were dripping from the tin roofs, reflecting the light from the torches inserted a dozen or so metres apart.

"Behold, this is Pentelia, I've been here many times because my father's one of the Elders Council, invited by the king to various meetings, councils and official celebrations. For the first time in my life I've come here without my family, alone."

"You're not alone."

She looked at me and smiled. Closer to the wall the guards could be seen marching back and forth, their helmets and blades of halberds were shining in the moonlight. We drove up to the gate and stopped in front of two guards, both had black-ringed eyes. They had a pot of coffee from the canteen, and sipped the hot drink.

"Welcome to Pentelia. For what purpose are you coming into the city? If you have bad intentions, then leave immediately." One of the guards recited the greeting text that he was ordered to learn by heart. Not knowing what to say, I let Melea answer the question.

"Our intentions are pure, sir. We're just passing by, we'll stay at the porterhouse, a day or two, and then go on our way."

"Fine. I'll send for somebody to escort you to the inn." Just as he said it, he put to his mouth a carved whistle, and blew; the sound was probably heard within the next two towers. After a while, a short guard appeared, looking at us angrily. As opposed to the others, it seemed his armour was bespoke. "Are they registered?"

The sentry stood up and made a silly face, muttering that he had forgotten, and gave us the thick book bound in black leather, hiding his embarrassment in front of me and Melea.

"I don't know my father's name," I whispered, trying not to look suspicious. She knew that for my whole life I had lived with my uncle, and he never told me his name, bah, forget the name, he never mentioned anything related to him. Melea looked at me furtively; her eyes reflected the glow of the torch.

"Think up a name," she hissed through clenched teeth. The sentry was listening to our whispers, so Melea had to bestow him with a smile.

The short guard looked at her registration fee. "Why didn't you sign up together with the rest of your family, missy?" Melea looked at him.

"Your father has been at the palace for three days.' The sentry was clearly waiting for an explanation.

"Oh... you know, sir, I had to stay and settle some things at home." Now it was my turn. Inscribing my name, and avoiding the blank space "Name of the father", I passed to the date.

"Excuse me, what day is it today?"

"What is this? You do not know?" The guard looked at both of us in surprise.

"Today is a red-letter day, Princess Sara is getting married to Count De Marge," he announced with pride, as if he was the father of the groom.

Now I understood why Melea had asked me to stay in the city.

"The most distinguished guests from all over the Land will be gathered here, tomorrow. Today we are celebrating."

Melea blinked at me, smiling without hiding the joy. We could not have arrived at a better moment, the great event meant many visitors, and this in turn meant that all the shops would be open. Oh, how well it happened, that our uninvited guests chased us away that night.

I handed back the book, the guard took it without checking and set it aside. We were guided by the short knight, who conducted us through the gate. A big wooden door with solid pieces of metal held on two mighty hinges, which probably weighed a lot.

I was amazed at the way the city was protected. All the doors were unbreakable; it would take a huge battering ram and many hours of attacking for the gate to be surrendered. The wall was cleverly constructed; there was nowhere to attach a hook with a rope for climbing. Every hundred metres there were defensive positions where the enemy could be attacked from above.

The knight walked in front of us without saying anything, the silence was broken by the rhythmic beating of hooves on the cobbled road. On the way to the porterhouse, I tried not to miss anything while the streetlights lit our way. We passed wide streets dotted with shops, merchant houses, ale houses, gambling houses and brothels. These last ones, even at this late, or early hour adopt clients with pouches full of ducats.

"I hope you will not guzzle all the money and do not spend it on whores." Melea noticed as I stared at one of the brothels from which came the laughter mixed with groans of delight.

"I have never been in a brothel."

"And I hope that you never will"

In less than five minutes we were there.

"Enjoy your stay in Pentelia." The short guard disappeared, turning into the darkened lane.

We found ourselves in the city – a place where we planned to start our journey. While dismounting the horse, I could hardly feel my stiffened ass, it was good to stretch my legs after a five-hour trip. The light at the porterhouse was lit, in such a big city it was a normal occurrence, the guests were coming and going regardless of the time.

The building looked like a typical homestead, where travellers could board and lodge. Wooden walls and a straw roof did not mean that the inside was in a bad condition. On the contrary, it felt very homely, as it said on the sign above the door:

Make yourself at home, travellers

On the wall was the price list:

A bed for the night -- 8 denars + meal

7 days -- 50 denars + meals

Breakfasts -- 2 denars

Dinners -- 3 denars

Suppers -- 2 denars

Glancing at Melea, I asked in a whisper, for fear that someone would hear, "Do you know the value of our yellow metal here?"

"Unfortunately, I don't." She looked around, and after a moment the master of the house came out. He was of average height, with a storm of black hair on his head. His joyful eyes were looking at us, judging our profession and the weight of our purse. His nose looked like it had been broken in at least two places.

"Greetings honourable guests. What can I do for you?"

"We'd like a room for two nights if there's something free."

He looked first at me, then at Melea. "Of course, naturally, where are my manners?" He approached Melea and kissed her hand. "How was your trip, I hope not very exhausting?" He smiled, baring yellow teeth like a horse.

"Thank you, it was not so bad."

The innkeeper whistled. After a while a stable boy appeared, now and then stumbling over the straps of his shoes, he could have been at most fourteen years, his tousled chestnut hair and aquiline nose gave him roguish look.

"Make sure the horses are fed and given water." The innkeeper grabbed Melea by the hand and led us inside.

The interior had a homely atmosphere, under the windows there were braids of garlic. The wooden floor was worn and threadbare, but swept and clean; Melea was looking around curiously at every corner. The fireplace in front of the door warmed the room, and from the kitchen on the other side of the dining room came delicious smells, if the scent was not deceiving me, it was a roast.

The owner conducted us to the elegant, carefully washed, oak counter and quickly stood on the other side. He smiled at Melea. I looked at him a little annoyed.

"I wish to ask you, single or double room..."

We answered the question before had finished. "Double," Melea said at the same time that I said, "single". We looked furtively at each other; somehow I knew exactly what her expression was trying to say. "We're just partners, we'll take a double room."

"I'm sorry, but we only have a single room with a large bed. I must say, it's a nice cosy nest." The owner winked at me. "The rest are occupied and reserved for today's ceremony."

Melea nodded in agreement, frowning slightly. "We'll take it." When the housemaster turned to take the key, she whispered, "You're sleeping on the floor". I looked at her in surprise, after all the training and a night skirmish she was making me sleep on the floor.

"Shall I include the meals in the price?" The owner gave us the key.

"Just breakfast, sir. Tomorrow's the wedding and..."

"Are you invited to the ceremony?"

"Well, actually we want..."

"Yes, we're invited, I know the bride quite well," answered Melea.

"Have you heard the rumours about the groom?"

"No, what rumours?" Melea looked curious, whereas the master of a house grinned once again with his yellowed teeth, glad that he could interest his customer in conversation.

"They say that in his youth he had a terrible accident. Two people were killed, including his father. De Marge wineries make excellent wines, but they're located too close to the Southern Wasteland and no one wants to deal with them much."

"How much do we pay, sir?"

"It's one ducat." He looked at us trying to guess who would pay. Melea pulled out her purse, dug out the tiniest lump and handed it to the host with a smile.

"I think that'll cover all the costs. Please ensure that the horses are ready for the next day."

"Thank you for your generosity." He bit the lump checking its authenticity. "Is there anything else I can do for you?"

"Please conduct us to our room, we're quite tired."

His smile faded and he snapped his fingers. The young stable boy appeared again taking our backpacks, it was nice to take a rest from the heavy burden.

The innkeeper grabbed Melea's hand, and led us through the narrow corridor; the oil lamps were barely illuminating the house, all the walls were decorated with simple paintings and furniture.

The innkeeper turned to the stable boy. "When you're done with the luggage, pour some oil in all the lamps, it's a bit too dark. God forbid, someone will trip over." He looked at Melea with an affected smile.

"Small scallywag, every day I have to tell him what to do, he cannot guess for himself. I have sent his elder brother to some master of the guild. Maybe I should hire someone else?"

Melea seemed to have sympathy for the boy. "Maybe you should teach him how to be a good host."

The housemaster was confused by her answer, and changed the subject. "Great property, isn't it? I inherited it from my father, a hardworking self-made man. Imagine, every day from dawn to dusk and..."

A second later the boy lost his balance, and flew forward with the two knapsacks. A belt buckle in Melea's bag broke, and almost the entire contents spilled out onto the floor, an extra pair of garments, underwear and some purses. The innkeeper noticed the bow, quiver and protruding hilt of the sword. He looked at Melea, who did not know what to say.

I had to save the situation. "We're merchants, hence we have to defend ourselves sometimes while travelling."

"Well said. A man may not feel safe even in his own house."
Melea knelt down and started to put everything back in the knapsack, pulling at the torn belt. The innkeeper immediately took it, and said that he would send a new one in the morning.

We walked into the room, which looked nice and comfortable just like the master of the house told us. He lit the oil lamp on the table.

"I hope that you'll rest here," he said bowing low, and went out.

Falling from exhaustion Melea threw herself onto the mattress, putting her hands behind her head, staring at the ceiling. I looked around the chamber, a table, two chairs, a tiny shelf with a pot, and a huge bed strewn with a simple woollen blanket.

"Do I really have to sleep on the floor?" I looked around the swept and worn parquet floor. Melea smiled at me, while the oil lamp attracted a small moth, which was hiding in the corner.

"No, I was only joking. I can give you the duvet and a pillow, if that makes you happy." She dropped them with one hand and lay down on the mattress covering herself with a blanket. "Sleep well." Melea closed her eyes.

I made my bedding and killed the light. The fuse of the lamp was making balls of smoke against the darkness in the room. I could not feel the hard wooden floor under the soft duvet; it was more comfortable than I thought. I fell asleep immediately, but within an hour, a shy whisper woke me up.

"Aron, can I lie down next to you?" she asked softly, peering over the edge of the bed. It turned out that the mattress was uncomfortable, hard as stone, and creaked whenever Melea turned from side to side. The sound kept waking her; even the biggest sleepyhead could not take a nap on such a bed.

"But you wanted to sleep on the bed," I replied sleepily, and after a moment she lay down next to me grabbing my hand. We had to sleep together, like we were stuck with each other. I could not say that I was unhappy, on the contrary, the nights in the city are cold, even in such cosy houses, and Melea's body was so warm. I opened my eyes, trying to see if she already was asleep, Melea also opened her eyes at the same time.

"Thank you," she whispered, and immediately fell asleep.
The next day she woke up first. It was a beautiful cloudless sky; the sounds

of the city waking up were increasing with every moment. The chatter of people passing by, carriages transporting goods of all kinds. Pentelia was second biggest merchant town in the north of the Land. You could buy a lot of things here, from ebony toothpicks to golden forks and silver swords, only in Scarborough Fair the merchandise was more developed.

I watched Melea get up and look out of the window. The rays gently fell on her fringe and eyes making them sparkle like droplets of dew on the petals of flowers lit with the first rays of the sun. She grinned, observing the street, where we arrived in the morning.

She opened the window and a gust of fresh air and the scent of flowers filled the room. The sounds were much clearer; the morning greeting of neighbours, negotiating merchants, patrolling guards, laughing children, beggars asking for alms and many others.

Amid all this confusion, Melea seemed to be interested in one particular conversation between the innkeeper and a traveller who had just arrived.

"The same storm had to catch him like us."
Melea observed both men enter the porterhouse. She left the window slightly ajar, took some gold and left the room.

~ Chapter .7. The oath. ~

Warend was standing waist-deep in mud, soaked to the skin, stiff and afraid to move. He unbuckled his belt with the scabbard and sword so that he would not sink so fast. The wind was attacking him from all sides, making him feel as though thousands of icy needles were piercing him to the bone. The cold and fear almost froze his blood. He looked around, trying to get out of this unfavourable situation. In the distance, he could hear an owl hooting. He cursed Jerch and the others who left him for dead. Each moment he was slowly sinking deeper and deeper. If he could not come up with something, the swamp would swallow him anyway and he would join Nakros.

He jumped when he heard a wolf howling at the moon. *Fight!* He heard an inner voice. *Don't give up.* Warend's eyes flashed, his mind began to move at a rapid tempo. There must be some way to get to the shore. Although he was touching the bottom with one foot, still he was sinking. *Damn muddy bottom.* He swore breathing calmly. Warend bit his lip and an idea came into his mind. He calculated his chances and planned everything exactly. His life was on the line, and he had only one chance. *If I can't get out of that mud above the surface, let me try to do it underneath.*

It would be difficult, but worth a try. Warend took a deep breath and was about to dive, when he stopped. He exhaled and closed eyes his for a moment. Strange images flashed in various directions. Now he was ready. *I'll have to hurry beneath the surface; can't hold my breath air for too long.*

Warend dived shivering from the cold. Groping in the mud, he tried to reach protruding roots and twigs. He let out a small breath. It was hard to feel anything under the thick mud. Lumps of earth and clay covered his eyes and mouth. Grains of sand were falling into his nostrils causing him to cough.

His lungs were demanding a new breath. He clenched his teeth and began to swim faster. The sand was scratching his nostrils making him snort, but he had to endure it. His dead comrade's leg appeared in front of his face. He grabbed it and bounced it away with full force. He pulled up emerging on the surface. A breath of fresh air did him good.

Finally, Warend climbed out of the deadly trap. He looked worse than the devil himself. Only his blue eyes betrayed that he was a human being. A thick layer of mud covered every inch of the survivor, who sat on the edge and looked down. *Thanks for your help, Nakros.* Getting out of there cost him no small effort. The only thing he wished for now was a hot bath, dry clothes and a hot meal.

He climbed up the hill, from which Nakros had rolled down. There was no trace of the rest of the band. He cursed them with all his heart. They left him in a swamp to rot. He clenched his fists; the thief code and the outlaw's pride told him to sacrifice everything to take revenge. Warend looked up at the sky to define which hour could it be. The dark night showed him that it was still far from dawn.

He started to walk towards the centre of the circle. He had not passed four hundred yards, when he saw a disagreeable view. Rekel was lying on the ground in a pool of blood and mud like a slaughtered pig. Warend did not want to leave his soldier like that. Maybe Rekel called him sluggish, but there was a reason. Indeed, it was Jerch who had led him up the garden path, or rather the swamp.

He took Rekel's sword and covered the body; he did not want to waste time looking for a shovel. Or maybe he was too tired to look for any tool. Exhausted, he walked exactly the same path as Jerch, barely dragging his feet. Clouds revealed a milky white moon, and it got a lot brighter.

Warend noticed the dark shape of a wooden cottage and a body lying in the doorway. He walked with his hand resting on the hilt of his sword. Nothing surprised him anymore. Even the great stain of blood that he discovered on his way. He knew immediately that it was Jerch's blood, he could see a greenish pus. Besides, he had been hit in the face with the severed hand.

The pilgrim deals with this dumb stripling again he began to laugh to himself. *What if I could join him? Offer him a truce and cooperation. With such a partner I would quickly make my money, buy back lost time on the leadership of those dunderheads.* His mother always used to tell him when he was young, "Son, remember, if you can't beat someone, join him." She was smart and wise. *I think I'll join that boy.*

He walked into the house and decided to shelter there for a couple of hours, just rest for a while and leave for Pentelia. Warend leaned against the wall and pushed aside the curtain, letting some light into the cabin. With every step, he lost an ounce of strength.

Warend went inside, he no longer cared if anyone was there or not, and closed the door. He peered into the room and saw a puddle of blood on the floor. *They got the elfgirl, killed her while asleep, those bastards. They were afraid to stand up to her, to face an open fight. I swear I couldn't act like that, like a lousy rat. She must've been a great warrior. Too bad she was killed in that way. A woman with such skills is extremely rare.*

Warend felt remorse, so he went out and closed the door. It occurred to him that the youngster might try to find him and get revenge for everything he had been through.

Why do I make so many mistakes? Warend was troubling himself. From the dark corner, a man came out playing with his moustache. Warend blinked a couple of times, trying to get rid of the ghost. He took two stones from his coat, which turned out to be flints, and lit a candle which was standing on a table.

"Rekel? Is that you? I just buried you." Rekel smiled at the sight of his frightened ringleader.

"You call this a burial? You covered my body with litter and sticks. You didn't even bother to find a shovel."

"I'm tired, give me a break."

"I'll haunt you until you kill that one-handed, brainless, lousy, nasty, smelly, pathetic..."

"I'd no idea that you had such a vocabulary."

"Kill him and I'll give you peace of mind."

"Jerch? Forget it. The purpose of my journey is Pentelia."

"Ah yes, you want to join the pilgrim. I wonder, after the events of the last days, if he would still want to talk to you, or will he kill you at first sight?"

Warend pulled a small clod of mud from his pocket. "If I give him this back, he won't kill me."

Rekel twirled his moustache and looked at the clod. "With this lump of shit you won't affect anybody. Anyway, I wonder if you're fast enough."

Warend closed his eyes, imagining the reaction of the courier.

"Till next time, sluggish man."

Warend woke up lying on the mattress along with the dead animal under a blanket. The candle in the kitchen was lit.

"Rekel, are you there?" Only silence answered him. "What a nightmare," he said and fell asleep.

This time he had an extremely bloody dream. He was hunting the members of his gang, killing them one by one, and although they were begging for mercy, he was slaughtering them all, leaving Jerch at the very end of the list.

Warend slowly approached his victim in an old tavern, where the giant was sitting at the table with his back to the entrance. Somehow Jerch immediately knew what was going on, he stood up rapidly and grabbed his throat.

Warend noticed with surprise, that the giant had a prosthesis, not an ordinary one, but one made from fine steel, and its metal fingers were crushing his windpipe. His eyes burst into tears, which made his image blurred. He did not have the strength to break free from the grip, choking terribly he could hear laughter from all directions, someone applauded, the others shouted.

"Kill him."

"Strangle that scum."

Warend regained consciousness and snapped out of his nightmare, all covered with sweat, he woke up just in time, there were still couple of hours till dawn.

Time to move on. He went to the kitchen where he managed to cook up a poor breakfast from things left in the pantry.

He was still thinking about his dream, about how he turned into a monster. Animal instinct turned him into a cruel murderer who was living just for revenge. Much like someone known to him. In the dream, he was similar to his brother. He shuddered at the thought and left the house.

The fresh, cold air made him feel much better. He began to calculate how long the journey would take. Without a horse it would be about a day. He noticed that the bushes in front of him moved. He dropped the backpack and grabbed a sword.

"Who's out there?" he shouted, but there was no answer. "Show yourself, I know you're there." From the bushes emerged a horse. Apparently Jerch carelessly left one animal. Warend could not believe his luck. He grabbed the backpack and approached the horse patting him on the neck. For a few minutes he struggled with the reins. The animal was tangled up in the bushes.

He was about to take the same route, when he saw hoof prints leading in the opposite direction. He dismounted and leaned over them, the tracks were fresh and clear. There was no doubt where they led. Warend looked at the opposite side of the clearing, clenching his teeth in anger. *The youngster should've chopped off his head instead of his hand*. He grabbed the horse's reins, circled the small morass and the rock from which the stream flowed, and noticed the traces of two horses that had galloped through there. The path was slowly coming to an end.

Warend went out of the woods and within an hour he was on the main route leading to Pentelia. He rode like crazy passing the merchants and the other guests who were invited to the wedding; he almost jostled a stout man who was standing by his carriage.

"Watch where you're going, ragged man," he shouted after him.

"Stop getting in my way you fatty." Warend growled and rode away.

The pot-bellied man looked at him angrily and said to his son, "You see son, what kind of people they are. Meet such a ruffian elsewhere and he will simply rob you or even worse."

"But Pa, we don't have a lot of gold, anyway," retorted his son, eating a hard-boiled egg.

"You know what? You really are senseless. From now on I'll watch how much you eat each day."

"Oh, Pa!"

"No, "Pa". If you want to become a good host, you have to take care of yourself. You've been indulging in eggs since the morning."

"I'm hungry. You make me work so hard since the..." He never finished because his father gave him a bloodthirsty look.

Warend stopped his horse, breaking with a screech of hooves on the paved entrance, dismounted and walked over to the guard.

"How can I help you, traveller?" Warend pulled a dagger from his belt and showed it. The guard looked only at the hilt. "Do you want an escort, sir, for a safer trip through the city?"

Warend looked him in the eye and replied coldly, "Lad, at your age safety was what we ate for breakfast."

He grinned, jumped on his horse and passed the Great Gate, over which hung the city crest. It consisted of five parts, four were square and each one had a colour of the roofs of the four districts. The fifth part was round and beautifully plated. It could be seen from far away almost like a lighthouse in the harbour at Grodlin.

He knew the city well as he passed the streets and the other alleys. Despite the early hour, people were bustling around, some were shopping, some going for a morning walk and others were finishing decorating the streets, and embellishing anything that could be adorned.

Warend drove into the Blue Roof District, with the intention of having a short nap at a friendly inn, eating a proper breakfast and then finding the courier. Along the way, he entered a gold merchants. He tied the horse to a wooden railing at the front of the door, brushing some more sand from his clothes. Fortunately, the label hanging behind the door proclaimed "Open".

The door creaked slightly and a bell rang. The interior felt cramped and stuffy. *Those windows have never been opened.*

"Good morning," came a squeaky voice. It belonged to the owner of the place: a small man with slightly greying hair and a big wart on his chin. He wanted to shake the customer's hand but as soon as he realized that it was all full of mud, he withdrew his hand, staring at him with narrowed eyes. "What can I do to serve you?"

Warend's hand reached into his pocket. He dug out a small pebble of mud. It quickly crumbled in his hand leaving a glowing piece of gold ore. The merchant rinsed the ore, weighed it and examined it for a while with his monocle.

"I can give you a maximum of ten ducats."

"Only ten? Other jewellers have told me that you buy gold at the right price," he lied hastily.

"That's right, dear sir. My price is still ten ducats. If you're not interested, please seek your fortune elsewhere."

Warend came up with another idea. He pulled a dagger from his belt with the royal emblem on the handle and showed it. "Shall I get a better deal with this?"

The merchant took off his monocle, frowned and stared for a moment at the royal symbol, looking suspiciously at Warend.

"All right, you win, sir, I shall give twenty ducats." He disappeared in the back. A moment later he returned with a purse full of ducats and dumped them on the slightly dusty counter. In front of Warend, he counted the change.

Warend took out his purse and poured everything into it. He tied it firmly to his belt and shook hands with the dealer. As soon as Warend turned to leave, the merchant wiped his hand on his trousers. The wooden door creaked again and rang the bell.

"Goodbye," said Warend.

This lad is profitable, indeed. With his luck and skill, and my mind, we could be a great team. I hope that we can somehow come to an agreement. He untied his horse.

While travelling a few streets away, the sun was glinting on the blue roofs giving the impression of a double sky and in some places colouring the cobbled street like a carpet.

The porterhouse hasn't changed since the last time I was here. Warend admired the street and the buildings nearby. He gave a quick glance at the price list. *Everything is more expensive.*

Out of the front door came the innkeeper, he smiled at the sight of the traveller.

"I'll be damned. Who have we here?"

"Is there room for an old friend? I'm tired and looking for a courier."

A window on the first floor opened and Melea stood there, looking around enjoying the view. She did not recognize Warend talking to the innkeeper.

"Again, some dark business? It'll bring you bad luck, mate," warned the innkeeper, patting his friend on the shoulder.

"Not this time." Warend took a ducat from his pouch and handed it to the host. He took a key from his pocket and passed it to the guest.

"Second room, first floor. I'm glad you're back, did you travel a lot?"

"You could say that. Take care of my horse, I have to rest." He went into the inn pushing the wooden door. A tear appeared in his eye, so many memories, so much time he had spent in the household. He knew every corner, each chamber.

Warend went upstairs climbing slowly. With each stair, memories hit him harder and returned with a vengeance. He did not even notice the woman who he accidentally bumped with his elbow. He turned around and tried to apologize, when he noticed something familiar about her long brown hair. *No, this can't be, she's dead, I saw the blood, they killed her while she was asleep.*

He went into the second room on the first floor and lay on the bed, exhausted. It had been so long since he had slept on a soft mattress. He stared at the ceiling for a moment thinking about the last few days and the significant changes that had taken place in his life. He scratched his dirty nose. *How do I find this lad here?* In less than ten minutes, he fell asleep.

~ Chapter .8. A venturer. ~

Melea left the inn, exchanging greetings with the owner. She had never walked around that part of the city alone. Every time her father was invited to Pentelia, she stayed close to the palace located in the centre. The city could be extremely dangerous, especially after dark when the alleys were swarming with criminals all lying in wait for their prey.

She had heard so many stories about muggings, even for a few pieces of silver. Not all of them were true, of course. Her father fed her with such stories to warn her about men and their unbridled lust for wealth. Melea remembered one particular story about a crippled pickpocket. Once, when she was much younger, she went with Sara and her nanny to the market. The woman was about to pay for something, when she realized that her purse had been stolen. Neither of the children had noticed anything, a moment of inattention and the money immediately changed owner.

Walking down the street and looking around for a gold merchant, Melea needed to exchange the ore for ducats; they would be much easier to spend. She crossed a few sidestreets clogged with different bins and barrels. Melea watched as people were walking briskly. Despite this early time, it was pleasant. There was no sign that this day might somehow be spoiled.

She headed to the main street of the Blue District, admiring multicoloured decorations, impressive, multi-floral garlands and all the posters that she passed along the way. The windows were polished and everything smelled of flowers. The guards were dressed in their elegant uniforms highlighting this special day, guarding the main street before the ceremony.

As many as five weapon stores were on this street, offering discounts. The exhibitions were carefully arranged in order to attract as many customers as possible. There was not a passer-by who would not stop even for a second just to look at the goods which were so wonderfully displayed. Today was a big opportunity to get rich, not only for dealers and merchants, but for collectors and customers too.

She stopped in front of one exhibition. Lots of rapiers, rows of sabres and swords, daggers and other weapons that you could only imagine. They were laying on red feather cushions like jewels. Her eyes immediately saw a bow with a wide chord, which she liked, the grip was wrapped with a piece of delicate skin to absorb sweat. With such a weapon, you could easily fight from any distance.

The next one had jewellery that attracted the eyes of many ladies. The products were meticulously made from any alloy, of various sizes, fineness and forms.

"Prices for every budget" proclaimed the sign above the door. *I'll come here if I save some ducats later on.* She turned right; the gold merchant was just around the corner. Melea pushed the wooden door gently which announced her entry with a bell.

"Good morning," welcomed the owner bowing elegantly. "How can I help you, madam?"

"Good morning." Melea approached the merchant, at the same time untying her purse and spilling its contents onto the wooden counter.

"I'd like to sell this gold."

The owner put his monocle on and turned one of the stones in his hand. "Hmm, interesting, I had a similar deal earlier. Just a few minutes ago one man sold me a lump from the same ore. He scared me with the royal emblem and I had to pay more."

Melea looked concerned. "How did he look?" She observed how the goldsmith cleaned the lumps, weighed them on the scales and calculated their price.

"He was filthy, probably one of the royal couriers. He showed me the dagger with the royal emblem. I can pay you a hundred ducats for the gold."

"One hundred ducats for five decent lumps?" Melea wanted to find out how much the gold was really worth. "How much did you pay to the previous customer?"

"Twenty."

"Twenty ducats for just one small piece?"

"It wasn't that small."

The goldsmith looked astonished when Melea looked into his eyes. "It that case, I ask one hundred and thirty ducats."

The merchant bit his lip and looked at Melea neither angry nor amazed. He knew that if he did not accept this offer, someone else would put their filthy hands on that fine ore.

"All right." He went to the back room and returned a moment later with the money.

But Melea's thoughts were elsewhere. She was thinking about the man who had spoken with the host on the street. Only one name was ringing a bell. She was pondering so hard that she barely heard when the merchant spilled the ducats onto the counter and counted out her due.

"Thank you, have a lovely day," she said leaving the shop.

With a hasty step, she turned into the street around the corner, the whole time thinking about one person. *He came after us to take revenge, I must warn Aron.* Without losing a moment she began to run. The ducats jingled happily in the pouch strapped tightly to the leather vest.

***

I stared at the ceiling with my hands under my hand. The usual street noises of the carriages, shouting pedestrians and merchants along with rushing animals hit my ears. I noticed that Melea had gone. I approached the window and smelled the heavy scent of the flowers.

It was going to be a great day; the sun was shining on my face. Nothing was interrupting that peaceful morning apart from the resonant snoring on the other side of the wall. I approached it and hit it a few times with my fist. The snoring intensified as if my neighbour was doing it out of spite. I started to hit even harder. Nothing happened.

Upset and annoyed I left the room and stood at the next door, clenched my fist and hit it with full force at least five times. The snoring stopped. I heard footsteps and after a moment, the door opened widely. My jaw dropped in amazement. It was not only me that looked that dumbstruck, my neighbour took a similar expression too. We were looking at each other in silence. I was about to step back when Warend quickly raised his dagger and held it at my throat.

"What are you doing here?" I felt the blade gently tighten the skin on my neck. I tried to calm my rapid breathing. "I could ask you the same thing. Last time I saw you, you were lying on the ground knocked down. You tried to rob me and kill me!"I tried to free my neck from his grip. Warend was holding it tightly, looking at me in surprise.

"To rob, yes, but certainly not to kill. It's not in my nature to kill a fellow courier."

"Courier? What courier?" I had no idea who this mad man thought

I was. Without saying a word, he grabbed me by the arm and led me to my room, holding the dagger at my throat the whole time. We had barely crossed the threshold of the room when I heard quick steps and a thump. The hand holding the weapon fell motionless. The knife blade stuck in the wooden floor, I turned around immediately.

"I left you alone for five minutes and already you're in trouble." Melea was standing over Warend's unconscious body and rubbing her elbow. She grabbed him by the leg. "Come on, help me. I can't shift this bulk by myself." I grabbed the body by the hands and we carried it into the room and laid it on the bed.

"How the hell did he find us here? He was sleeping in the next room."

"You're lucky that I found you," she said triumphantly.

"He said he didn't want to kill me, he took me for someone else."

"Who?" She fixed her gaze for a moment on Warend.

"He called me a courier." I picked up my dagger from the floor and turned it in my hand. Warend again began to snore loudly. Melea also ceased to like it after a while, so she approached the bed and revived him. He blinked rapidly and looked at her.

"You..." he began to mumble.

"Yes, it's me." She smiled, small glimmers shone in those almond-shaped eyes.

"But... but, you're dead," he stammered. "I saw the blood, they killed you on the mattress."

"Apparently, I've woken from the dead. You assaulted us, or rather your band attacked. Where have you been all this time? Were you afraid to cross swords with us?"

"I was standing waist-deep in mud, sticking to everything and trying not to sink," he tried to hide his shame behind a cynical smile.

"What's all this about a courier?" I broke this conversation letting them know that I was still there waiting for answers.

"Don't tell me you're not one of them," he growled angrily. "Show me the dagger." Melea vigorously shook her head in protest.

"I won't do anything stupid," he promised, so I went over and passed him the dagger. He smiled triumphantly and pointed the royal emblem. "Explain this, then."

Melea squinted at the symbol. "This is the royal coat of arms; I've seen it thousands of times." She looked at me with astonishment. The look on her face explained all.

"I don't know how this symbol got here, it's an old dagger. I took it from the buttery on my uncle's farm."

"Maybe your uncle was a royal courier?" asked Warend.

"I wish. He was, is and always will be a farmer. Uncle despises other occupations and professions. Providing cabbage and potatoes for the town he considered to be the way to make money." An idea popped into my head. "Hand it over."

Warend obediently gave it back, rubbing his head. "For the third time I get it from you in the head."

"Next time try to look behind," Melea replied, smiling and along with Warend looked at me.

"It's not a crest, look." I scratched it gently with a fingernail and a piece of the sword shaped in the beak of an eagle dropped out. "It's just grease and dirt." Warend made a face as if a bolt of lightning had struck him.

Melea began to roar with laughter, she could not get out a single word out. "So, you...all the time...oh no, I cannot..." tears were flowing down her face. Warend looked at her and began to laugh as well.

"And what actually did you do in that mud, Warend?" Melea sat on the floor and rubbed her wet eyes.

"I fell into one of the forest swamps, trying to save one of my comrades. The rest of the gang left me there to sink and rot. Your good friend..." he smiled in my direction. "...Jerch, left me there." We looked at him in disbelief, listening to the whole story. Melea did not want to admit that she felt a little sorry for him. Warend explained that he returned to headquarters, gathered a band and without rest, they set off. He told us of the hard and arduous journey through the forest, and how Jerch had mocked him in front of everyone.

"I'll kill that bastard," shouted Warend, clenching his fists.

"Fine, we both wish you good luck, but for now you can tell us what we should do with you." I turned the dagger in my hand.

"I want to join you," he said bluntly.

There was a moment of complete silence. Warend was waiting for my reaction; Melea frowned slightly and looked at me. I did not really know what to do. On the one hand, how could I trust this man? He wanted to seize my fortune, and his former band had almost ripped my guts out; on the other hand, the experience of someone like Warend was priceless. I had a feeling that this could be the beginning of a great friendship.

"So you want to join us?" Melea folded her arms. "We have to forget about everything that happened and welcome you with open arms?"

"More or less, yes."

"Please don't get me wrong..." I started slowly, "...but yesterday you robbed me." I had not forgotten about the piece of gold.

"There you go, mate, the money from the gold buyer." He took out a purse from a dirty pocket, Melea observed him for a moment in surprise; neither of us expected this.

"I only spent a ducat, you can count the rest, everything is there." Warend looked me in the eye. "I secretly hoped I would find you first in that cabin. I knew Jerch wasn't listening to my orders. I never had any intention of killing you, the word of the robber."

"So why do you want to join us?" Melea asked.

"My mother always was telling me, if you can't beat someone, join him," he answered calmly. Trying somehow to convince us more, he continued, "Maybe you don't know, but once I was just like you, having adventures. I used to work briefly as a royal courier, but it was too boring and predictable. I was trained a little in the art of theft."

After a while I realized that the purse of ducats, which I was holding in my hand, was pinned again on his belt. Melea apparently noticed it too. She began to play with a lock of her hair.

"All right, you have some skills, but don't you think that you're a bit ol..."

Warend did not let me finish this sentence. With an agile movement of his hand, he snatched the dagger from Melea's hand and set it up on my throat again. She shivered and froze in an attack position staring at the assailant. Warend's facial expression implied that he would not hurt me.

"Old? Is that the word that you wanted to use?" He looked at Melea and moved the blade from my neck.

"There's life in the old dog yet," he said through clenched teeth and stuck the dagger in the floor. "I'm not as old as you think." Suddenly I felt great respect for Warend.

"I apolo—"

"Don't apologize. Now you know that you shouldn't judge people by their appearance. So, what's our goal?"

"Whoa! Hold your horses, mate," said Melea. "If you want to help us, there's one condition, forget about Jerch and the rest, they're not worth it."

"But..." He wanted to say something, but Melea was uncompromising, so he nodded his head in agreement.

"We'll share the profits into three equal parts."

Sitting on the bed holding my hand on my neck, I was barely listening to what they were saying.

"Aron." Melea looked at me angrily.

"Yes, in three parts."

"When do we leave?" Asked Warend more excited than we were.

"Shall we first fill our stomachs, then get dressed up and go shopping and then go to the wedding?" Melea was looking at Warend's dirty apparel.

"Done." We answered together and left the room. Each of us washed in the bathroom and went downstairs to the dining room.

The servant brought our food to the table. We greedily ate the specialties of the inn, fresh smoked ham and warm bread.

"Do you have any specific plans, which direction do you want to go?" Warend cut a piece of pig leg.

"Not yet." It was hard to answer with my full mouth, I swallowed a bite of sausage that I had in my mouth. "We intend to plunder every possible place to find the booty. I mean the mines, caverns, mounds and old temples, where chests are filled to the brim with gold just waiting until someone takes care of them."

"Very practical, I like this plan, short and easy to remember." Warend rubbed his hands with excitement. "How about a boat trip to the north-west of the Land? It's full of caves, barrows, old ruins and abandoned altars, waiting for someone to eventually discover them." Melea stopped for a moment to chew a crust of bread and looked at Warend, who had encouraged us on.

"I've heard of unimaginable treasure, about chambers full of gold and gems, I'm not talking about tombs, but old forgotten treasures of many fraternities. As you know, I was engaged in acquiring this type of information." He took a sip of mulled wine with roots and continued. "Chests of gold are good for pirates and treasure hunters. What do you say about the powerful artefacts so much desired by merchants and nobles families? With your gold Aron," he pointed to a purse tied to the belt, "we can buy quality equipment necessary to plunder any place and get away from there in one piece."

"Adventure is awaiting us. Let's go and spend some gold." At these words my companion smiled at me.

After the meal, we went upstairs and Warend went to brush up properly. We took our coats, purses with ore and ducats, and went shopping. Warend showed us around; some time ago he used to work in the same inn, some merchants even knew him by name. We all agreed that our priority would be to purchase weapons.

Walking into the first store on the main street, the seller was glad to see three customers in the morning. When Warend entered the shop, the owner recognized him and came out from behind the counter to say hello, giving him a warm hug.

"These are my partners." He used the word "partner" because friend was too strong. The balding vendor smiled warmly. "Warend's friends are my friends. How can I help you?"

"We'd like to buy some weapons," we all said at the same time.

"Right. Before we begin, I would like to ask, defence, attack or adventure?"

"I think the adventure." answered Melea looking uncertainly at Aron and Warend.

"Excellent choice. I have lots of adventure tools. What are you specifically interested in? Swords, sabres, daggers, axes, spears, bows?" He was listing the products one after the other.

"Something tells me that we'll be spending some time here," said Warend. "Maybe you can serve the lady first?"

"Of course." He smiled at Melea and took a measuring tape from his pocket. "With your permission?" The seller bowed gently. Melea nodded and smiled while the seller measured the length of her arm, then a hand, and at the end the length of her forearm. All was carefully noted.

Melea was standing at the centre of the store, blushing a little, Warend was watching the weapons on the counter. The seller calculated everything and put his quill behind his ear.

"Right then. First, the primary weapon." He went behind the counter and pulled out a sword wrapped in a cloth. It was superb. It seemed to be forged specially for her hand. The blade reflected light and was broad with a slender hilt. Melea drew the sword and raised it. The weapon seemed to be as light as a feather. She was delighted. She put the sword on the side and waited for the next one.

"I see that you're satisfied?" asked the seller with a wide smile. Melea nodded. He took a short weapon from the counter, a small dagger for self-defence. It could easily be hidden anywhere. Melea was girded with a black leather belt. On the side, she pinned a scabbard for the sword and at the back a sheath for the dagger.

"I'm thinking, but I could be wrong, that you like throwing

weapons."

"Sir, you're incredible."

"Please, call me Wolter."

"Melea."

"Would you be so kind and lift your left hand? That's right." He clipped a small leather sheath to her left arm. From a distance it was nothing unusual, but you could not say that about the contents: ten deadly darts, sharp like the fangs of a monster.

"Can I try it?" Melea pulled one out and threw it at a stuffed moose on the wall behind two candelabras. The blade struck right between the eyes, Wolter looked astonished and began to clap.

"Thank you for your cooperation, Melea."

"I'm really grateful that I was helped by such an expert."

Wolter beamed, while Melea bowed and sat on the chair next to me.

"Now it's your turn young man." He turned to me and smiled. "Come on, don't be shy, I won't bite." The seller repeated all the measurements and calculations. "I'll find something suitable for you as well." He went out again to the back, while Melea was admiring her new weapon, and   Warend was comparing the hilts of two axes. Everything was made with meticulous care. Even the leather scabbards and belts were decorated in some amusing shapes. Wolter came back with a couple of bundles under his arm.

"The primary weapon." He gave me a sword, it was quite light, maybe not like Melea's, but it was pleasant to feel the weight of that blade. I lifted it with one hand and started waving rakishly.

"The blade is sharp as a razor; the alloy is unique and very strong." Quickly I got used to the hilt. Pleased with the primary weapon I put it aside, hungry for more surprises.

Wolter handed me a dagger, how he guessed that I never use short swords, I really cannot say. The dagger was amazing. I could brandish it without any problems, scrolling it between my fingers as if it was an ordinary knife. After a while, I threw it at the moose, the same as Melea, the blade never reached the scalp of the animal. In fact, the dagger fall over the candlestick on the left side. Melea just shook her head and Warend apologized to the shopkeeper that I still need to work on accuracy.

Wolter rejoiced to my satisfaction and approval, he smiled and approached the wall where there were even more weapons.

"I presume that you could use a bow as well." Wolter took one from the top shelf with a boat hook standing in the corner. "Oak wood, perfectly bent and specially crafted, bowstring very easy to strain."

I grabbed the bow and stretched the string as tight as I could. It gently gave a stretch. After a while, I received a leather quiver full of new arrows. I was about to shoot, when Wolter protested, handing me the last thing. "And finally, this little knife. It has a retractable blade, after it folds itself it looks like a wooden comb.

"Sir, you're an expert of weapons and human needs." I thanked him for everything and sat down next to Melea, now admiring my purchases, eying my new sword blade.

I was pleased that Warend led us to this very shop; Wolter was an excellent merchant. Warend did not have to stand in the middle of the store. The seller hid the measurements, calculating everything in his head. After a while he handed him a brand new sword with a shiny hilt, an almost tailored short blade, double headed battle axe and war hatchet. Once Warend grabbed it in his hand, he swung it, which whizzed across the room and sunk in the poorer looking moose.

All the weapons were collected, and it was time to pay. Warend only had nineteen ducats in his purse, Melea had about seven times as much and my purse still contained some fine ore. Not knowing the price of the weapons I knew how much to pay. Without waiting for the final price, I gave the seller my two largest lumps of gold.

"That's too much, I can't accept it." Wolter was embarrassed and his hands were shaking. I could not see in him any signs of greed or avarice, unlike most of the sellers and merchants.

"This is also a reward for your great help." I explained closing Wolter's palm, in which the gold gently glinted.

"Besides, you sold quite a few decent weapons, you deserve it." Melea interjected with a smile on her face.

"Thank you for your generosity young man."

"Please, call me Aron."

"Thank you Aron, Warend couldn't have chosen a better partner."

We walked out of the store onto the street bathed in sunlight. We thanked Wolter for all our purchases and his help. He said goodbye, squeezing Warend warmly.

We had not gone five steps when I said, "We can't go further with these weapons. It would look too suspicious."

Melea looked at Warend. "He's right. We'll have to take them back to the inn. I'll do it," he said. We handed him all the purchases and he rushed to the inn, turning into a side street.

Melea looked slightly surprised. "I guess he won't flee?"

"No, he'll come back. What do you think about him?"

She looked at me for a moment, trying to answer. "He's all right, I suppose. The idea of artefacts is not that bad, after all, and he showed us this shop. With such weapons, we can even go to the top end of the Land."

"I guess you're right."

We went slowly along the street to a small square with an impressive bell tower. The first shop on the corner was a jewellery store where Melea stopped for a moment to look at rings and other assortments. I saw that something was drawing her attention; it was a gold ring in the middle of the exhibition. She stared at it without blinking. I left her quietly and went to the store. The entrance was just around the corner, Melea did not even notice.

"Good morning," welcomed the seller.

"Good morning," I replied, checking whether Melea had noticed that I had disappeared.

"Can you see that ring, which is being observed by the lady?"

"Of course, I shall bring it for you." He went to the back for a moment and returned with the trinket.

"Ninety silvers, please."

"I'm sorry, how much?" I could not believe it.

"Ninety silvers, nine zero," repeated the seller with a smile on his face.

"Ninety silvers for that piece of gold?" *Robbery in broad daylight.* I checked one more time what Melea was doing.

"That's right, dear sir, ninety silver coins for that golden trinket."

"I'll give you fifty, I must save a bit for my journey."

"I understand. Ninety silvers, please." He was unimpressed with my requests, emphasizing the word "please" with such forced politeness that made me sick. I took a ducat from the pocket which I had flicked from Melea's purse and laid it on the counter, in return receiving a nicely wrapped ring and a large silver coin; the profile of the king's head was barely visible.

I walked out of the store, throwing hostile glances in the direction of the counter and stood next to Melea, who stared at me puzzled and surprised that I had disappeared without a word. I grabbed her hand and gave her the package; she immediately opened it and looked like a little child who had been given an unexpected birthday gift. She put it on her pointing finger and admired it. Melea looked at me and then unexpectedly kissed my cheek.

"Thank you." At the same time, around the corner came a breathless Warend. He approached us and rested on his knees for a moment, catching his breath.

"All hidden in the room, now we can move on and buy some equipment. We'll need backpacks, rope, lock picks, sleeping bags, camping set, climbing set and much more for such a journey." He looked around slowly comparing the stores in the area. "Unfortunately, we won't find all these things here, we'll have to go to the Green Roof district. Luckily it's a south-western one, not so far."

We passed a small square and crossed the main street admiring the stands with street food, the smell made us feel hungry, kiosks with cheap jewellery, shelves with necklaces, charms, rings and bracelets. A shoe-shine boy was offering his services for half price.

The district was packed with all kinds of shops, beer houses, public houses, exhibitions and everything that could satisfy guests with silver and ducats. At the end of a long side street, we came to one of the main streets of the city, leading right through the centre. There were several such streets all over Pentelia, all crossing at one place – the palace, which stood in the centre of the city.

With each step, we encountered even more fanciful ornaments made from flowers and wild plants, hanging between buildings and lanterns. Beautiful garlands, winding back and forth, a multi-coloured semicircle forming a distinct way from one town house to another.

With a bird's-eye view, the city looked like a meadow adorned with its spots of green curls in many directions, forming snails and other shapes that you could only imagine. The most fascinating thing was that each district had these ornaments in accordance with the colour of the roofs. But on the main roads leading to the palace, they were all mixed. Ornate paths made of fragrant jasmines, cornflowers, daisies and roses.

We walked down the main street to get to the Green Roof district, passing the merchants, guards and townsfolk scurrying to their ordinary duties. Warend turned into a side street, where the horizon looked like the city was on fire, the amazing effect caused by the sun reflecting off the red roofs, it was not a bloody red but delicate, reminiscent of a gentle campfire illuminating the night.

Warend led us between narrow streets full of different people, orphans playing a war of sticks, whores lurking at the morning customers, street musicians tuning their instruments, and a variety of street vendors.

For a silver coin I bought an ounce of roasted nuts in honey, a sweet and pleasant crunch.

We went to the main shopping square. At first glance, the shops seemed to be the same as in the district of blue roofs, but Warend claimed that he knew what he was doing. He led us to the best assortment shop in Pentelia. I opened the massive wooden doors with iron fittings on both sides and let Melea walk in first.

The interior was filled from floor to ceiling with all sort of diverse equipment. In the corner stood a chest, from which protruded rods, on the other side of the room were rusty hooks on which hung piles of iron pans and pots. From behind the counter came a seller with a hearty fake smile plastered on his face.

"Good morning," he said, pulling out a handkerchief from his sleeve and blowing his nose loudly.

"Good morning," Warend smiled widely. "We'd like to buy some travel equipment."

"How long will your trip take?" He did not take his eyes from Melea's breast.

"Best quality equipment only."

The seller shrugged and went into the back room for a moment, returning with a big wooden box. Inside was a whole bunch of new items, starting with a small skillet and pan, a set of ropes and much more. Not to mention a handy folding shovel, snare, two pick axes and a small wood saw.

"We'll also need the rod with the toolbox, for camping, conquering, exploring, sneaking, stealing and more." The seller brought everything from the back, pulled out his handkerchief and wiped his wet forehead.

"How much does it cost?" I asked expecting some giant amount.

"Hmm... let me think. This class of equipment, for ninety-nine ducats, we will make a deal." He was biting his tongue, scared that he had given too high a price.

"If you add these three backpacks with sleeping bags we'll take it." Warend reached out to nail the contract.

"Deal." The seller shook Warend's hand. Fortunately this time Melea had a proper amount of ducats, she moved aside for a moment to calculate the due on the barrel. We packed everything into our new knapsacks and left the shop.

"We still need to buy clothes and then we'll have everything we need," said Melea.

"There's a shop with some robes." I pointed to a big house with a wooden banner in the shape of the shirt.

"Actually, it's a laundry," said Warend. "The garments can be bought on the other side."

We walked across the street and began to circle the building. Through the windows I could see piles of dirty pants, shirts, dresses, aprons, jumpers, nappies, socks and underwear that all the residents of red roofs must leave here.

The double door was open. Inside the store, a few clients were hanging around in search of suitable clothes for today's ceremony. The piles of clothes in the laundry were nothing compared with the assortment here. Lots of shapes and materials for men, women, children and the elderly, both fashionable and unfashionable.

I chose a pair of dark trousers, couple of shirts, a leather vest with silver buckles, a pair of comfortable leather shoes and nice coat with deep pockets. Soon I had picked my robes and observed while Warend and Melea compared clothes, trying on and adjusting their sizes. Melea picked a dark green attire; Warend chose a red shirt, leather trousers and a new vest.

The clothes were our least expensive purchase. We left the shop laden like donkeys. My uncle's gold that I worked so hard for all these years was nearly spent. Together with Melea and Warend by my side, I felt that it was an exceptional investment towards a long lasting partnership.

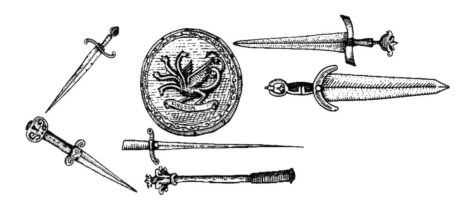

~ Chapter .9. The wedding ceremony. ~

The clock on the tower chimed eleven, in about sixty minutes the ceremony would begin. People were slowly finishing their shopping and duties, and the sellers were hanging out signs that read "Closed". Everyone returned to their homes to get changed or otherwise prepared. We went back to the inn and took a closer look at our purchases. The knapsacks actually contained a lot of useful things: a foldable brass lunette, an exact map of the North Land, a set for camping, climbing, adventuring and much more.

Warend grabbed the lunette with a slight interest. He went to the window and looked at one of the instrument's ends, putting his right eye into the hole and closing the left one. He looked at the tenement opposite.

"All our purchases are done. We can hit the road straight away." Melea unrolled the map and smiled at the sight of the city.

"We're not staying for the wedding?" Warend was repacking his knapsack in a more comfortable way.

"That's a great idea." I replied, searching for something in my backpack. "I mean, how often we will have the opportunity to participate in a similar celebration? Besides, it will be a mine full of information about treasures and other possibilities." Warend nodded and Melea bit her lip.

We changed and went out into the street. I had never seen so many people in one place. The procession had already started and was going to the main entrance of the royal palace. Townsfolk came out of their homes elegantly dressed, with smiles on their faces. All the streets were filled with guests and many travellers. It looked like a human stream gathering in the middle of the city where the church bells were calling the faithful for mass; everyone was rushing to the palace.

Finally, we went to the main street, admiring the contribution of the townsfolk. The whole city was clean and decorated, it was a pleasure to look. Everybody was enjoying the day for which so many had been waiting. We joined one of the groups and walked slowly.

The towers and turrets of the palace dominated the roofs of Blue District. It made a huge impression on me, its white and golden dome sparkling proudly, gleaming in the sun. The flags on masts and towers were dancing happily, poked by invisible fingers of the wind. Together with the walls and moat it looked like one big impregnable fortress.

We were gradually approaching the gates of the palace, passing the green market that was closed until tomorrow. Since then, there was a prohibition on the sale and exchange of goods. Warend pointed to a queue of carriages, which were waiting for entry into the side gate. They came from various parts of the Land, some of them were simple, and some sophisticated, gilded and silver-plated.

***

For many people, it was their first time in the capital. Those who managed to enter the palace were immediately sent to the first available seat. In spite of such a large number attending, the Great Room somehow housed everyone.

The proud ruler was sitting on his throne looking at the approaching people. His daughter was getting married; at this very thought, a tear flowed down his cheek, reaching the bottom of his greying beard. He had tried to be a worthy successor to his father, doing so much good for the citizens; he limited slavery, prevented rampant wars between villages and cities, minimized taxes, and banished the wild barbarian clans and tribes. The king was a tired man, but fully deserved to be called a good ruler.

On the pedestal stood an altar, where the priest Vitorius, an older man, and a loyal and devoted friend of the king, was praying. He had crowned Horen at his ceremonial coronation.

The priest remembered that day, as if it happened yesterday, where a similar number of people were standing in the Great Room. It was not as elegant then, but it still had charm: collar beams and rafters made of finest oak wood, stunning, enormous stained glass windows showing the XII important events in the history of the Land.

The king looked pleased that so many honourable guests from the entire kingdom had arrived for such an important celebration. Vitorius looked at him in the same way as he did many years ago, with sadness and joy. Horen lived to see his only child Princess Sara, he was so proud of his daughter, who diligently studied under the guidance of best teachers. She was familiar with horsemanship and fencing. From such a little girl who used to run merrily in the palace, she had grown into a charming lady and one day would officially be the queen.

The time is flowing fast, thought Horen. Vitorius ended with a prayer and went towards the king. To start a conversation, the priest cleared his throat, but with so many people chatting it was rather inaudible. He cleared his throat again, this time much louder, still nothing. Horen was deep in his own thoughts; one in particular did not give him peace of mind. It was concerning his future son-in-law. The king feared that his daughter had made her decision too rashly. Vitorius gently poked the king's shoulder, which woke him from his trance. He looked with absent eyes at the face of the priest and smiled sadly.

"Vitorius, I'm afraid," confessed Horen.

"What are you afraid of, my Lord?"

"I'm afraid that my daughter made a hasty choice. After my death, an uncertain man will sit on the throne. I tried so hard to be a good ruler and to have a worthy successor." He looked at Vitorius with slightly glazed eyes.

"Did I deserve this title? Tell me frankly as a devoted servant and friend."

"Yes, Sire." The priest answered without hesitation. "Why are you having such gloomy thoughts? Your heart should rejoice; it's the happiest day for your daughter; she should see happiness on her father's face, not sadness and thoughtfulness."

The king, bit his lip, "I had a disturbing dream last night, so realistic that once I woke up from it, I was scared to close my eyes again in case the dream came back or became real. Do you remember what my brother Serner did after he lost the duel?"

"He left the city in grief and anger, deciding to build his own kingdom, the Southern Wasteland," answered Vitorius.

The king nodded. "While leaving Pentelia, he promised he would dethrone me. I have seen my brother leading a huge army, which was able to take control of all the Land. I've seen a dreadful glint in his eye, a desire for revenge as strong as it could be, and his hatred towards his younger brother, who took the throne and all the honours. I'm afraid that my brother will come soon."

"Give up these thoughts, my Lord." Vitorius, patted the ruler on the shoulder. "It was only a dream. Tomorrow I will send you the prophetess; she might be able to answer your questions and concerns."

"Thank you." Horen smiled uncertainly.

"Count De Marge will be a good ruler, you've taught your daughter many virtues, and she will lead her husband when necessary."

"I don't know, Vitorius, she gave her hand to De Marge when he asked her, without a second thought. This decision may affect the fate of the entire Land. You know that the consequences of that marriage may be irreversible."

"That's true my Lord. Sara has changed, but she's still your beloved daughter, who's grown up into a wonderful princess."

"For some time, I felt as though she could not reveal all the truth to me."

"Sire, that's impossible, everything will work out, you'll see." Vitorius put the skullcap on his head.

"You're too nervous, my Lord, exactly the same as the day of your coronation." Both men smiled. They had been through so much together; true friends who could count on one another in any situation.

"What if you're wrong? What if the Count only cares about the title, power and treasure, not the love of my daughter? What should we do, then?"

"Then, dark days will come to the Land, as dark as the Southern Wasteland. There will be no rescue."

"Let's hope that it doesn't happen," replied the king.

***

There was panic in the princess's room, where the servants were making the final touches to her wedding dress. The white dress reflected the sun's rays like a silver shield, which contrasted perfectly with her raven- black hair and blue eyes. She was smiling, but her eyes betrayed her. Only her father would have noticed it.

"Princess Sara, please stop turning around, just a few tweaks and everything is ready," said one of the servants, bustling around to make this important ceremony a successful one, and make the bride look heavenly. The finishing touches were done and tucked, and the lace was sown. One of the servants turned a large mirror with a crystal and silver frame. They gazed at her with admiration; she looked perfect, smiling and holding a nosegay.

Sara stepped down from the stool, on which she had been standing for more than half an hour. "I look like a big snowflake. Does this dress make me look fat?" She turned sideways to the mirror and looked from every possible position.

"Oh no, not really, my princess," answered one of the servants.

"You look stunning, my dear," said Nanny.

Someone knocked on the door and Nanny opened it. There was a young man in a green robe decorated with gold-coloured threads, and the royal coat of arms proudly embroidered on the chest. The page stood in the doorway like a statue, unable to look away from Sara. They all looked at him and waited for the message which he brought.

"Dalbret," shouted Nanny. The boy did not even blink; all the servants looked at each other.

"Dalbret!" That shout was even heard two floors below. He was about to start talking, when behind him stood Count De Marge. He looked at the bride and grinned. All the women present in the room covered their mouths with their hands, and the page quickly closed the door.

"Has nobody ever told you that it brings bad luck if the groom sees the bride before the ceremony?" asked Nanny.

"I'm sorry," he muttered. "I just wanted to say that everything is ready and we're waiting."

"We're coming," replied Sara, covering her face with a white bridal veil made of lace. It did not dim her charm, but, on the contrary, underlined her delicate and pretty face.

With a slow pace, the attendants went down the corridor and stairs to the Great Room. They stood in front of the big door and waited. Someone gave a sign that the bride was waiting; an organist began to play the march.

Massive gates adorned with iron flowers opened. The princess appeared in the threshold, the guests gasped in admiration.

As soon the princess crossed the entrance, the hall became silent. Sara looked so innocent, and as pretty as a spring morning. All those gathered in the Great Room were stunned.

Only Baroness Virgil was unimpressed. "Duh! No big deal," she snorted. "How can she be dressed like that for her wedding? Too little decency in that dress. At my wedding, I looked much more modest." She put the pince-nez on her nose, and watched the others react. Some guests were entertained by her comments; others did not want to listen to them.

Sara and her bridesmaids reached the middle of the Great Room, and the organist began to play a beautiful melody composed for this special day, perfectly expressing the mood of joy and happiness. Smiling and a little overawed by the amount of guests, Sara walked slowly towards the altar. Behind her were two flower girls who were holding her veil along with a bunch of garlic and wheat.

The bride passed one of the merchant's family, near where Melea was standing. They have known each other since their youth; they used to play together when Dermont, Melea's father, was in the capital. However, Melea was not looking at Sara. Her eyes caught a tall, greying man on the other side of the room who had similar features and pointed ears. Her father, the same man who a couple years ago threw her out of the house for disobedience.

The king sat down on the throne, proudly watching as his daughter approached the altar. Everyone was nervous so Sara gritted her teeth and kept moving, restlessly crumpling the bouquet in her hand. Count De Marge, dressed in a black robe sewn to order, was already waiting, grinning from ear to ear.

***

Meanwhile, on the south side of the city, around hundred heavily armed soldiers were passing the gate, dressed in black and in appalling helmets and ripped robes, which had long falchions at their sides. They drove the horses like the wind. They crossed the main street led by the person who everyone least expected. The inevitable had begun.

***

The organist finished his composition and the guests gave a thunderous applause. Sara went to the altar at the end of the Great Room, where Horen looked at her with unbridled joy with a couple of tears streaming down his cheek. He wiped them quickly and smiled at his daughter, clapping along with the others. She also gave him a smile, as he passed her hand to her future husband. They turned towards the altar, where Vitorius was standing, girdled with a four-coloured sash with the coat of arms of Pentelia. He raised his hands, and voices gradually quietened. There was complete silence; even the baroness refrained from commenting on the dress of one of the ladies.

Vitorius observed the whole room; it was just like it had been at Horen's coronation. The sun was shining through stained glass windows making multi-coloured shapes on the floor. The bells began to toll and the priest turned to everyone.

"My dearly beloved, we are gathered here to join the sacred bond of these two young people."

The priest was talking about the relationship, and especially the role in such a high position in the Land. It seemed that the Count was not excessively interested in the priest's preaching; he was staring blankly around the Great Room.

The ceremony was interrupted by a great rumble. Something huge and heavy fell to the ground, Silence filled the room and the people looked around anxiously.

Into the Great Room ran a young page clutching his stomach, his hands and robe were all red. He fell over and hissed in pain, the wound was deep, and the blood was trickling between his fingers, splattering the carpet. The page was crawling painfully moaning and groaning with pain, his dilated pupils begged for mercy all around. No one spoke, no one helped him, after couple of metres the page fell down dead.

A few ladies screamed in terror, others were yelling and clinging to their husbands. Horen looked at Vitorius, his son-in-law and finally at his daughter. He was the only person there who knew what had actually begun. He had seen this scene so clearly last night. Horen felt dazed for a moment and closed his eyes, he knew what was about to happen.

All the stained glass windows began to burst, spraying shards of different colours onto guests. They burst one after the other from left to right, letting in the southern sun and fresh air. Through the windows, you could see the blue, red and brown roofs. There was silence again. The calm before the storm.

~ Chapter .10. The duel of the kings. ~

Everyone froze. They listened to the heavy iron boots banging on the stone floor of the hall, causing a tiny tremor. The guests fell back sharply against the walls, someone inadvertently bumped into a vase on the edge of the table, which spilled its contents while crashing to the floor.

At first I thought it was Molten running with my uncle because they did not want to miss the celebrations. Baroness Virgil and the other noble ladies were crumpling their handkerchiefs in nervousness.

The guards, surprised and scared at the same time, did not have the slightest desire to draw weapons as they stood among the guests listening and waiting. A few people thought it was only a show, arranged to entertain the guests. Unfortunately, the bloody page lying on the carpet was very real.

The king, Sara and the Count were staring at the door. Outside, someone blew the horn alarm. With that dying sound, at least eighty heavily armed men ran into the room, moving as one. We could not see their faces; the armour was protecting them. They all ran forming battle lines and surrounded the middle of the Great Room, pushing people into the walls and corners.

I did not know who they were or what they wanted, but it seemed that they were great troublemakers. Black soldiers stood in battle formation with outstretched arms. Spears, swords, halberds and axes reflected the sun. The squad stood still squinting menacingly, waving their dangerous weapons and roaring wildly, wanting to scare the vast majority of people crammed inside.

Horen stood up immediately, and with anger in his eyes he commanded a small group of guards, "Soldiers, grab your weapons! I won't let anyone spoil this occasion."

The guards drew their swords and turned to hold the invaders back. However, their weapons could not compare with heavy arms and fitted armour. The captain of the guards, a young and brave Bren, ran to his opponent, swiftly dodged an approaching axe, and plunged his sword with all his strength into the gap in the helmet. The blade pierced the head stained black, blood dripped onto the floor. Standing a couple steps away an evil arhet pushed the captain and swung his arm, ready to strike.

"Enough!" shouted the king but nobody listened.

Something sharp pierced the captain's breastplates and came out the other side. Bren staggered, spitting and choking with red gore. Finally, the captain looked straight at me with agitation. Those who noticed this anxious glance stepped aside as if I was infected with something or, even worse, was one of them.

I did not know what to think or say. The captain fell to his knees, while the assailant violently pulled the sword from the body and immediately cut off his head with a single slash. The blood gushed from an artery in all directions. Several ladies screamed in terror when the red drops began to run down their faces. Baroness Virgil grabbed the nearest bottle of wine and took a mighty sip, fixing her eyes on another dead body. The rest of the guards stepped aside to a safe distance, forming the battle array, but no one was willing to attack and lose their lives as the captain had done.

Melea squeezed my hand, terrified. The marriage of her friend had been interrupted; two innocent people were dead. Nobody knew what the invaders wanted.

Sara broke the silence. "Father, what's this all about? Is it a play?" She turned around for a moment surprised to see her fiancé running to the servants' entrance, closing the door behind him.

***

The Count passed the corridor in a hurry, looking behind to see if anyone was following him. He closed the door and started down the winding stairs carved into the rock. The south tower was the appointed venue to meet once it was all over. He was about to open a locked door when he heard a voice behind him.

"Going somewhere, sir?" asked the page.

"They sent me here." The Count lied quickly, taking out a handkerchief from his sleeve and wiping the sweat from his forehead.

"Who sent you?"

De Marge took out a short rapier from its scabbard and stabbed the page. The boy dropped the candlestick. He looked at the blade which was piercing his body and fixed his gaze at the Count as he slid to the ground.

The murderer quickly hid the sword, picked up the body and hid it in a barrel which was standing near a solid wooden door that was heavily bolted.

He went out into the yard covered by one side of the palace wall; on the other side was a shed with gardening tools and behind that a tidy three-metre high hedge. The Count closed the door and leaned against a rock wall.

It's all going according to plan. I had perform my task.

***

The princess was clearly demanding answers, so she repeated the question. "Father, what does it all mean? You came up with this?"

"Not at all, Sara." A hard and icy voice broke the silence with remarkable ease. Everyone looked at the front door. Only His Majesty did not have to do that, he recognized the voice after the first syllable. Horen closed his eyes, so afraid that his dream was coming true. Standing on a pedestal he looked in the same direction as everyone else. He had not heard this voice for a long, long time.

A tall man sauntered into the Great Room. His long dark hair was flowing in the wind blowing through the open door and the smashed stained glass windows. All those standing closest withdrew far away from him. Women covered their mouths with their hands, and Baroness Virgil adjusted her pince-nez. Her eyes widened. Again, she grabbed a bottle of wine and took a healthy sip. Other ladies pointed at the newcomer, cursing him in whispers. Fear was spreading quickly like a disease passing on from one guest to the other. The small army of arhets – the invaders – enjoyed the view.

A long leather coat was sweeping across the carpet, and dark armour decorated in incomprehensible symbols gave a sinister look. The man's face was grey, like ash, as if life had been sucked out of his body. His features were hard and ravaged by the south wind, and his eyes were two dark glimmers that circled the entire room. He focused on the crowd, hall decorations, the dead page, and finally the royal family standing on the other side.

"That's Serner, the king's brother," whispered Warend, Melea nodded and looked around anxiously, none of the guests had spoken loudly, fear and shock paralyzed them all. The guest who arrived had not been invited. For over twenty years he had not passed these thresholds. Finally, the brothers looked into each other's eyes.

"Greetings, dear brother," said Serner with a cruel smile on his face. "It's been ages." Having taken another few steps, he relished the horror painted on people's eyes. "As you can see, I haven't forgotten about you or your daughter's marriage." He paused, enjoying the growing tension and dread of the other guests. The Grey Lord smiled at the sight of the terrified bride.

"I've brought the gift." At these words one of the subordinates pulled a jar of dark green liquid out of a large bag. Inside was a rotten, chopped off head. The arhet threw it in the direction of the altar. The jar burst into hundreds of pieces, and the contents spilled on the floor. Guests were shocked and several ladies lost consciousness, landing in the arms of their husbands. The guests and visitors were waiting for Horen's reaction, while Serner continued, almost snorting with laughter at the sight of the unconscious and frightened.

"I also came for my property!"

"What did I do to deserve to entertain you under my roof, brother?" asked the king.

"I have crossed this threshold long time ago, now I came to get back what I lost years ago. Give me back, what you have taken!"

The brothers stares crossed like two swords. Their furrowed and grave faces fought each other. All the guests looked first at Serner and then at Horen as they spoke.

"The throne belongs to me," said Horen gritting his teeth and clenching his fist. "You have an impure heart, filthy and evil, you would bring only total anarchy, leave as quickly as possible!"

"I've barely arrived, and you already want to get rid of me?" Serner asked sarcastically. "Is that the way you treat your elder brother?"

"I'll treat you the same as you've treated all the people in the south of the Land. You've taken their possessions, and burned and slain many innocent lives. You're not worthy to sit on the throne; you deserve to rot in the hell that you've you created."

No one dared to interrupt. Baroness Virgil rubbed her glasses to get a better look at the situation, Melea stood on tiptoe observing the lonely bride.

"Let's drink a toast to the young couple." Serner walked over to the table, grabbed a bottle of vintage wine, and poured himself a cup, spilling some on the pearly-white tablecloth, the red drops creating flower shapes like the blood all around.

"Drink, get lost and never come back." Horen filled his royal chalice, the wine gurgled wildly, splashing over the edges of the vessel, like the waves of the red sea. He raised his cup and poured its contents into his mouth, shedding a few drops, which disappeared into his thick greying beard.

Serner watched him carefully, his dark eyes sparkled with unbridled joy. In one swift movement, he took the sword from its sheath. Every pair of eyes looked at the blade. It was not an ordinary sword; in the sun's rays the blade sparkled in three colours, it was perfectly polished and sharpened, the sword of all swords.

Horen also paid attention to it, he felt like the back of an axe had hit him with a force of a thunderbolt. He felt a burning sensation in his chest and closed his eyes. It was the sword hewed by the order of their father. In the entire kingdom, only two existed. Two swords for two brothers, yet no one could have guessed that one would turn against the other. The king had ordered his blade to be split into pieces and hidden somewhere after an unpleasant event, which he did not want to talk about to anyone. Apparently Serner's sword had been re-forged again to wreak havoc and destruction.

Horen drank his wine; his burning throat motivated him to fight. He had managed to beat Serner once, thus he could do it again. Horen descended from the pedestal, drew his weapon holding it up like a banner and passed the royal guards.

Sara ran to the king and grabbed his arm, trying to stop the clash of the brothers. "Father, please don't. Calm down."

He was not listening, anger was written all over his face. Horen wanted to kill his brother, sink the blade into his body and let him suffer terribly; he deserved it. With a slow and dignified step the ruler stood up opposite Serner.

"The king is dead! Long live the king!" Serner intoned ominously and slightly bowed his head.

"Die, then!" Horen held his blade firmly and crossed it with Serner's sword. They both tried not to blink, and breathed steadily, striking each other, the characteristic shrill sounds echoed through the Great Hall. Serner pushed all his weight onto the defending Horen, their faces only inches apart.

"The Land is mine!" roared the Grey Lord and stepped on his brother's foot with his heavy boot.

"Over my dead body." Horen clenched his teeth and brutally pushed the attacker. He withdrew against the sweeping strike of his brother and almost lost his balance. One of the guards tried to help His Majesty, he pushed through the array of arhets and stood behind Serner ready to strike, but the king reacted immediately with anger painted on his face.

"Step aside, this is my fight, my matter and my honour." The soldier obediently turned around, watching the hostile invaders.

Horen deftly wrapped his weapon around his brother's blade and wrested it. The sound of metal rolled through the entire room, bouncing off the floor and walls.

The ruler was about to inflict a decisive blow when he felt a piercing pain in his leg. Serner had taken the dagger from his belt and stabbed his brother in the left thigh. The blood immediately stained his white trousers, and a small trickle dripped into his shoe.

Horen took the blade out, clenching his teeth. His opponent deftly grabbed the sword and began to attack, constantly cutting like a mad man, turning and striking again and again, without the slightest care whether he hit chest or head.

Horen had difficulty parrying Serner's stronger strikes. He could not hold the sword as vigorously and firmly as earlier, the pain in his leg was teasing him unmercifully, and blood was dripping down from the open wound. People watched as their ruler was bravely fighting, despite his strength beginning to leave him.

Melea noticed that the king was defending himself slowly and weakly. She was not the only one willing to help, but she could not do anything, no one could. It was supposed to be a great ceremony finished with a dance and shared common meal, not a duel with invaders whose fear had paralyzed everyone.

Horen grabbed the sword with both hands and charged on his brother, who had not expected such an attack; he was convinced that was the end of the fight. Oh, what a marvellous sight, admiration mixed with fear erupted from the face of the Grey Lord, who did not know how to defend in such a situation, he fell with a crash again. Horen stood over him and without hesitation raised his sword to finish his opponent, when he stopped.

A terrible pain appeared from nowhere; it started in the stomach, and quickly spread to his whole body. Horen clutched his chest, as if a burning sensation was tearing him to pieces, his mouth filled with blood, and sweat appeared on his forehead.

The king could not catch his breath; the fear in his eyes showed that something was wrong. He looked at his daughter and then at the guests. No one knew what was happening, no one had the courage to stand up and help him. Taking this opportunity, Serner got up immediately and struck his brother in the chest knocking him down.

The princess moaned softly, while the crowd froze with shock. Their ruler had been defeated, bleeding like a pig in a slaughterhouse, his shirt was slowly changing colour from pearl white to crimson rose.

"Forgive me..." whispered the king, and lost consciousness. The arhets howled loudly, looking with admiration at their leader.

There was a high-pitched scream, Sara immediately ran to her father, checking his wound to make sure he was still alive. A desire for revenge on her uncle consumed her. She picked up her father's sword and dashed at Serner, with tears flowing down her cheeks. Every part of her wanted to humiliate, to punish, to hurt, to destroy, to kill, however, Serner pushed her away as if he fought with a child. The princess fell down right next to her father, looking at the aggressor with hate and regret.

"Murderer, I'll kill you." Tears ran down her cheeks, she clenched her fists until her knuckles turned white, no one dared to speak. Serner looked venomously at his niece.

"My dear, don't take it personally. Your father wasn't fit to be king, and you're not going to be any better than him, kindly give me back the throne."

"I'd rather die than ruin what my father has built."

"And what did he make?" cried the executioner. "He was a political puppet ruled by the Council of Elders, people who have no idea what to do. Nothing more than lies, inventing worthless decrees hindering the lives of normal people, they had promised so much, but did nothing. Horen was an ordinary politician not a ruler." His voice boomed throughout the room.

Sara could not answer these accusations. She tried to put into words what her father was trying to build; she felt the ideas but to express them was so difficult. She covered her face with both hands; tears were streaming down.

"I'll come back and take over this throne. Then you'll feel the true hand of the right ruler." Serner waved his sword and the armed arhets ran out of the Great Room as quickly as they had appeared.

The guards immediately rushed to attack, some of them blocked the entrance, but Serner's guards killed them easily. All the black figures ran out of the hall and left the palace, their horses were waiting in the courtyard.

"What shall we do with Count De Marge?" asked Terdes, Serner's right hand. "He's performed his task."

"We'll leave him here, I have instructed him what to do." replied the Grey Lord.

"As you wish, Milord. Soon, all this will be yours, the people are weak, they cannot defend themselves; we shall take over all the Land, piece by piece."

Serner laughed shrilly. "Prepare the army, heat the furnace, forge the swords, and sharpen their blades, there will be many throats to cut." The arhets roared wildly.

The riders mounted their black palfreys and moved down into the main street, through the deserted city, stirring up fire and destroying whatever they found.

From all the watchtowers and barracks the guards ran with glaives, fauchards and crossbows. They did not manage to put the bolts on the string before the villains had passed.

They reached the last gate, the horses manes and tails were dancing as they galloped, while the wind was whistling in their ears. The afternoon sun was a shining triumph in honour of Serner, who had managed to end Horen's rule.

~ Chapter .11. The prophecy. ~

Count De Marge was waiting for his companions at the southeast tower of the palace. The wind was flapping his cloak held with a silver clasp in the shape of the letter "R". A few drops of blood dripped from the blade embedded in a sheath at his side. He walked back and forth wondering if everything had gone to plan, if so, soon he would not be a Count any more, but someone much more important, one of the governors of the Land.

When Serner had persuaded him to take his side, he was so proud to be asked to help with the fall of the monarchy. The Grey Lord poisoned his mind about Horen's incompetence and told him of his evil plan to take control; he told a sufficient quantity of lies, so the Count diligently completed his tasks.

De Marge recalled that moment as if it had happened yesterday, when he swore absolute obedience, offering his services to the Ruler of the South. He smiled at the thought of this task, remembering how he had to attend all those balls, making himself visible at high society salons, where the rich were pretending to be richer, and the wealthiest were talking about those poorer than themselves. Passing along the corridors he cleverly eavesdropped on whispering groups. Thanks to his father's position and name, he easily worked his way into their company and plucked Sara's rose.

The Count ran his tongue over his lips remembering that moment, her sweet kiss and smooth thighs. The crafted wine worked perfectly, he seduced the princess and almost took advantage of her that very evening, had it not been for that damn chaperone.

The second task was much easier. On the night before the wedding, he was supposed to pour a special powder into the royal cup. This herb was named lentra, it was incredibly rare and its properties equally scary. The powdered extract had to be mixed with liquid. When it was drunk, it spread throughout the body causing a fever and giving a feeling of internal turmoil and decay. The burning heat caused a terrible suffering and there was no known cure for this poison. You would have to be dishonourable to even think about using it.

The events of the previous night flashed by. The Count had got out of bed slowly, so the mattress did not creak too loudly, and put on a comfortable pair of slippers lined with rabbit skin. The prevailing darkness made him feel calm. De Marge lit a candle and placed it on the bedside table, his eyes flashed, it was the opportunity of his lifetime.

He wrapped himself tightly with his night robe and put the tiny pouch filled with crushed leaves in his pocket. He had to prove to his ruler that he was worthy of the second throne in the soon-to-be conquered Land.

He remembered Serner giving his conditions. "You have to give up everything, your name and title, possessions and faith, weakness and fear. Only such governors will truly be worthy." The Grey Lord put a hand on the kneeling one, his dark eyes almost immediately sensed a pang of doubt. "You don't want to disappoint me, my dear R—"

"Of course, your Greyness." De Marge bent his head low and had tears in his eyes.

Sitting motionless on the bed, he wiped his eyes with a handkerchief and listened. Nothing out of the ordinary. At the bottom, he could hear the final preparations. Quietly he opened the door and stuck his head out. The torches inserted into wall-handles were burning wildly, as if sensing the motives of the groom and trying to warn someone.

The traitor moved on tiptoe and went out. He moved silently on the red carpet, while his tense nerves and muscles caused him to sweat. He reached the bottom of the stairs and went down to the Great Room, where all the helpers were finishing the decorations. De Marge was lucky, no one had seen him and he managed to pour the contents of the pouch into the royal cup. He returned quietly to the second floor where he heard a voice behind him.

"Monsieur le Count, what is sir doing at this time? Please go back to bed, tomorrow is a great day." One of the pages looked at him in surprise.

"I had to go to..." He began to think frantically about something, any simple idea, his stomach rumbled suddenly. "To empty the potty." He muttered finally, drying his forehead with the sleeve of his robe. "Too much wine and the chef overdid the pepper," he added looking at the suspicious young man. "Good night," he said and closed the door behind him.

De Marge leaned against it and listened to the young man's retreating steps. He breathed a sigh of relief, satisfied that nobody knew what he had done; everything had gone according to plan. No one would blame the death of the ruler on his son-in-law. He was proud that he had faithfully served his master, imagining himself in a black crown lined with rubies, sitting majestically on a throne, holding a sceptre and giving orders and decrees.

The time was running out quickly. He looked around constantly waiting for his master to join him. Not knowing what was going on, he opened the side door at the bottom of the tower. Just in front of him appeared three guards with weapons pointed at him. Surprised, De Marge looked offended.

"What are you doing here, sir?" asked the guard at the centre of the formation.

"I just..." He did not know how to excuse himself this time. A trail of blood caught the attention of one of the soldiers, who bent down and began to trace it.

"I saw one of them trying to break in here. He leaped from behind the door and killed a page." Everyone looked at the bloodstains. One of the guards opened the lid of the barrel and jumped back immediately.

"Where is that arhet?" asked the highest in command.

"I must have scared him," he mumbled, while his eyes shot at his scabbard.

"Sir, would you please show us your blade?" These words hit him like a thunderbolt.

"But I..." *Oh damn, what to do, what to do.* His mind could not come up with any idea. Soon his act would be brought to light. How could he forget such a detail? One of the guards had already approached and pulled out a bloody sword from the scabbard.

Drops of heavy sweat began to run down his forehead. He was almost shaking with nerves and looking around impatiently. His guilty look was so clear that the guards did not have any problem guessing what had just happened here.

"Arrest him!" shouted one of the soldiers. They tied the Count's hands with rope and led him back to his would-be wife. The return of the groom sparked a flurry of whispers and comments.

***

There was panic in the Great Room; guests were told to leave the palace. Anxiety and terror were tangible and in many corners, we could hear sobs and moans. Lots of guests going out from the hall had tears in their eyes at the sight of their ruler lying lifeless on the floor. Sara was weeping with her head on His Majesty's breast. Melea slowly stepped out of the crowd to comfort her friend, but the guards would not allow anyone to approach the centre of the room. No one was allowed to go near the body.

The room slowly emptied. Warend and I exchanged horrified glances and headed for the exit. It was to be a great celebration, they said. Nobody would have imagined that such a disaster could happen on such a day. Baroness Virgil did not say a word as she left the room, sending a last kiss to the ruler. Farewell gestures were quickly sent by the other women, with handkerchiefs in their hands they started to leave.

The turn came for the three of us. We walked slowly towards the massive doors, when I felt someone's hand on my shoulder. The fingers were tightly clenched, and I could not get free. A couple of people whispered something, looking at us.

"Guards. Guards. Arrest this man, he's one of them, I saw how Bren recognized him as a spy. He participated in the conspiracy." Everyone stopped and watched. However, the man tightened his grip, still shouting and calling to others for help; more hands held me down, Warend and Melea protested.

"What are you talking about? He's with us." My comrades looked at me, when four guards approached quickly.

"We saw how Bren stared suspiciously at this man a second before he died," said someone.

"Yes, I saw it too," confirmed a second guest.

"And they're with him." The third pointed with his fat toe at Melea and Warend. A further argument made no sense; the guards took me and tied my hands behind my back.

I was led to the middle of the Great Room. Everyone looked at me, some even started to hurl insults and curses, here and there I heard shouts.

"Murderer!"

"Hang the traitor!" shouted one woman.

Melea and Warend tried to settle the situation, but nothing could be done. I stood with bound hands and could only wait for justice.

A fumbling De Marge was brought into the centre of the room. His scruffy hair testified that he had resisted all the way.

"How dare you," he shouted. "I'm a Count, the next King of the Land! Release me at once, or you'll pay with your lives."

"You'll perish first, scum!" someone shouted.

"We hang traitors like you immediately, without a trial!"

All the guests left. In the Great Room only a handful of people remained. No one spoke to each other. Vitorius approached Sara and gently stroked her head, like a father. He applied his hand to king's forehead and closed his eyes. But after a while he stared in amazement at the body.

"He's alive." He said it loud enough for everyone in the room to hear it; they all looked in his direction. Melea and Warend stood in the vestibule looking carefully.

Vitorius wanted to say something, but stopped in mid-sentence, his voice choked and took an ominous low tone. The colour of his skin had changed, he was kneeling facing the vault of the Great Room. Terror seized the guards, who jumped back in panic, the princess immediately shifted away. Finally, Vitorius spoke.

"Verily, I say the darkness will embrace the whole Land and shatter it, but do not fear, and do not lose your hope. Behold your king, who must defend and protect us with his own hands, the defender of the Land who will set forth for the elements, but beware of a traitors who has the power to tempt and enslave us."

He had barely finished the last sentence when he fainted, his pale face covered with small drops of sweat. The event caused quite a stir. Melea looked at Warend, the guards looked at one another, and Sara looked at the unconscious Vitorius. No one knew what the words of the priest had mean.

"Vitorius." Sara rolled his body onto his back and began to slap his cheeks, he woke up quickly in a cold sweat.

"What does it all mean?" Sara shook her head.

"What you are talking about?" replied the priest. "I've no idea what happened, I passed out."

"You said that my father is alive." She looked at him with eyes full of tears. "You said something about the king's saviour."

"My child, I don't know, really." He answered embarrassed, putting his hand to the king's forehead again, his eyes widened.

"Quick, take him to the royal chamber! Call for Iwar at once!" ordered the priest. "Maybe there's hope."

The guards brought the golden curtain folded in four. They gently laid the ruler's body on it, lifted it up and went to the back of the Great Room, to the second small door.

While Sara was passing the traitors, she looked at De Marge and me. "To the dungeons with those traitors!" The blue flames of her eyes were blazing with anger. She looked into the eyes of her would-be husband and then she looked at me. I tried to remain calm, believing in my innocence and justice in the world. Sara's eyes were full of hatred and grief; I could see how much she wanted to avenge her father and send us to another world.

The guards took us into the hallway and turned right, leading me slowly, the Count walked behind with a similar escort. Our footsteps sounded dull on the floor, each corridor was narrower than the other, the torches were burning uncomfortably.

The royal entourage turned left to go to the king's bedroom on the fifth floor.

The Count coughed loudly and sounded like he was trying to spit phlegm in the guard's face. Winding stairs carefully carved in stone led the way down a few levels below the basement. A damp, musty smell hit my nostrils straight away, the dungeons looked like a big cave where they tortured and detained convicts. My journey had hardly even begun and I had already ended up in the slammer.

New torches had been lit and the fire flared cheerfully, our shadows moved on the walls performing wild dances. On both sides of the tunnel, stood all sorts of tools for torture and killing, hooks attached to rusty chains hung from the walls and the ceiling, and at the end of the hall we could see bars and cells, several of them already had guests.

When the first inmate passed by the guillotine, the blade easily dropped, cutting a piece of thick twig lying between the pillory. It did not make any impression on him, but on the contrary, fear choked my throat with its invisible hand. The executioner smiled grinning and rubbing his hands, the guards apparently were amused too, laughing at each other and pointing at me.

They opened the gate and pushed me into one of the cells, De Marge occupied the next one. Unlike me, he was squirming terribly with the guards, insulting and cursing them all, he looked like he had lost his mind, his eyes were circling wildly in all directions and his mouth was foaming like a mad dog. The guards locked two bars and came out of the dungeons, leaving us alone with the warden and other inmates.

"Soon you will not feel like betraying." The warden walked over wiping his hands with the dirty rag that he had just used to oil the guillotine. Smiling from ear to ear, he asked me, "What have they locked you up for, boy?" He threw the rag into a corner and sat down on a stool in front of my cell. I sat on a small haystack staring at the ground.

"I'm innocent." I had no wish to talk to that man. I was supposed to hit the road and begin my journey, now I was in deep shit depending only on Melea and Warend, waiting here for the verdict.

"Ha, ha! Really? As a matter of fact, we're all innocent here, of course, in our own way of thinking. For instance, week ago your cell was occupied by one funny fellow, he used to steal horses and cows from the farms; he claimed he was innocent because he needed them, so we cut off the thief's hand. You've no idea how it changed him. First he became awfully softened, he dished out everything he had stolen and joined one of the brotherhoods. Believe me or not, our methods can straighten a man, you're all the same, when someone gives you the finger, you avidly take the whole hand." The executioner was staring at the cell next to mine. De Marge was struggling inside, hitting his fists on everything indiscriminately; his hands had already begun to bleed.

"Surely he's gone mad for good." He was enjoying himself observing the insane inmate kicking his bedding and throwing the haystack around his cell. The executioner had probably not seen such entertainment for a long time.

I could not stand the noise, even though my ears were covered. I got up and walked to the side of my cell, beckoning De Marge, who obediently approached. I grabbed him by the collar and banged his head into the bars. The prisoner moaned softly, staggered and fell.

The executioner looked at me with surprise and respect. "I've never tried to calm prisoners like that before; I always use chains and other heavy equipment." He smiled and gave a quick look at the whip, hanging by the wall. "Apparently the simplest of resources will suffice. What's your name, boy?"

"Aron." I sat down again on my bedding and began to speak to the hangman. My description of my cousin Molten amused him indeed, he snorted with laughter and nearly fell off his rickety stool.

The executioner listened to my story from the beginning. I did not mentioned Warend and Melea, though the news about the whole event in the Great Room shocked him.

"And what do they call you, guard?"

"Regh. I'm not a guard, I'm a warden." He took a piece of cake with apples and offered me some, it was quite fresh. "Once, I was also a prisoner like you, the king made me one of his servants but under one condition, I can't leave this dungeon and the palace until I fulfill my debt to the king, serving him as an executioner and a conservator here below. It's not easy to keep order," he added, looking around. "These tools are in constant need of oiling and wiping, some of them I constructed myself," he boasted proudly thrusting out his chest.

"Which ones?" It was the first time I had spoken to an inventor. Regh stood up and walked with a limp to the wall shelves, where there were a couple of books, an oil lamp and a chain. After a while, he returned with an object and showed it to me.

This shackle was no different from the usual ones that hung here and there attached to the walls. It was made of wood and at its side was a butterfly knob. By screwing it the torturer could easily break the ankles or wrists of criminals, I could only imagine the pain when the bolt sank into the leg. The thought of rattling bones made my hair stand up; torture is the worst thing in the world.

After an hour of discussion and demonstration of all the tools, they brought the food. The servants were carrying eight trays; they put everything on the dusty table and left in a hurry. No one liked the smell of the palace dungeons nor their inhabitants. For many people that particular scent was associated with skeletons and torture. Other prisoners began to knock cups on the bars, so Regh quickly distributed the trays, giving one to me. He was about to take another one, but he stopped; De Marge had not yet regained consciousness.

The warden sat down in front of my cell and began to eat his meal; I looked at my tray with bad feelings. The very sight of it was discouraging; it was some sort of soup or stew of an indeterminate colour. I put the vessel away, hoping that the second course would be better, but hell no! Here, a piece of meat that was no tastier than baked shoe leather. I would not be surprised if the cook entered and demanded his property back. None of it was suitable to eat.

I looked around, the prisoners on my left were not fussy, some closed their eyes, others held their noses, trying their best to fill their bellies.

Regh looked at me and grinned. "You'll get used to the food, boy. It's only a matter of time." He looked around to see everybody busy with their meal. "There you go." He furtively gave me a piece of chicken and two tomatoes. "Don't expect this every time," he added.

"I understand, thank you."

After the meal I handed over my tray, the neighbouring prisoner looked amazed at my barely touched food and moved closer.

"Warden, please don't throw that tray."

"Did you like the slops?" Regh asked in astonishment. "Yesterday you damned everyone for the conditions in the palace dungeons. Hunger is an excellent teacher, you know." Smiling he walked over to my neighbour, who stretched out his hands greedily after the tray. Regh was about to give it to him, when he stopped as if someone had thrown a spell on him.

"My dear Tezil, you know that prisoners are only entitled to one ration, I can't give it to you, I'm sorry." He moved away, chuckling heartily. Apparently he loved to entertain himself in that way.

"Give me that tray! Give it to me!" The prisoner began to kick the bars, lashing at the hangman like a famished beast. The rations we were given would not have satisfied anyone. Regh had to take the whip off the wall and calm his jailbird. The idea of staying here for much longer was not filling me with optimism. I wanted to get out of here as soon as possible.

The prisoners gave their trays back and returned to their previous activities. Some were counting how many stalks of grass made up their bed; not all of them were so educated, the fifth prisoner could count only to three. On the other side, one lad was struggling to do up the straps on his boots, while the rest found other ways to try to kill their boredom.

Sitting on my bedding and chewing the last bites of chicken, I was wondering how to occupy my thoughts, so I asked Regh to lend me a book. Just looking at the other prisoners made me sick, my other neighbour took off his shoe and quickly crushed a cockroach that crawled into his cell, as he made a mark on the wall, I counted it and it all added up to thirty-eight strokes. In the meantime the warden slid a book to me; red leather, I looked at it, terrified, I already knew what the title was. Uncle had made me read it and almost learn it by heart.

"Only try not to be caught, otherwise we'll both be in trouble."

"Of course. Thank you." I turned the book and the first page was "About planting and ploughing". It was a guidebook for farmers written by an unknown author. Great, nothing better could I have asked for! All the information contained in the book I knew already. Uncle, along with Molten, had made me study it to carry out my duties on the farm. My uncle surely wrote the book, when I was turning all those pages I found several phrases and expressions that were similar to the ones he used.

My eyes had hardly begun to follow the text, when I heard the servants entering the dungeons, bringing another meal for the warden and taking the trays away. Regh came up to me with a tray, looked around carefully to see if anyone was watching and handed me a piece of chicken. "Here, take some, you'll need it later." He advised me to wrap the meat in a cloth to prevent worms.

I began to read him one page after another, while I was reading I had forgotten where I was. He was interested in life in the farm, and mentioned that as soon as he repays the debt to His Majesty, he will move away and begin a new life as a farmer.

"How does the plough work?" The warden stopped me at times to ask questions, giving me the pleasant feeling of being a teacher. Perhaps my pupil did not understand but somehow I had to repay him for his help. I have found knowledge a great treasure. I explained to him all that I knew myself, or rather what my uncle had tried to instill in my head so badly.

In the dungeons where there were no clocks, Regh knew what the time was. By looking at the amount of oil burned in the lamp, he could tell the time to the nearest ten minutes. I was so lost in the book, that I had not noticed when my neighbour opened his eyes. He got up quickly and looked around wildly as if awakening from a terrible nightmare.

"Uh-oh, our madman woke up," said Regh with a smile. "Rise and shine, fish!" These words must have hit De Marge like thunder. "Where am I? What's going on here?" He looked at us as if he had seen us for the first time in his life.

"You're in the palace dungeons and I'm your warden." Regh explained calmly.

"Oh God, It was you! You did it!" shouted De Marge.

The executioner looked at me, waiting for an explanation.

"How could you? He was your king you heartless son of a..."

"Tell me right now, what has this man done?" asked Regh, approaching the cell.

De Marge accused me, pointing. "Murderer! Kill him, flog him!"

I could not believe my eyes and ears; This mangy upper-class rat was lying and twisting the truth.

"What are you talking about?" asked Regh.

"This lad is responsible for the king's death." De Marge was clenching his teeth, while sparks were gleaming inside his mad eyes.

"That's a lie!" My words echoed on the walls and ceiling. For a brief moment, I felt as though everyone was watching me; I looked at my neighbour with hatred.

"Tomorrow you'll be hanged, yokel, and I'll be free as a bird!"

"Regh, don't listen to him, he's lying." I gritted my teeth in anger, punching the rod and tearing off a little skin from my knuckles, De Marge only giggled.

The hangman did not say a word, gazing at me, trying to assess whether I actually would be able to do something like that. I wanted to kill my neighbour, maybe after that crime they will be able to punish me justifiably.

I tried to defend myself, but was not sure if my words had reached the warden, who left locking himself in his tiny little room. Through the gap under the door, I saw the light. After a while, Regh went into the tunnel and began to extinguish the torches and lamps one by one.

"Good night," he said and turned off the only source of light in the cell.

The ghostly darkness prevailed; my eyes became accustomed to seeing white streaks of light on the dark walls. I heard Regh stumble a few times along the way back to his place. Everyone roared with laughter as usual. He took off the whip from the wall and smacked blindly towards the cells. Maybe it was dark, but I could feel anger bubbling inside him.

One of the prisoners was hit in the face with the whip, the thin strap with the lead ball at the end cut his face just below the eye, blood began to drip slowly to the ground. The inmate screamed. The warden hung the whip on the wall and went into his room, slamming the door behind.

Voices raised again.

"Hey you!" someone screamed.

"You two, fishes!" called someone else.

"What crime brings you here to this pit?"

De Marge took advantage of the situation to humiliate me again. "I'm just passing through but the other one has contributed to the death of the king." The news astonished everyone; all the prisoners were listening, and decided to have some fun with me. Their favourite scapegoat had gone to sleep, so I had to replace him.

"Ooh, the death of our Majesty, I suspect that you'll not live till tomorrow noon, mate," comforted one of the thugs.

A second one was trying to make me feel better. "He may not live, but before they'll take him to torture, phew, I mean the hearing." Everyone laughed.

"I wonder if they've already send for Lord Deuchas from Scarborough Fair. Last time he visited us, he killed one fellow in the meanest way. They tied him, grounding his jaws with a wooden instrument, and then they poured salt into his throat." He laughed, spitting on the side, several prisoners swallowed loudly.

"After half an hour he confessed everything, even that he slept with the princess. Unfortunately, they didn't believe him, he died like an animal." Everyone laughed except me. I curled up on my haystack, hearing the laughter and giggles.

It was so dark that I could not see the tip of my nose. Somewhere, water droplets were hitting the rock floor. I could feel carved miniature grooves with my fingertips. I wondered how many drops had fallen from the ceiling and hit the spot to create such a cavity.

I pulled out from my pocket a piece of cold chicken and began to chew it with the small tomatoes, which were left from earlier.

I started to think about Melea, and wondered if she was sleeping now. Had she managed to prove my innocence?

"My journey can't finish like this," I whispered. Melea and Warend, they were the only hope for my situation. If they want to save me, they will have to talk to the princess. And to do that, Melea will have to speak to her father. Only he can lead her to Sara. Everything depended on that meeting. I closed my eyes, and hoped that everything would work out.

Sentence of
death

~ Chapter .12. The Council of Elders. ~

"What they will do with him?" Melea was trying to resolve her deepest and darkest fears.

"The Count is waiting for his sentence, locked in the cell in the dungeon."

"She's not asking about that coward and traitor, sir."

"Oh, the other one... same thing. The Council of Elders will gather soon, and they'll decide whether your friend will be hanged or beheaded."

"But we can testify that Aron's innocent," she insisted. "He was with us all the time; we came here for the wedding. I'm a special guest of Princess Sara."

"You could be the king's stepdaughter as well, but we're talking about treason. Connections won't make any difference. For the Council of Elders you need to have a serious argument, tangible proof."

"Thank you for your help." Melea and Warend both headed for the exit.

"We have a couple of hours for that. I suspect that they're going to execute both of them in the Main Square tomorrow morning." She looked at Warend, keeping up with his step.

"Where are we going?"

"We need to find my father, he's a member of the Council. Maybe I can persuade him to free Aron, or even beg for a meeting with the princess. Only she can repeal the Council's decisions."

The guests had already disappeared with hope deep in their hearts for their ruler who had fought for the Land. Melea and Warend went out of the palace into the courtyard, where a few more guests stood in silence waiting for more news.

The guards and servants lowered the flags and banners at half-mast, working in silence. Among the handful of people standing around, Melea recognized Helor, once her neighbour. Long blond hair tied back in a ponytail with a piece of green ribbon, piercing dark green eyes and a slim figure distinguished him from the other guests standing outside. Dressed in an elegant robe, he was adjusting his gold necklace. Melea approached the elf, who looked at her in surprise.

"Greetings, Helor." She smiled, looking him in the eye. He was a little confused.

"Melea, what are you doing here? What if—"

"I need to speak with my father. Only he can convince the others of our comrade's innocence. Do you know, perhaps, where I can find him?"

"He's in his room, preparing for the Council of Elders. They're discussing the future of the kingdom and today's traitors."

"Aron's not a traitor." She raised her voice. "We were together all the time, we can vouch that he is innocent."

"In the registration book he didn't give the name of his father." Helor said calmly. "He was in the palace and we even don't know who he is. I'm afraid he's the prime suspect after Count De Marge."

"I can explain his background, he didn't write anything in the blank space because he's never met his father."

"Wonderful. Another bastard that no one would regret."

"How dare you talk about him like that. You don't even know him." Melea barely stopped herself from slapping the elf's face. "He was brought up by an uncle on a farm."

"A peasant and farmer," snorted Helor.

"You think you're better than him, decking yourself with gold and expensive robes?" Embarrassed, Helor lowered his gaze.

" Your father's in his room on the fourth floor. He assumes that you will come to meet him."

These words hit Melea like a bolt. Someone must have mentioned to him about the registration fees when they entered the city. Warend grabbed her arm, and with an apologetic smile left with her.

"I know you don't want to meet your father, but it's the only way."

They went back to the palace and were about to cross the threshold of the gate, when their entry was blocked by three guards, they crossed their glaives and did not move.

"Where you two going?" asked one of them.

Warend patted his sides looking for the dagger then remembered it was in the porterhouse, without it, it would be difficult to get into the palace.

"I'm Melea, daughter of Dermont, a member of the Council of Elders. I'd like to speak to my father." The guards stood still for a moment. After a while, they uncrossed their weapons and Melea entered. Warend followed her, but the glaives crossed back again, just in front of his nose.

"And you, where d'you think you're going?" Warend gritted his teeth. "I'm her servant." He pointed at Melea standing in the hall and giving him signs. However, the guards were adamant.

"The young lady can handle it alone without you, dog," the tallest one answered dryly. There was no choice; Melea had to go alone.

Warend left the guards, passed the entrance and quickly walked to the left wing. He began to walk very fast, not paying attention to anyone, his coat flapping behind him.

There's no way I'm missing anything. He circled the palace from the garden side, heading to a side entrance at the end. He used to work as a courier for the ruler, so he was no stranger to the palace and knew some of its secret passages.

Warend turned into a cranny in the wall, the gap was well covered, hidden in the shadow of the outbuilding roof; the sun's rays never reached that spot. He had done it so many times, it was almost like a habit. He pulled one of the stones triggering a complicated machine, the gears turned slowly moving the stone block. When it stopped Warend opened a small door leading into the palace.

The tunnel was small and narrow just like many others secret passages. He knew only three of them, but once he had heard that there was a whole bunch of them. They led from one room to another in a different wing of the palace, some of them even far away from the city where the royal family could safely escape during a siege.

Warend turned right, feeling the wall with his hand and found the handle of a torch. He lit it with two flints that he always carried in his pocket. The flame brightly illuminated the path, cobwebs were hanging from the walls and ceiling. *The Council will meet soon; there's no time to lose.* He went ahead without lingering. A trip to the porterhouse to collect the dagger would only be a waste of time.

The tunnel began to descend rapidly for a few yards, so Warend had to crawl on bent knees. After a couple of minutes, he felt hot, he was breathing harder and sweat was covering his face. Without hesitation, he turned right at the intersection of the path. He smiled at the sight of the ladder, which appeared at the end, and started to climb quickly taking two rungs at a time until he reached the metal flap on the top.

***

As Melea was climbing the neatly decorated stairs, she admired the gold-plated brass flowers, which were running down the walls from the top. They matched the beautiful red carpet covering the floor. She recalled her carefree times; years full of fun and games with the princess. She missed

Sara. Whenever she used to depart from Pentelia, she used to descend the stairs with other children to join her father. Now, she must face him alone.

She climbed up to the landing in the middle of the fourth floor; there was a wooden chest of drawers, with red curtains hanging at the sides. The wind was gently moving them passing through half-open window shutters. Melea walked over to the curtains and raised them. The view of the city buildings was impressive; she could see the Red and the Green Roofs of the city districts. She closed her eyes imaging that Aron was at her side, waiting for an audience with the princess. For a second her eyes were fixed on a small crack in the window frame. It had been made a couple years ago as Melea was leaving Pentelia. She associated herself with this place; it had so many good memories. She walked along the corridor of the fourth floor, where the Elders occupied almost the entire left wing.

Melea entered into a long corridor, which looked different to the others, the carpet was green, the furniture and paintings were unusual, and potted plants were standing along the walls. The king had tried his best to give his guests a domestic atmosphere. She passed all the doors with initials, looking for her father's. Slowly she approached the end of the hall, where the green curtain with gold tassels hid large windows. The last door, not much different to the others, had an engraved plate with the letter „D".

She did not have time to knock; the doors opened. Melea stood boldly, fixing her eyes on someone standing at the table, someone with long, dark brown hair. The elf was pouring wine from a blue jug, while his green coat was shimmering in the sun.

"I knew you'd come," said Dermont. He turned to have a closer look at his daughter, his eyes lit up and the cup of wine fell to the floor. He was trying not to blink; he had not seen his daughter for a long time.

"Hello father." Melea went inside and closed the door. Her face was impassive; she did not care about the meeting. The only motive behind it was to free her companion who was behind the bars in the dungeons.

***

Warend had reached the ladder that led to the north-east tower. *That metal flap must weigh about twenty stones*. He tried to push it open, but to use his shoulder, both hands and his head. He heard a heavy scrape as he lifted it and daylight immediately lit the tunnel.

Closing the passage, he heard footsteps approaching from behind the only door. Without thinking twice, he jumped to the wall hiding himself against it. The sound was becoming louder. After a moment, the door creaked and one of the pages came onto the roof of the tower mumbling an order.

"Why is it always me who climbs up that damn tower to keep an eye out for that damn mast?" The page had a fear of heights; he walked carefully, trying not to look straight ahead. Approaching a small flagpole he began to untie the knot.

Here's my chance. Warend slipped into the corridor, moving as quietly as he could. He went down the stairs to the lower floor. Looking around, his last visit to the palace had taken place a couple years ago; the hallways looked similar, they only differed in width and colours of the carpet. If he only could find a map or a guide, a reference point from which he could move on. Getting lost in the palace was not difficult.

Warend passed a door to the right, a corridor on the left side and finally he entered a room. He did not notice the plate on the door carved with the letters „BV", the initials of Baroness Virgil.

He gently closed the door behind him, now he could hear quiet snoring. Looking around the room, he froze. On the great four-poster bed asleep the venerable woman. He turned to leave the room, but it was too late.

The woman shook nervously and seemed to be waking up. He could do only two things: hold his breath and hide under the bed. Warend leaped under it, catching his right leg on one of the supports. The baroness opened her eyes, looking around like a small child awakened from a nightmare, checking whether the monster that she dreamed about was not lurking nearby.

She screamed, "Guards!"

Warend could not stand the noise, and covered his ears. That scream could wake the dead. Lying under the bed, he prayed to get out of this situation. He could hear several guards climbing the stone stairs. The baroness sat on the bed with her legs curled, the blue downy duvet was covering her body like armour, only her head was peeping out. Her small spectacles slid down her nose at the end.

Bang! Four guards burst into the room, holding their weapons ready; looking around to see what was making such an uproar.

The baroness was able to say only one word, "Rat!" She squealed with fear, covering her head with the duvet. The guards laughed like small boys, Warend was not amused at all. That meant only one thing, soon one of them would look under the bed; it would be the end of his adventure. He looked around slowly; the four shoes circulating the room meant that escape was out of the question.

Warend felt something run up his left leg and shuddered. *A mouse, I'm saved.* He grabbed it carefully but firmly and tossed the animal to the edge of the bed, the mouse ran out. One of the guards noticed it and immediately grabbed its tail.

"Baroness, here is your monster," said the guard, and the rest laughed, putting away their swords. She whimpered softly, "Take this hideousness out of my sight. Right now. Get out, all of you. This is my last night in the palace. I'll never come back here," she announced adjusting her spectacles.

"Never say never," whispered the shortest one. The baroness look at him furiously and the knights quickly left the chamber, closing the door behind.

"Laughing at an older lady," she snorted angrily and vanished behind the side door.

That was close. Quickly slipping out from under the bed Warend jumped towards the doorway with three small steps. He grabbed the handle and heard footsteps. He waited for a couple of seconds listening carefully, nothing except silence.

One detail caught his eyes when he left the room. A gold medallion on the table; he knew that symbol well. The Council of Elders uses it. That meant Melea must be somewhere nearby, on that very floor.

He passed the main hall of the fourth floor and turned to the corridor with the green carpet. He came to the end of the hall and knocked on the door with the initial D.

"Come in." He heard after a moment, opened the door and entered. Warend had not taken one step when suddenly a blade was at his throat. He raised his hands; his eyes swept down the sword to the hilt and, finally, the elf holding it. He had chestnut eyes, and looked old and wise. Warend did not dare move.

"He's with me," explained Melea grabbing father's hand. Dermont looked at his daughter and withdrew the rapier.

"Are all elves so vigilant?" asked Warend putting down his hands.

"Nowadays, I'm afraid most of us are," said Dermont and smiled slightly. "I see that my daughter has still not told you about us."

"No, sir. However, I can say that she's a true warrior."

"I've no doubt about that." Dermont looked at his daughter, with a hint of pride and sorrow at the same time. "I acted rashly and injudiciously throwing her out of the house. I'm not sure if I deserve her forgiveness." Melea was helping herself to the wine.

"Melea told me about Aron and you. In a few minutes, the Council of Elders will be gathered. You can go with me as guests, but you mustn't speak for any reason unless they ask you." Melea and Warend exchanged understanding looks.

"In other circumstances, we would sit down at the table in the Great Hall, enjoy the wedding and chat about elves and other matters. Unfortunately, we don't have time for that. Maybe they'll set your companion free, I make no promises, but I suspect that you won't convince the Council of Aron's innocence. For that you should speak to the princess, she hasn't seen you for a long time, Melea, and was asking about you." Warend noticed how the eyes of both elves met for a moment.

"Let's hope she'll listen to me." Melea put back her empty cup.

Dermont put his medallion on the chest observing his daughter carefully and wondered if his apology was accepted. He deeply regretted and was ashamed of his act, if only had he known how the story would turn out, he would not have thrown Melea out of the house.

"Follow me and remember you mustn't speak under any circumstances."

They walked down the stairs to the Great Room, and met a young man carrying a large straw basket full of jars with coloured contents. The man stopped, bowed to Dermont and looked at Warend and Melea with curiosity.

All three of them went down the stairs and passed the same soldiers still guarding the main hall. They looked at Warend with surprise wondering how he got there.

The Great Room was already prepared for the meeting. It was hard to believe that such drama had happened here just a couple of hours ago. The staff had managed to clean up half of the room. Eleven chairs stood in the middle, on the red carpet, the Elders were already sitting on most of them. They all wore the noble garments from their region. They were whispering among themselves about their lives. Warend spotted that they all had a gold chain with a medallion, the emblem symbolizing membership of the Council. It was a scroll, quill and the sword with the letter „L " in the middle.

It was a great responsibility to belong to the Elders. Members were selected from all six parts of the Land with the exception of the Southern

Wasteland and the Rocky Mountains. Each part of the Land chose their two candidates every three years. The Council gathered once a quarter to discuss matters of the utmost importance: taxes, duties, acts and prices of all commodities, it was the political and economic machinery of the realm.

As they walked into the room, the Elders looked questioningly at Dermont. He calmly looked at every member. Dermont sat on a chair in the middle, and Melea and Warend took their places outside the circle. A moment later Baroness Virgil entered the room wearing a blue dress, the expression on her face was more cloudy than usual. No one knew whether it was because of the king or the incident with the rat. Somehow, the rumour had spread around the whole palace. At the sight of her, Warend burst out laughing and covered his mouth with his hand. Melea looked at him.

"I'll tell you later, look, they've already begun."

The doors of the Great Room were closed. All the members took their place and Vitorius stood in the middle. Usually the king would stand there, but Sara had asked the priest to lead this meeting. She did not have that strength, constantly watching over her father.

"Welcome. We gather here to discuss recent events. We all made a pledge to protect our kingdom."

"And what about those two?" asked one of the participants. He was of small stature, dressed in a purple robe, pointing at Melea and Warend.

"They're with me," said Dermont. "I can vouch for them."

"Then we can start," said the priest and smiled at Melea.

"As you know, our ruler is lying unconscious in a fever. We suspect that he won't live till tomorrow. Authority of the Land will go to Sara, his rightful heir. We can't let the throne go to Serner. As we all have seen, he became an evil king slayer." He bowed his head and glanced at Warend and Melea.

"Brother attacked brother, brother killed brother. One of the captured traitors contributed to it. The first one is Count De Marge. The accused was found in the south tower, along with the body of one of the servants. The evidence indisputably shows him as a murderer. Why did he leave the royal family during the attack? What was he looking for at the tower? Many questions still remain unanswered."

"The second traitor is a young man who Bren, the captain of the guards, looked at curiously, apparently recognizing in him a spy and a traitor. We checked the registration fees and the night before the ceremony Aron arrived with Melea, daughter of Dermont."

At this point, the entire group looked at the elf who was just sitting quietly on his chair and listening. Several heads glared at Melea; they stared at her with undisguised curiosity.

Vitorius continued, "Aron didn't write the name of his father. We must assume that he's a spy, and had something to do with the attack. He—"

"Aron is innocent!" shouted Melea. All heads looked up at her; even Warend looked in amazement and tried to silence her. Dermont said nothing, staring at the red carpet piercing the Great Room like a big bloody wound.

"Young lady, have you been notified that you mustn't speak until the Council allows it?" asked Baroness Virgil, frowning slightly and clenching her lips.

"Yes, I have baroness." Melea stood up and looked at the Council. "May I have permission to speak?" Several people began to mutter.

"We are listening," said Vitorius, trying to calm the existing situation.

"Aron is innocent. He didn't write the name of his father because he has never known him; he was raised by his uncle on a farm. We arrived at the city yesterday, and he was with me and my comrade the whole time. Aron is loyal to His Majesty and the Land."

"There's no mention of Aron in the general census," said one of the participants, smirking.

"Because his uncle had never introduced him as a family member. Aron spent his whole life working on a farm almost like a slave. A few days ago he escaped and I know he would never hurt our king."

"Fine. For now let's resolve what to do with De Marge. He fled instead of defending the royal family and killed an innocent man."

"Death for treason and murder!" shouted one of the participants.

"Who says yes?" All eleven hands shot up.

"Good." Vitorius, looked around.

When they were about to put their hands down, the governor from Ewrod wearing purple shouted, "Death for both!" A couple of heads looked at him with surprise and admiration.

This time Warend could not stand the pressure of the silence. Without waiting for permission, he stood up and shouted, "For God's sake people, he's innocent! Have you not heard what she just said?"

"The evidence isn't convincing, it's only her word," said the hostile man in purple.

"Death for Aron. Who says yes?"

Everyone was waiting for the result of that vote. The first hand went up, then another. They all looked at each other and in turn began to raise their hands. Dermont was next in line, and he was the first one not to vote. The following two members also abstained from raising their hands.

"So, it's eight to three," announced Vitorius with a distinct hint of regret. "Capital punishment by hanging will take place on the Main Square at dawn; this time we'll skip the interrogation and torture."
The judgment pierced Melea's chest like a dagger. Tears began to roll down her cheek.

"So, let it be, the meeting is dismissed." The priest tapped the official cane on the floor.
Dermont exchanged glances with the governor of Ewrod and approached his daughter. "I warned you what the verdict would be, now everything's in Sara's hands. Thank God she wasn't here, otherwise, she would have to accept the will of the Council." He pointed at the man in purple. "It seems that some people really want to hang Aron as well as De Marge."

"Why?" Asked Warend, trying to comfort Melea.

"I don't know. Karles and Gildam have been members of the Council of Elders since a couple of sowings. They came from the southeastern part of the Land, the closest located to the Southern Wasteland."

"If only we could find some clue, or evidence," said Warend.

"As soon as you find it, come to the royal chamber on the fifth floor."
Melea and Warend got up right away. They did not wish to waste any more time. The Great Room doors were open again. Vitorius thanked everyone and approached Melea.

"Greetings, my child. I'm so glad to see you in good health. So many years have passed."

"I wish I could be happy as well. Our comrade, Aron..."
The priest interrupted her gently. "I know that boy is innocent. But nothing could be done, the fault belongs to Gildam, he demanded Aron's death."

"What about the prophecy that was revealed?" Melea did not want to surrender without a fight.

"Sara told me what happened after the duel. The Council of Elders is rigid; it won't acknowledge that there was a prophecy. I feel that the death of the boy will not do us any good."

"You have to talk to Sara," repeated Dermont. "It's the only way. Look for evidence, something tangible otherwise nothing will change."

"In which room was the Count sleeping?" Warend was curious to see if he could find something interesting in there.

"Third floor, right wing, right above the Great Room." The priest closed his eyes for a moment.

"Hurry up, we'll go to see Sara." Melea walked slowly, small pieces of glass were crunching under their feet. Lying on the floor they resembled multi-coloured crystals, which a few hours ago were illuminating the interior.

The sun was slowly going down, so they both ran to the stairs quickly climbing the first two floors. The spiral stairs could be dangerous. Melea remembered how once she almost tripped over running away from Sara.

They reached the third floor, walked down the hall and stood in front of a wooden door. Warend pushed it hard; it did not want to give way. Something was blocking it from the inside. He took a swing and kicked the door around the handle. A crashing sound echoed in the corridor. Melea opened the door and the candlelight illuminated them.

"What are you looking for?" They heard a familiar voice and jumped with fright. Inside in the shade Gildam was looking at them nervously and scratching his nose.

"You tell us what you're doing." Melea looked at him with undisguised hatred.

"I just..." He was not sure how to explain this situation, so he tried to put on a brave face. "I just came to pick up a book that I borrowed, before the king's death."

"His Majesty isn't dead yet," said Warend.

"Indeed," Gildam admitted viciously. "It will be a great loss, such a ruler. Both traitors must pay for what they did."

"Aron isn't a traitor," said Melea through clenched teeth.

"It's only a matter of time when my men will interrogate him and force him to plead guilty." Melea felt like she had been slapped, she clenched her fists with the intention to beat him black and blue. "How dare you..." Warend put a hand on her shoulder.

"I see that I'm not welcome here. I'll come back as soon as you finish whatever you're planning to do. I'll see you at the execution at dawn." He left, his purple robe fluttering behind him. Melea relaxed her fists. "I want to kill him."

Warend had never seen such an angry woman. To change the subject, he asked, "What are we looking for anyway?"

"I can't tell; anything that could set Aron free, some document maybe?"

"No, it won't work. They'll think we forged it or something. Besides, do you think that Serner would issue a contract or bill of exchange for the ruler's death?"

"You're right, it must be something else. Let's think... How could De Marge have contributed to the attack on Horen?"

"I'm more than sure he's a traitor."

"Somehow he weakened the king."

The answer came to them quickly. "Poison!"

"Did you see how Horen reacted when he drank his wine?"

"Of course. The Count poured some poison into the royal cup. We need to find the poison, I only hope Gildam wasn't faster than us."

"No, he wasn't." Warend answered quickly and confidently. "His expression said everything; he hadn't found what he was looking for."

They looked around the brightly lit room, searching potential hiding places. So much furniture, so many places to hide. They had no idea how this particular poison should be kept.

"We need to look for a small vial or some kind of pouch."

They both began to ransack the room. Melea started on the bed, Warend from the cabinet. She found nothing in the sheets, so she stood on the edge of the bed and looked at the canopy, also nothing. Warend went through all the books one after the other, but all in vain.

Melea knelt checking under the bed and found a medium sized trunk locked with two locks, it was impossible to break them. They were like an integral part of the lid.

"We need to find the right keys, I've a feeling that our evidence is inside." Warend pulled out a thick book bound in brown leather. He grabbed the cover and shook it upside down. Out fell a small iron key, he handed it to Melea. She tried the first lock and it opened straight away.

"It'd be great if you could find a second one."

Warend checked other shelves and its contents, unfortunately nothing was found.

"Perhaps it's somewhere else?" said Warend, looking through the last book.

"If the first key was in a place like this, the second key should also be easy to find. Look around one more time."

They hunted frantically, looking everywhere. Unfortunately, they only found a mouse's skeleton. Warend raised the bed in case the key was lying under a wooden rack.

"That two-faced bastard took it," shouted Melea and hit her fist on the wall. As soon as she spoke those words, Warend realized. "That's it." She looked at him in surprise. "What? You know where the key is?"

"Observe this one." He took it from the first open lock. Now Melea had no trouble understanding what Warend meant. It was a very sly trick. The key looked normal, but after looking closely they could see that not only the stem but the base of the key could also open the lock.

Melea knelt beside the trunk and put the key in the other lock. She twisted it, opened the lid and poured the contents onto the bed.

At first glance, there was nothing special; an old sword, some scripts written in an unknown language on papers and cards, leather pants, an elegantly decorated gold-plated crank, and a white coat and robe.

Warend stared at it all, speechless. Why would you keep such worthless junk in a locked trunk? Something was not right. Only the robe seemed to be new, soft venomously green woollen. He searched the pockets and found a leather pouch. He opened it, and showed Melea.

"We've found the proof."
Melea sat down next to him on the edge of the mattress. She looked closely at the purse, sniffing the contents; the burning vapours immediately spun her in her nose and she winced slightly.

"That's it." She pointed to the stuff. "Horen was poisoned with this herb. We have to show it to Sara and…" But she did not finish the sentence.

The door was once again broken down. Three armed soldiers ran into the room, behind them Gildam was smiling evilly. He pointed at them, and with a commanding tone, shouted, "Get them! They're traitors! They contributed to the fall of His Majesty. Snatch that purse from her."

"Over my dead body!" shouted Melea, looking at Gildam with hatred. She put the purse into her cleavage and stood in an attack position raising her fists. Warend grabbed an old sword lying on the bed and pulled it from its scabbard.

The guards rushed him first; he tried to keep his distance, waving with the rusty blade. Melea hit one of the guards with full force in the back and he fell down hitting the wall. She quickly ran to the door, but the midget Gildam was blocking her way. "Interrogate this!" and Melea punched him on the cheek.

The other two guards were stunned. They had never seen a woman hit a man like that. Gildam stumbled and nearly fell, trembling. He fled without looking back at Melea.

Warend used the prevailing confusion to throw his weapon and escape with elfgirl. Climbing the steps as quickly as possible, they heard the soldiers heavy gait.

Each step is closer to victory and freeing Aron, thought Melea, looking out of the window. The sun had gone down; they had been so busy that they had not noticed how quickly the time has passed.

They reached the corridor leading to the royal chamber. Warend noticed that this wing was much more dignified than the other ones. On the walls hung portraits of previous rulers of the Land hung in beautiful gold frames and between each pair of images an oil lamp was burning. The red carpet shimmered softly from the dancing flames.

After a while they stopped, encountering five heavily armed guards, the elite of the royal army, personal guards of the king. Their captain had paid with his life during the ceremony. The soldiers crossed glaives and axes. Others pulled out swords and stood in an attack position. They were ready to give their lives for His Majesty lying unconscious on the bed. Melea faced the human wall, Warend stood beside her.

"Father!" The only person who could let them pass was Dermont. He quickly walked down the hall and approached the guards. "Let them pass."

The guards obediently parted to the side. Melea and Warend went on. They crossed a few rooms and finally walked to the royal chamber, the door was slightly ajar.

~ Chapter .13. The decision. ~

Sara would not leave her father's side, while the body, wrapped in a golden curtain, was carried out of the Great Room. The king looked like a dead saint on a pedestal, and behind him a retinue of followers. The man loved and adored by so many had fallen in the duel with his brother, now everything was lost. The fate of the Land was uncertain and unsafe. Darkness slowly enveloped the thoughts and hearts of the people. The news about the king spread all over the kingdom in a flash.

They took his body to the royal chamber on the fifth floor. Along the way the servants bowed their heads as a sign of respect and sorrow, many of them wept. Sara was holding her father's hand, his palm was cold, as opposed to his forehead that was burning with hellfire. Horen's breath was feeble, the wound on his leg and chest were bleeding slightly.

They put him on the bed and left the room with downcast heads. The royal medic arrived immediately, sat on the edge of the bed and began to look after the sufferer. He had been here many times when Horen had health problems. Sara looked at him with puffy red eyes.

"Iwar, can you do something?" A few tears spilled down her cheek and splashed onto the bed.

"Yes, but I'll need your help. Bring me cold water and some cloths. We have to stop the bleeding and cool down that burning fever. I'll go to my room for more medication; it looks more serious than I thought." Sara made a horrified face, these words dug deep into her flesh, freezing her blood.

"The wound isn't dangerous, however, the poison is. If only I knew what substance he's consumed, I could set to work at once, we need to hurry. I'll be right back, stay here and make cold compresses for him." Iwar quickly left the bedroom and went down the hall. He passed servants gathered at the stairs.

"Go, please, the king needs a rest now."

"Is he alive?" asked a young servant girl, her face glistening with tears.

"The health condition is critical, not a moment to lose." Iwar answered hurriedly, turning around and speaking to the soldiers, standing on the other side of the corridor.

"You, take the heavy weapons and stand here on guard. Don't let anyone in except members of the Council, I'll be right back."

The guards rushed over to the armoury, while the medic went to his room on the other side of the palace on the third floor.

Vitorius walked briskly down the empty hallway on the fifth floor. The lack of guards at the king's bedroom surprised him. Even the servants were not watching the door. He went into the room, brightly lit with oil lamps and candles. At the opposite wall from the entrance stood a wide bed. Sara was sitting on a chair mopping her father's burning forehead. She took off his shirt and applied the bandages to his chest and then his leg. Vitorius walked over and sat down next to her.

"Sara, we need to talk. You have to tell me exactly what you heard in the Great Room when I lost consciousness."

Sara put another compress on her father's forehead and looked at the priest, she was sick of this day. So many preparations before the wedding, then the interrupted ceremony, De Marge was a despicable traitor. Then her uncle had suddenly appeared in the palace and attacked her father.

"What does it matter? My father lies here almost lifeless; if not for you no one would take care of him."

"I know Sara, but I assure you, it's important. It was about the future of the entire Land. Please tell me what you heard." The priest encouraged her with a gentle smile. Staring at her tired face, he was listening carefully.

"You mentioned something about the darkness that will rule the Land, and that among us inside the room there was a traitor and the future ruler of the Land, a saviour of some kind."

"The saviour will be the new king?" The priest wanted to know all the details of the prophecy.

"I don't know. I think you only mentioned two people, a traitor and a future king."

"Is that all I said?" The priest looked even more puzzled.

"Not all. You said something about the elements and some kind of key, I don't remember. Please, stop questioning me."

Vitorius looked anxiously at the king and, closing his eyes, tried not to harass the princess. "My dear child, are you sure about this? Please, you must lead the Council of Elders. If they decide on the execution, it could seal the fate of your kingdom." Thoughts were swirling in his head.

"I won't preside over any Council. Not now, when my father needs my help. I won't leave him like this." Sara turned to change the compress. With a quick movement of her hand, she wiped the tears from her blue eyes. Vitorius bowed his head in agreement and left. Just one thought tormented him concerning the saviour of the Land. He stopped at the bedroom door and looked at Horen's face as if he was looking for inspiration.

"If they want to kill both of them, we have to be careful. One of the captives may be our saviour or even the next king. Do you know this young man, who was arrested along with Count De Marge?" The priest looked at Sara.

"I don't know this traitor," said Sara dryly. "I don't care. In a few hours, they will both hang, they deserve it."

"De Marge, perhaps, is a murderer and traitor. He left His Majesty and, worse still, he left you; he killed the page and tried to get away with Serner. There's no doubt about his treason. I don't see any guilt regarding the other one; he was only charged because Bren looked at him suspiciously. Let's be rational, we all succumbed to great emotions. We can't draw hasty conclusions. One mistake could affect the whole Land. Imagine the Grey Lord on the throne."

Sara looked at Vitorius with unconcealed anxiety. A horrible thought occurred to her, what if the last chance was lost, and her uncle ruled the kingdom? Sara imagined the situation. Serner sitting on a throne with his weapon in one hand and a sceptre in the other one, his triumphant smile turning into ruthless laughter. A shadow flooded the whole kingdom, together with chaos and anarchy. Races from all over the Land fought each other for no reason. Servants killing their masters, children killing their parents. She could not allow this to happen; she will fight to keep the kingdom. That would be the will of her father, he fought till the end.

Vitorius knew exactly how Sara was feeling at this moment.

"I'm going to lead the Council. We'll see what the Elders decide. As soon as we've finished, I'll inform you about everything."

***

Iwar swiftly ran into his room. He opened the door so hard that it almost fell off its hinges. *There's no time to lose.* He dashed across the room and opened the door on the other side; it also creaked. He lit candles and quickly went inside. The shelves were full of different jars and gallipots with pickled animals, dry insects, and vessels full of dried herbs and leaves; it was a paradise for alchemists and herbalists. In the middle stood a long table with apparatus for making concoctions. Above the

140

fireplace hung a small pot where something was bubbling slowly.

Iwar put his magnifying glasses on his nose. His teacher had given them to him when he completed his education. Without them, it was hard to read descriptions of the contents of the jars. He scratched his nose and began to read aloud. From time to time, he firmly grabbed the jars and put them on the table. After five minutes, he had gathered fifteen vessels, placed them safely in a straw basket and left the room without closing the door. The king's life was more important than formality, so he walked quickly up the stairs to the fifth floor.

On the way he came across Dermont who was accompanied by young elfgirl and a man. The medic bowed his head to the elf as a sign of honour, at the same time grabbing a moment to look at them all. Everyone passed in silence; Dermont looked at the medic and closed his eyes slightly. Iwar understood the gesture, something awakened him, so he increased his pace. Jumping two steps at a time, he reached the fifth floor, while the jars rattled in the basket, protesting that he should slow down. *Last hallway, I'm getting closer. Everything is in my hands. More than twice I've helped His Majesty recover from other problems. But never from such predicament.* It was true, Horen had never been poisoned before.

Sara approached Iwar to help him sort out the basket. They moved the table from the wall and sat next to the bed. They put the contents onto the counter and opened the lids. Finally, Iwar pulled out a small bowl with a mortar, he gave a chopping board to Sara along with a sharp knife and herbs that resembled chives.

"Cut them into small pieces, then soak them in a deep bowl, and use the extract to wash your father's wounds and forehead." Sara's hands were shaking; she cut the index finger on her left hand, she put it in her mouth, while Iwar crunched a mix of different leaves in a mortar. He was rubbing them hard and fast amazed at his work, holding the bowl tightly in his left hand and preparing the dried leaves with his the right one; they had a pleasantly soothing scent. If you closed your eyes you could smell a wild meadow. However, the reality was quite different; pain and suffering, hope and help.

Iwar poured the powdered herbs into a glass of water with a few pinches of powder from a small purse; he stirred it and put it down for a while, looking at the princess rinsing her father's wounds with chopped leaves. Despite the bleeding finger and burning pain, she continued and would not stop, seeing her father suffering motivated her like nothing else, no force was able to stop her saving the kingdom. She sat next to her father and bent his head so he could swallow a portion of the concoction.

If only the medic knew what poison had been used, he would act immediately and prepare the appropriate mixture. Sara observed Iwar hoping that her activities would help relieve the suffering.

"We've done everything we can," he wiped his sweaty forehead with his sleeve and closed the rest of the jars. "Let's hope our efforts weren't in vain." He looked out the window at the darkish sky, where the clouds covered the stars and yellow-milk moon.

They heard footsteps in the corridor; someone was approaching quickly, passing the guards who did not resist.

Dermont entered the room. "The meeting is over." He looked sadly at Sara and the unconscious king. The princess needed a moment to realize what she had just been told.

"What is the will of the Council?" asked Sara, soaking another cloth in a bowl of the extract.

"Both culprits will be hanged in a couple of hours. You have authority in the Land." With these words, silence surrounded them, the medic carefully wiped his hands and looked at Dermont.

"Who were your companions that I passed on the stairs?"

"Melea, my daughter, and her friend."

These words aroused the Princess. "Melea is here?"

Dermont could see a glimmer of joy in her eyes. A friend from the past, someone whom she trusted implicitly.

"Why didn't you tell me before?"

"She arrived in the city yesterday with the second one who was recently arrested. We only know his name."

"Aron," whispered the princess.

"Princess Sara, you have to listen to me about this man." He began to tell her the whole story, just as Melea had told him. She was the only one who could give the acquittal order.

"If only they could find some evidence," said Dermont.

"I must speak with Melea, where is she now?"

"I've sent her into De Marge's chamber, maybe she will find something there that could free their companion."

"Who applied for the death penalty to Aron?"

"I believe it was Graf—"

Sara broke him in the middle of the sentence. "Was Graf Gildam present during the prophecy?" Her intuition was telling her that something was wrong and so far it had never let her down.

"I think so."

"Father!"

They heard shouting in the hallway. Dermont immediately recognized his daughter's voice, left the room and approached the heavily armoured guards.

"Let them pass." The guards obediently gave way to Warend and Melea.

"We've found the evidence, a purse with the remains of the poison. It was De Marge who poisoned the king."

"Well done, there's still hope for the boy."

"Maybe there's still a chance to save His Majesty as well," suggested Warend and they all ran into the royal chamber.

Sara soaked another cloth in the freshly prepared extract and cooled her father's brow. Looking at the entrance she saw Melea, in less than a second, a smile appeared on her face. It was the gift she had been waiting for. She got up from the bed and ran to her friend. They jumped into each other's arms, hugging as if they had not seen each other in ages. Many summers had passed since their last meeting.

Melea smiled. "We've found evidence." She pulled the rolled-up pouch from her pocket. "Aron's innocent, this pouch was in a closed chest under the Count's bed."

Iwar jumped up quickly taking the herbs to investigate.

"My greatest respects, Princess Sara." Warend knelt and kissed Sara's hand. She bowed slightly and returned to her seat. His gesture would have been accepted more warmly if her father had not been dying.

"It's been a while," began Sara, holding Melea's hand. "Please, sit."

"Yes, indeed! There's a lot of good memories to recall and a lot of new stories to tell." She noticed that her father was listening.

Dermont and Warend watched the medic tip the extract onto a sheet of paper and stared at it for a while. First he performed the same test as Melea, leaning forward and gently sniffing the leaves, which gave a caustic odour. He winced immediately, and realized how much His Majesty must be suffering. Scratching his head and imagining thousands of needles searing the limbs and other organs, he remembered one of his lessons, years ago, when he had dealt with a similar plant.

Iwar froze, with thoughts swirling in his head, he already knew that there was no hope, the medicine was not that advanced to help His Majesty recover. That night was the last one for the ruler. He gently looked at the

143

princess, who would find out sooner or later.

Dermont did not wish to disturb, but subconsciously he sensed the result of the analysis. For a moment, his eyes met the medic's who shook his head almost imperceptibly. He did not want to extinguish that spark of joyful hope. The loss of the father may be too much of a burden for young Sara.

Melea touched the king's forehead, it was burning; herbal wraps were powerless against such poison. Sara was changing compresses now and then, praying that her actions would help; she would not give up easily.

"Has my father told you about Aron?" asked Melea.

"He mentioned about his escape from his uncle, and how you met him and came here."

"He's innocent, pardon him. Please."

"Why is it so important to you?"

"I bonded my fate with him." Melea began slowly. "We met in non-typical situations; I saved his life and discovered that he is much like me." The friends looked at each other. They had spent so much time together that each knew what the other was thinking.

"Do you remember how we used to play as children?" asked Melea. Sara closed her eyes and returned to those carefree and untroubled years.

No one had heard the crowds gathering in the Main Square, the noise penetrated the windows and the open doors, escalating every moment. All of them were in deep conversations, but only Iwar felt its effects. Strange, odd voices came to his ears, hateful screams and roaring voices.

"Kill them! Hang them! Torture them! Off with their heads!"

Iwar frowned angrily, it was hard to concentrate in such conditions. Once again, he tried to recall everything he had been told about the lentra, but the image of his lessons with the master had disappeared. Realizing that the noise was not disturbing anyone, Iwar left the room trying to figure out the source of that din.

~ Chapter .14. The execution. ~

The sound of a loud smack could be heard down the corridor, like a piece of raw meat falling onto the floor. None of the soldiers had ever seen a woman strike a man in that way. They lowered their weapons with admiration, while Gildam stumbled and almost fell down and moaned softly. Putting his hand on his cheek, he turned and ran as quickly as his short legs allowed him in his long uncomfortable shoes.

He was running, not looking behind; Vitorius's prophecy was occupying his mind, some of its words resounding through his brain. *Is it possible that the prophecy was about this young shaver?* He imagined the face of the prisoner. *Or maybe he was also considered a traitor.* One thing was sure, thanks to this action he will become Serner's right hand, but the first step was to get rid of Aron. He would love to dismiss De Marge from the governor's position as well, ruling not only in Ewrod, the capital city of south-east Land where he was held, but also in Horeb. And yet, he was instructed to initiate the execution on the count and just before his death give him this innocent-looking bundle. He moved faster. On the southern corridor, he met a group of soldiers, which gave him an idea.

"Guards!" Everyone stood to attention, staring at the midget. "The Council has agreed that the two traitors will be hanged on the Main Square. Send some heralds to the city and assemble as many people as you can wake. I'll write what you have to say on a scroll."

,,*By the order of Her Majesty, Successor of the Land, Princess Sara, both traitors: Count R. De Marge and his confidant-spy Aron will be hanged by their necks till death in one hour on the Main Square. It will also be a warning to those who break the law of our Land. Death for treason*''.

"Get out on the streets and decry this royal proclamation. We have traitors to be hanged in one hour. Remember, Princess Sara is counting on you." With these words, the knights spurred into action, ran out of the palace and read the announcement which had been handed to them.
In many houses the doors were opened at the news that the culprits would perish in such a short time. An increasing number of people were coming out of their houses, with the desire to watch the execution.

Gildam was standing on the balcony, on the third floor, rubbing his hands at the view of a growing mass of the people gathering in the Main Square, crowds were coming down every street, gathering around.

The activity in the Main Square looked like preparations for a performance of troubadours. Several knights brought all necessary equipment to prepare the wooden platform with the gallows and tied loops. A couple of guards, with the help of several servants, placed torches every few metres, their fire danced gaily with the wind in that cloudy and sad night.

The gallows made a great impression; it was three and a half metres high, built with sturdy, solid beams and trunks. Together with the platform it created a spot that was visible from any point on the square. The bearing beam had four smooth carved notches, where the rope ran through; it could easily lift up to seventy stones. The crowd watched as two ropes hung on opposite ends of the beam and two stools were placed beneath them.

"Graf, sir, everything is ready," said one of the page boys, but the midget was not listening at all, looking at all the people as if he was already ruling the entire Land, standing proudly on the balcony and holding a sceptre.

"Sir, we're ready!" Only this shout tore him from his dream. Graf's eyes flashed reflecting the dancing fire of torches, giving him the appearance of a mad man. Satisfied, he watched as the last available spots in the cobbled square were filled and the guards together with pages were scurrying around like ants.

People were impatiently waiting for the execution, so to make it more enjoyable someone quickly organized a theatre troupe, actors standing on the platform were playing comedic roles, but not many people laughed at them. Gildam turned and tied up his greasy hair; his purple robe fluttered in the cold night wind as went inside the palace and headed to the dungeons.

Executioner, do your duty, he thought grinning happily and turned into the hallway leading to the southern spiral staircases. On the way, he passed Vitorius, who stopped him for a moment in a corridor.

"Where are you going?"

"I'm going to talk to the prisoners. I shall be the one who breaks the news." With these words Gildam sneered. He loved to bring bad news, especially if someone was suffering and frightened. It gave him unbridled joy.

"All documents have been set. I must speak with the princess about the Council's decision. She must have decided about that boy Aron." This information shocked the midget, and a shiver ran through him. "That boy has been considered a traitor, he's guilty."

"You really think so?" asked the priest.
Gildam tried a different approach. "Why trouble her grief-stricken mind with such trifles? Sara's under great pressure, I'm certain she will decide on capital punishment for both traitors."

"I have a different opinion on this subject," said Vitorius.

"Really? They'll be executed, preacher, whether you like it or not." He turned and walked quickly to the lowest level of the palace, the dungeons. He passed the guards who only looked at the symbol hanging on a chain around his neck, ringing quietly with every step.

"The Council have decided?" asked one of the guards. Apparently most of them were interested in the results. All the soldiers stationed there liked to gamble and bet; the flat rate had risen significantly, so everyone stared at the midget, who scratched his nose and said with grace, "Both traitors are about to be hanged on the Main Square."

Four soldiers jumped with joy, they did not give a damn that in a few minutes both prisoners would be hanged. The winners ran to the corner where the profits were divided into four equal parts, the others looked at them with envy. Gildam just rubbed his hands, glad that he had brought so much joy with such sad news, however, the main event was waiting for him in the cells.

***

We were lying on our straw bedding; I was chewing the last piece of chicken, which I got from the executioner. I swallowed the last bite and noticed a man coming in our direction. His purple robes were lightly fluttering behind him, and he had a big smile on his face. He stopped in front of our cells, folded his hands behind him and began to recite.

"In accordance with a resolution of the Elders Council, we sentence you both to hang till death for treason of the Land, which led to the death of our beloved ruler. The penalty will take place in..."

He was keeping us in suspense, though he noticed at once how we were shocked by the verdict. The midget looked at me with malicious eyes and laughed wildly.

The awareness of near-death did not make much of an impression on my neighbour. De Marge disappointed the midget's expectations, just lying on his side with his head on his hand. With his second hand, he was picking at his teeth with a piece of hay. In turn, I was trying to control my fear. I knew that Melea and Warend would find a way to get me out of this situation. There was still a lot of time.

"... five minutes!" He finished with mad joy. In that moment my last hope was shattered. I stared blankly at the floor, speechless and distraught by this decision. Tears shone in my eyes, it only remained to pray for a quick death, and hope that within five minutes everything might change.

***

Iwar was looking through a magnifying glass at the leaves, but he could not concentrate. Something was making too much noise.

Sounds like a crowd, what crowd? He thought for a moment, and turned round. Warend was speaking to Dermont, and Melea and Sara were taking care of Horen, discussing the last few years. They were so busy talking that no one even heard the chanting crowd outside. Iwar hurriedly ran into the hall, where he could see what was going on the Main Square. People were gathered demanding the traitors to be hanged.

"Quickly, downstairs!" shouted Iwar. "The execution will begin in a minute!"

They all looked at him, to make sure the vapours had not intoxicated him. Warend approached him asking if everything was all right, when suddenly he stopped.

"Princess Sara, we have to go at once. Only you can stop this execution," said Warend.

"Iwar will take care of Horen. If we don't stop the execution, the consequences could be tragic," said Dermont.

"There's no time to lose," answered Sara and they all ran out into the hallway, heading towards the stairs. Around the corner they came upon Vitorius, who was surprised that they had all left the royal bed so suddenly.

"I just met Gildam. He went to inform the prisoners about the death penalty."

"No Vitorius, he wants to kill them, especially Aron."

Melea shuddered at Dermont's words. "Does Gildam have authority in the palace? To perform the de—"

"The death penalty?" The princess finished the sentence for her.

"I'm afraid he does."

Melea's concerns were confirmed. "Gildam is also a traitor. We found him in the Count's room, he was looking for something." This message made a huge impression on the priest and Melea's father.

"Run!" shouted Vitorius, taking the guards with him.

**

Gildam was observing me, enjoying my fear. He turned his head and looked at the Count, tapping his finger into the grating to attract his attention.

"De Marge, you, here?"

The Count jumped up suddenly. He grabbed the bars and faced him, their noses separated by about six inches. I tried to listen to every word; maybe someday it would help me save my skin. Both traitors tried to whisper as quietly as possible.

"Get me out of here." The Count's eyes shot in my direction, checking whether I could hear. De Marge lowered his voice, "Have you found it? The key was in the brown, thick book." Gildam almost imperceptibly shook his head and whispered so softly that I had to read the movement of his mouth.

"The companions of your neighbour have forestalled me, unfortunately. They managed to provide the pouch of poison for Princess Sara."

The Count's face turned pale.

"I do not want to rot here. The agreement with Serner—"

"Shut your dirty mouth. Give me one good reason why I should help you."

The prisoner frantically tried to think of something, but his mind went blank.

"I thought so. I'll let you hang first. Thanks to me, it won't be the guillotine, so you'll not lose your head."

The condemned man swallowed hard, while the midget pressed firmly a small leather pouch into his hand, he blinked and left.

The Count hidden quickly the bundle in his coat pocket and began to kick and hit the bars. "Come back here you two-faced bastard. You cheating rotter!"

Gildam stood in front of the guards. "Escort those traitors to the Main Square. I've wasted enough time already."

149

The gate of my cell was opened and one of the soldiers pulled me out. They tied my hands behind my back, while the Count was yelling and cursing horribly.

"You're a traitor and a coward!" Gildam suddenly slapped De Marge so hard that he cut his lower lip. A drop of blood ran down his chin.

"Don't you dare call me a coward."

They led us through the Great Room. Gildam walked in front of the cavalcade, then De Marge, tightly surrounded by guards, and then me. Looking around the room I could not believe that a few hours ago such drama had taken place right here. With every step, I approached the exit of the palace without any idea what was awaiting me, except death of course. The crowd was whistling and jeering insults, the chants were ominous, full of hatred and swearing.

The whole Main Square was illuminated, especially the wooden platform in the middle. Walking through the main gate, the guards glanced menacingly at us. They formed a passage for us straight to the scene, except that my performance could be admired only once. I noticed the gallows and two loops on both sides of the beam. I stared at one of them, hypnotized, aware that soon it would be put around my neck. Fear choked me and I could not swallow. Panic was hatching inside me like a beast, which I could not control.

Gildam proudly walked passed with a smile on his face, leading the procession of death. The guards could barely hold back the masses of people. With each step, I could hear insults directed at me and the Count.

"I didn't do anything wrong! I'm innocent!" To be honest, it would not matter among all those people, whose hearts were blinded with anger. They had stopped thinking about their dying king, they just wanted revenge, execution of the traitors whether they were guilty or not.

We approached the pedestal and the guards pushed me up the wooden stairs, which creaked with every step. Only six people climbed: me, De Marge, Gildam, two guards and the executioner. Gildam read the short announcement prepared for this event.

"Citizens of Pentelia, by order of the Council of Elders, I hereby announce that both traitors, Count R. De Marge and the spy Aron shall be hanged by the neck until dead for their actions. Executioner, proceed."

The guards helped us to stand on the stools. The hangman approached the first accused man and put the loop around his neck. He checked it twice, improving the grip. Regh tried to take off the scarf around the traitor's neck, but the prisoner protested. Gildam looked into the Counts's eyes and it seemed to me that he winked at him.

"May you rot in hell!"

"One day we'll certainly meet there," admitted Gildam.

"Hangman, proceed with your duty," he roared, and Regh kicked the barrel.

De Marge had only time to shout, "Damn you!"

The beam creaked softly and the rope firmly hung under the weight of his body; he hung motionlessly. The people applauded and whistled, glad that one of the traitors was dead.

Fear began to twist my guts on every possible way. In a second, I began to lose control of my body. Regh looked at me sadly, standing behind me and waiting for a command.

Although he had a mask on his face, his eyes were full of sorrow and pity. He shakily grabbed the rope and put the loop on my neck adjusting it carefully. I felt like the devil himself had come to strangle me as the knot slid down clinging to my neck. With watery eyes, I gazed at the chanting crowd, having blinked, my eyesight focused on the last person I expected to see, my uncle. I could not believe my eyes, he was standing right there together with Molten and both were pointing at me with their fat fingers. They seemed to be disappointed rather than sad.

Gildam shouted to Regh, "Hangman, proceed with your duty!"

With these words, my heart turned into a stone, nobody and nothing could hold it back. Regh did not move from the spot, staring sadly at his feet, sensing that I was truly innocent.

"Hangman! In the name of the king, proceed with your duty!" yelled Graf clenching his fists and spitting with anger. Regh stood motionless, he could not do it.

"Stop the execution!" Someone shouted. The midget looked startled. He heard the least expected voice at that moment, Princess Sara was standing at the gate together with Melea, Dermont, Warend and Vitorius.

With the corner of my eye I could observed them slowly approaching the platform. Fear gripped Gildam. "Now or never!"

He dashed to my barrel ready to knock me off, on the other side far away, Melea instinctively grabbed a bow from the guard's hands and drew an arrow from the quiver hanging on his back. I closed my eyes and prayed for her accuracy.

The midget was close by, I could see his desire perfectly: to knock me off the damn barrel. Graf pushed the executioner away with his elbow, who fell from the platform into the crowd while Melea put the arrow on the bow. She pulled the bowstring tightly holding the fletching between two fingers, index, and the middle one. She held her breath, closed one eye and aimed.

Gildam was just in sight. Melea released an arrow, which whizzed in our direction. The crowd froze, watching it all in silence. I closed my eyes, at the very moment when Gildam kicked my stool.

Too late. I bit my tongue and wondered what would happen next. *Where do I go and is there any way back? The moment of death, is it painful, will my spirit leave my body?*

Just as I was losing my balance an invisible fist twisted on my neck. The arrowhead cut the rope, while I fell off the stool and landed on the platform with the noose around my neck. Thanks to Melea and her reliable accuracy, I was taken away from the arms of death. Nothing was able to distract her, it took great skill to aim from such distance, in front of so many people.

Gildam did not look back, he rushed from the platform and disappeared somewhere in the crowd, knowing that he had to escape the hand of justice, which would try to seize him in Pentelia. The crowd looked at him in disbelief, giving him a way to escape.

Melea and Warend rushed to help me. They quickly climbed the creaking stairs and pulled me to my feet, smiling at the sight.

"What took you so long? I could almost hear death knocking at my door." I grinned at them with tears of joy in my eyes.

"We couldn't let you go off so easily, we've a lot of treasures to dig. Come on, let's go and bow to the princess." When Warend removed the loop, the stone that had stacked up in my heart disappeared.

De Marge's body swayed a little in the wind. All three of us looked at that traitor. Fortunately, for me, I had not joined him.

"He had it coming," said Melea and spat on the stairs. Instinctively, I looked again at the place where my uncle had been standing. There was no sign of him. I wondered if it was my imagination or if he had actually stood there to watch my execution. He vanished as quickly as Gildam, to be honest, I had completely forgotten about that scabby rat.

We approached a small group surrounded by guards with torches. Vitorius started walking towards the centre of the square and calmed all the people waiting for answers. He climbed onto the platform and explained why the second execution had been stopped, he mentioned the poison in the traitor's room, and that the whole procedure had taken place against the will of the Council and the princess. The gathered people were passing this information on, after a while there was no doubt who was to blame.

The Main Square slowly began to empty. People were leaving, talking among themselves about what had happened. Pages and guards began to collect the torches and fold the pedestal. The body of De Marge was put into a coffin and taken away to the cemetery. Just like my friends, I fell in love with the adventure, becoming a free and innocent man.

***

Gildam dashed away with bloodshot eyes, heavy anxious breath and a rapid heartbeat. He did not expect that the execution would be halted at such a moment. Passing the people who were standing on his way, he swore under his breath. He stopped and turned around, watching as Melea and Warend liberated their friend from the deadly loop and released his bound hands. Aron was walking down the wooden platform. Within a split second the anger turned into panic, which filled his whole body.

If he had not wasted time having fun with them in the dungeons, things could look much different now. The terrified eyes stared at the would-be dead. Why did he not kill him in the cell, this young blood was considered a traitor; no one would have asked any questions? One stab with a dagger and the execution would not have been necessary and there would be no trouble. *I have to tell Serner about the prophecy.* Gildam pushed a short man out of the way and quickly turned the corner of the tavern on the opposite side of the entrance to the square.

The sign swung in a gentle breeze, the melodious sounds scared Graf, who thought the guards might be after him. His face was covered with sweat and his anxious eyes were shooting in various directions. He had punched the wall several times to calm his nerves. He tore off a piece of skin on the left hand, in a place of the abrasion appeared blood.

He turned into a dark alley. *Thank God that I have a supply of gold.* The purse pinned to his belt rattled merrily, without it he could be in a serious problem. Suddenly the way was blocked by two men, who were attracted by the sound of ducats. *The knights from the palace?*

He jolted with surprise, but he was wrong, they were just ordinary rogues in ragged robes. The first thug had a nasty scar passing along his right cheek. In place of his right eye, Gildam noticed hurriedly stitched skin, the wound had to be recent, the horrible scabs were protruding in a few places. Gildam tried to pass him, but the taller one blocked the way, his grin revealing his brownish teeth.

"Spare us brothers, some small coins, sir." Gildam took a closer look at them, noticing they did not look like brethren.

"Give us some silver, sir, we have not eaten for days," repeated the second one approaching.

"So get to work, and stop bothering me." He tried to walk around them. Both robbers frowned angrily. One of them pulled out a short carved skewer and tried to stab his throat. Gildam deftly grabbed the aggressor's arm and without a second thought stabbed his opponent's neck. His pierced windpipe pissed with blood like a slaughtered animal, the wounded man tried to say something, but choked with his blood flowing from his mouth with a thick trickle. Gildam violently pulled the spike from the neck and tried to attack another rogue, who fell on his knees, begging for mercy. He noticed a strange tattoo on the back.

"Forgive me, sir," he squealed. He took off his hood. "Spare my life, you'll find me useful, I'll do whatever you want, I can be your humble servant."

"It just happens that there is something you could do for me," said Gildam with a sparkle in his eye. There was still a chance. "Come closer."

The thug walked shyly and listened to what to do, while his eyes widened, and a dangerous smile appeared on his face.

"Take that money. Get some new clothes and weapons," Graf, handed over a few ducats.

"Of course, sir. I'll do everything I can."
Gildam grinned, patted his servant and went on his way.

***

Slowly I approached the princess, knelt and kissed her hand. Melea explained to me exactly how to behave in front of such a noble person.

"I've heard about you, Aron." Her voice was full of melancholy.

"Thank you, your Grace, for stopping the execution and letting the innocent man go."

Vitorius finished his speech and we slowly entered the palace. The torches were burning everywhere, illuminating our way like lighthouses helping ships searching for a way to port. Our destiny was a royal bedroom; we were all praying in secret that it was not too late.

~ Chapter .15. Dance macabre. ~

The body of De Marge was swinging slowly, hanging limply on the line waiting for someone to take care of it. No one paid any attention; the people were satisfied with a single execution. Everyone present at the square focused their attention on Vitorius, who walked onto the platform and began to explain Aron's innocence.

He pointed at the Count's body. "This man has committed a terrible crime; he has united with Serner, betrayed our king and poisoned him." The priest wanted to use the word "killed", but hesitated to use it in the presence of Sara, besides Horen was still alive in his bed. People began to disperse towards their homes, with their hearts full of grief, just a tiny glimmer of hope was glowing somewhere at the bottom of it.

A slightly hunched gravedigger named Kalham approached with the carriage, while the servants began to clear up the Main Square. The pages were bustling in every corner picking up the torches, pennants and flags while the moon lit up everything with its milky-glow rays. Only the gallows with the culprit were left in the middle.

The undertaker, who was wearing a straw hat and black coat, unloaded the coffin and climbed the pedestal. *That bloody platform. Why is it always cracking under my shoes?* He hated this sound as much as the sound of dirt sprinkled on wooden coffins. It reminded him of his sad work as an undertaker. It was the worst act of his profession, in his opinion, climbing the stairs, removing the convict and transporting it through a town full of people. The gravedigger walked over to the body, loosened the knot at the neck and held the deceased traitor with both hands.

The body was unusually warm, which somewhat surprised the undertaker. He grabbed it under the arms and lifted it down the stairs. Whenever he was digging the hanged ones, they were cold, barely tepid; any signs of life had left them. Without thinking about it, he threw the corpse into the beech coffin and peered into the toolbox on the carriage.

Someone stole my hammer, he noticed, scratching his head. *Bloody thieves.* Kalham spat on the ground and tried to put the lid on but it was a little too big and barely fitted inside the narrow walls of the coffin.
In that case, the nails are unnecessary. He kicked the lid again and called one of the pages. They both loaded the coffin on the carriage.

The tired boy wiped his forehead with his sleeve; he had spent the whole day bustling about. Finally, a moment of peace came to let him eat a sandwich with ham and a ripe tomato. "Bury him at the far far end, where the rest of the traitors are rotting."

Kalham looked at him with pity. "My dear Dalbret, I always bury traitors away from other tombstones."

"Yes, but the princess has requested me personally to bury this one as far as possible." Boy divided his meal and shared it with the old man.

The gravedigger scratched his nose and climbed onto the carter's seat. "Are you coming with me?" Dalbret thought for a moment and sat down next to the old man, enjoying his company.

"Cover the coffin with that black coverlet, please."

"Can you tell me why you do it?" asked the page, going to the back, tidying the black leather hood of the carriage and covering the coffin. "That's why people say you are a... queer fellow."

"I don't care what people are saying. I want to be fair to the dead and their souls. I cover the coffin so that their spirits won't haunt in the city. This black coverlet is reserved for traitors and murderers so that their souls will have no possibility of returning." The undertaker gave a quick glance at the passing women who cursed their cargo. "You see, when I was travelling all around the Land, I saw many traditions and customs. Each part of the Land has its own way of burying the dead. For instance in Tahalat some people give their dead to be devoured by vultures, others burn the bodies and keep the ashes in special urns." The page looked at Kalham and listened to him intently.

The carriage slowly drove out of the Main Square, turning into one of the main streets, where the crowds were returning to their homes. The road was illuminated enough, so they did not have to light up extra lanterns. Some townies frowned at them, surprised that such a traitor could be buried with the others at the graveyard. They would prefer to dump the body to rot somewhere at the edge of the forest.

"No wonder the princess ordered us to bury this fellow at the far end," said Kalham. Everyone stared in silence at the load covered with a hood, no one commented on such a strange habit, as they had before.

"Why are these people looking at us with such hostility?" asked the boy.

"You can feel it as well, can't you?" The passenger nodded.

"People are looking at our client; we're carrying one of the greatest traitors since Horen became our king."

Kalham and the page did not speak until they reached the western gate of the city. Dalbret suddenly turned round frightened. Something creaked terribly behind him, the coffin lid popped out. The wind blew under the black coverlet, making the carriage look like a troubadour's tent.

"Hold your horses, boy, it's only the lid. I haven't nailed it yet, someone stole my bloody hammer. If you catch anybody with it, tell me straight away. You'll recognize it by the groove on the hilt, the shovel and the letters K and U."

"K and U, Kalham the undertaker. Sure thing, I'll keep my eyes open. Ouch."

"What happened?"

"A speck of dirt hit me in the eye." He wiped it off with the sleeve of his shirt. Kalham was rubbing his eyes today as well. During the ceremony, he wept as he watched Horen suffering. If only he could, he would have saved his king. However, at his age, it would not be feasible. The man recalled the fear that paralyzed even the guards; everyone who came face to face with Serner succumbed to such fear.

They passed the old rotten tree on which hung a plate with an arrow and the word „Cemetery". The scenery was creepy, especially at this time when it was still dark. Kalham put an ear of rye into his mouth, he offered one to his passenger, but the boy refused.

Finally they reached the stone gates with the embedded metal plate, where the Grim Reaper stood with a scythe in his hand in the majestic parade of skeletons; all dead eyes watched them enter. Dalbret shuddered and almost fell off the carriage. The undertaker caught him and put him firmly in his place.

"Why are you so scared?" He looked at the boy with a father's anxious expression. The page looked like he had just seen the devil himself.

"Those eyes," he mumbled. "I just saw bloody tears flowing from the Reaper's eyes." The boy's jaw quivered and his eyes shot at every suspicious dark corner.

"Silly, it's just your imagination. I brought you here unnecessarily, you're exhausted, go back home."

"No. I already told the butler that I'd help you, besides, I hardly ever get a chance to be out of the palace."

Kalham was looking at one of the graves, sighing heavily. It was the tombstone of his wife; she died about fifteen years ago at a young age. The undertaker had not been married for long, a few months after wedding, someone asked his wife for some alms. A young thug tried to snatch her pouch, she fought with all her strength, but finally the horse hit her. Kalham had no children and strongly desired to father a son, a successor to his work. Grave digging was a profession passed on from generation to generation. Dalbret took over the reins and led the horse further.

Rancorous with his loss, Kalham was looking for the culprit. Despite the presence of many witnesses, no one had seen the face of the malefactor. The only characteristic sign was a tattoo on his left shoulder in the shape of a red lily, the symbol of one of the brotherhoods, which have their pilgrim houses throughout the Land. He swore on his knees in front of the dead that he would take revenge on the man who took her life. The old man closed his eyes and thought about his Liliana.

Along the way, they passed various tombs standing straight like sentries on watch; they were all were set up by the Kalham family, from the oldest to the most current ones. Sepulchres made of marble, granite, red brick and other metals or various stones. Many people bought a place in the cemetery in advance.

In the middle stood burials, mounds and tombs of distinguished citizens of Pentelia, on the left and right were merchants and craftsmen; there were plenty of those tombs. At the back were the graves of the ordinary people, at the far end on the left side was a separate area for traitors and the condemned.

De Marge was the thirteenth villain buried by the old man. The carriage turned and stopped at a small gate, a slat with an engraved snake was nailed to one of the rails, a symbol of traitors.

Kalham jumped out of the carriage and opened the gate. Taking a shovel with him, he began to dig a hole; Dalbret stared at him for a moment and after a while suggested a change.

The cold, heavy air was not helping at all, just like the moon, which hid behind thick clouds, and the sky took on a greyish-blue colour reminiscent of steel. They had to light a lantern to illuminate their work area. The ray fell at the place where the shovel was digging another grave.

Now and then the page wiped his forehead on his sleeve. *What on earth brought me here*? He cursed himself in secret, digging some damned hole. He could have been lying in his comfy bed. Kalham understood his emotions perfectly, sitting on the carriage and finishing the sandwich. He tucked the tomato in his vest pocket for later.

Half an hour later everything was done, they both untucked the coverlet and pulled out the heavy coffin with its ill-fitting lid, which silently fell on the soft ground. The gravedigger was a superstitious man, he spat three times, having no wish to deal with the souls of his customers later on.

They put the coffin next to the dug pit and the lid next to it. The custom ordered all traitors to be deprived of their head. Kalham grabbed a shovel and stood over the body pointing it at the Count's neck.

"I don't want to see it." Dalbret stepped aside facing the other way; he simply did not wish to see the blood and massacre.

When Kalham was about to raise the shovel high, suddenly his hands shivered and it was not the weight of the tool. Undertaker's eyes turned white, his pupils widened in horror while he stared at the breathing corpse.

Kalham was powerless and his mind refused to move a muscle. With his own eyes he had seen this man executed, he had stood in the first row when Regh kicked the Count's stool from under his feet.

De Marge opened his eyes, stood up immediately, and smashed old man's head with the coffin lid. He drew a dagger from his boot and stabbed the unconscious man knocking him onto the packed earth. Alive by some miracle the Count spat the dark-green saliva and approached Dalbret, who did not feel the blade pierce him like an animal. Somewhere on the horizon lightning flashed ominously. The page turned around and noticed the blade covered with red, his mouth filled up with dark blood and he fell down, lifeless.

De Marge looked around anxiously; fortunately, no one was there. He grabbed Dalbret's body by the ankles and put it in the coffin, which he buried. Sweating terribly, he had to unwrap the scarf around his neck. He stroked it gently. It was cold as steel; his neck was wrapped with an unusual, extraordinary piece of metal. It was a sash that the Count had worn since his youth. He tapped it and recalled one nasty story.

Many years ago during the hunt he was wounded, an arrow struck him in the throat. The shaft almost slashed his windpipe and there was no hope. Bleeding, De Marge was taken home, no doctor could cure him, all medicine and methods were powerless. After one night, his mother broke down and his father lost his temper. Their son was slowly dying in his own bed and they had to change the bandages so often. One of the medics suggested a metal headband, which proved to be excellent.

During the execution, the loop of the gallows was not squeezing the traitor's throat, only a piece of metal. It was simple enough to pretend to be dead and for such a villain as De Marge it was not too hard. Everyone assumed that he was dead and buried, no one saw him, those facts pleased him.

I need to hurry. He untied the horse from the carriage, threw off the heavy leather collar and mounted the bareback animal, which ran like hell towards the south Land. As soon he reached the border of the eastern forests he would be safe, there was no time to lose.

Kalham opened his eyes slowly. He touched his wounded head and had a look at his cut vest. Instead of the body, the count stabbed a tomato. Fortunately, the undertaker was wearing a mail, that iron shirt had saved his life on more than one occasion. He got up and flicked the dust off himself.

"Dalbret! Dalbret!" He looked around carefully, but there was no sign of him. The old man noticed an empty carriage with no horse and a small pouch with the remains of strangely fragrant leaves. Common sense was telling him to warn Princess Sara as soon as possible and to apologize to the boy; it was an unnecessary trip for him.

He picked up the find and slowly walked towards the gate of the cemetery, breathing heavily. A strange aura that he sensed in the air confused him. His eyes glazed slightly and blurred his image. Lethargy slowly took over the old man's body; he miscalculated his strength and passed out by the gate. The Grim Reaper was standing at the entrance, dancing with a grin and empty eyes.

***

Wandering through the palace in the company of the princess was an amazing experience. Everyone bowed to us. We walked down the hall and into the Great Room, while Vitorius explained what we needed to do next. "We must write down the prophecy as quickly as possible, analyse it exhaustively in every possible direction."

He said to one of the helpers, "Make a list of all those present during the uttering of the prophecy, I want to have it in front of my eyes in ten minutes." The bearded guard nodded obediently.

"Let me know who were standing closest when I was in a trance."

"It's not necessary, Vitorius." All eyes turned towards Melea. "I wasn't standing closest to you, but I remember almost everything."

"Fine, my child," said the priest and moved on, his voice bouncing around the empty hall. More than twelve hours ago, it was crowded with people eagerly waiting for the coronation and wedding ceremony.

As soon as we passed the threshold of the Great Room, the priest stopped. "Please, someone tell me, was Gildam present during the

160

prophecy?"

"I am afraid so," said Dermont. "He was scared and tried to run out like the others, but I noticed he was standing behind the curtain." The priest looked concerned. "So Serner will find out. He'll do everything in his power to stop the future defender of the Land and break the binding treaties." Everyone stared gloomily at Vitorius, who looked tired.

The bearded guard approached him. "Here it is: the list of all those present."

Everyone looked at the list written on the yellow piece of paper. It was not as long as he had expected. There were names of the guards and members of the Council. The silence was interrupted by a page who ran inside the Great Room.

"Princess Sara! The king woke up." The princess looked at those around her and ran towards the stairs.

***

"Son, how many times have I told you not to stray away from the path?"

"But Pa, it's a great shortcut."

The sound of the slap echoed through the nearby forest; the boy started to rub his skull.

"You and your damned shortcuts. How are we going to get home now?"

"Don't worry, we'll find a way, somehow..." The son looked around anxiously. "Why couldn't we stay longer at the exe—"

He did not have time to finish the sentence. A horse with a rider jumped over a blackberry bush and nearly ran into the carriage. The startled horse threw his rider, who fell off and for a moment could not catch his breath.

The father held the animal reins. "Watch where you're going," he yelled in the direction of the rider lying on the ground. "You want to kill us both?" But he lowered his tone when he noticed the opulent robe and medallion on the man's chest. "I... I beg your pardon... milord." He helped the midget up.

The man quickly took five ducats from his purse and gave them to the carter.

"Keep this money, you haven't seen me. Don't spend it all in one place." He mounted his horse and set off at a gallop.

Father and son looked at the golden coins glittering in the darkness. "Are they real?" The shining gold had made the younger man euphoric.

"Of course you sheep-head, why would they be fake? We're going back to the city." Satisfied, the father took hold of the reins and sang an old song he had learned from his papa.

The farmer has a great big farm
As soon as cock crows he's working in a barn
What the nature shall give to use
Forage for the horse, seeds for the goose
Hard work does not quiet down,
Work is in full swing, all around

The son accompanied his father by hitting a stick on the board, enjoying this song, once he had even tried to learn it by heart but ended up only on the first line. His father swore that he would teach him the song no matter what.

They rode one furlong further and slowly approached the city. They drove close to the old oak tree with a sign and the word „*Cemetery*". Some cries attracted their attention; someone was lying on the ground and calling for help. The travellers stopped right in front of the stone gate, where the Grim Reaper looked at the new arrivals, with his dead eyes and an enormous scythe.

The father and son quickly jumped out of the carriage and ran to the old man. They laid him on his back and gave him water from the leather goatskin; the old man greedily lapped it up. The son pointed to a cut on the man's shirt.

"Can I give you a lift to the town?"

The old man said nothing, he shook his head slightly and immediately lost consciousness.

"I wonder if they've buried the bodies?" asked the son.

The father shook the reins and the horse quickened his pace.

"Of course. They wouldn't let those traitors stay too long in this town. I suppose they chopped off their heads, and now the souls are suffering torments in hell."

"Oh really?" shouted the son, excited about the idea of cutting off heads. He put his hand to his neck and pretended to cut it off, making a strange noise.

~ Chapter .16. The king is dead. ~

The news cut the silence like the brightness of flint-sparks in darkness. Sara ran ahead, and we followed her, one floor after the other without stopping, everyone was worried about the king who had regained consciousness.

I ran together with Melea and Warend, the red carpet was muffling our quick steps. Asweturned round the corner, the door to the royal chamber was wide open and the light was pouring out of the room, cutting through the soft twilight at the end of the corridor, the torches had been out for a long time.

Sara burst into the room closely followed by the three of us and the rest. His Majesty was conscious with his eyes slightly open. Iwar was sitting next to him the whole time. Bathed in the light of countless candles, he was applying compresses to Horen's burning forehead, holding the right hand of His Majesty. Sara timidly approached the bed, while the rest of us stood at the back. The king's eyes opened wider at the sight of his daughter and his mouth twitched strangely. The ruler was suffering terribly because of the poison circulating inside his veins. The princess sat down next to her father, grabbing his hand.

"I'm here," she said with a quiet voice. Horen smiled even wider clenching his teeth; each movement caused him immense pain.

"You have such a delicate hand." He stroked her from the wrist to the thumb. "You have your mother's hands."

"I know. You're always saying it." She looked at his ailing face and her eyes filled with tears.

"Why are you crying?" Horen squeezed her hand gently stroking her wrist.

"I don't know what to do. How can I help you?" The teardrops crowded into her blue eyes. "You're suffering and..." she burst into tears, sobbing like a child whose toy had been taken away.

"Don't cry, my child. You should be proud of me."

"I... I am proud. I feel sorrow; you're leaving me now, when I most need you. We won't see each other again, and..."

"That's not true." He shook his head gently. "We'll meet on the other side. The time has to come for every one of us, mine came now,

I won't live to see the morning."

Sara looked sadly into the king's eyes, full of pain and distress.

"Death, Sara, is our destiny. It will always accompany us wherever we go. It's an adventure that must take place, like a mystery that everyone will discover."

"But I don't want you to leave now, not now when such danger is threatening us." She gently put her head on his chest and the tears flowed more abundantly, Horen stroked her hair.

"Don't be afraid. You're clever enough to embrace ruling the Land. I was a similar age when I sat on the throne. Besides, you won't be alone. You have wonderful companions who won't let you down and, of course, you have me." The Princess looked with surprise at her father. "You're dying. How can you still be with me?"

"I am in you," he said calmly and put his hand on her heart. "I've always been with you and always will be." Horen smiled while Sara clung to his hand gently and kissed it.

"Have I been a good ruler?"

Sara looked at him, "You were a great ruler, you still are; people love you, you fought to the bitter end, for all of us, for your kingdom and even though were poisoned, I knew you would chase away my uncle."

"I believe in you, my child. Today, together with my ancestors, I will hunt in evergreen forests and join the endless feast." He closed his eyes for a moment.

"Let the one who was innocently accused approach," said the king loudly enough, so everybody could hear.

These words pierced me through and through. Six days ago I was carrying bags of manure many furlongs from here, and now I was about to stand in front of the king himself.

I swallowed hard; Melea put her hand on my shoulder and smiled warmly, which gave me courage. With timed steps, I approached the bed; Sara stood up. She touched my right arm delicately and for a second looked into my eyes. For me, it was much more than a normal apology. Behind those blue eyes, there was hidden despair, suffering and fear. But after a while I noticed a flash of hope, a spark of faith and a fire of strength, I sat down in front of Horen.

"Hello, dear boy," said the king calmly. "Look into my eyes, please." The ruler of the Land was lying next to me. I stared at his suffering eyes, bright, energetic and wise; eyes of a real king. The voice of His Majesty awoke something inside me, giving me faith, hope, courage, strength and wisdom. It was a strange feeling.

Horen smiled benignly. "What's your name, my boy?"

"Aron, your Majesty." I bowed my head as a sign of respect.

The king stared at me the whole time, trying not to blink; his expression was so calming. When he held out his hand to me, I shook it without any idea what to do.

"You have a good handshake, firm and kind. Hard work, as I see, is not foreign to you. What is your profession, Aron?"

I smiled, uncertain of what I should say. The news that I had escaped from my uncle's farm would certainly surprise and amuse him.

"I used to work on a farm, my king."

"With your father?" The king began to ask more about everything.

"No, your Majesty, with my uncle. I've never met my father; I was brought up by my uncle."

"I see. And he also made you read the book with the red leather cover, *About Planting and Ploughing*?" I almost fell off the bed, for a split second, I felt exposed. How the hell did he know that I read that book, even today? He seemed to be amused by my reaction.

"Can you use a sword?"

"Yes, your Highness." I was wondering about the purpose of these questions, and His Majesty looked deeply into my eyes again as if he noticed something there.

"My daughter has chosen good friends. Watch her Aron; I'm truly sorry that we didn't have an opportunity to talk earlier." He patted me on the shoulder in a fatherly way. I grabbed his hand and kissed it with honour and respect. Something in my heart was breaking; that man was dying, someone wonderfull was suffering, and there was nothing we could do about it. This sadness filled my heart, two tears rolled down my cheek.

"Come here Melea." His voice was gradually flagging.

Dermont and Vitorius exchanged glances and both listened to their ruler. Melea approached the bed and sat down in my place. She looked at the face of the dying king.

"I've know you almost from the cradle." He smiled as if their last meeting had taken place just yesterday.

"Whenever you came here with your father, I treated you like a second daughter. I was so pleased that Sara had such a beautiful childhood full of joy, games and fun; she had found a faithful friend for life."

He caught her hand and squeezed firmly. "Take care of each other."

Melea kissed his left cheek. Gently rubbing her eyes, she stood next to me.

I embraced her gently and hugged her.

Warend did not have to wait for an invitation; he approached Horen and kissed his right hand. Keeping a distance, he did not know what to say. The view of the miserable king shattered him.

"Come closer to me."

Warend shyly sat on the edge of the bed, with an expression full of sadness. The king fixed him with his glare, just like me, maybe his eyesight was not as good, but he still recognized his people.

"Bow down, I won't bite you," encouraged Horen, smiling warmly. Warend obediently bent. We all watched as His Highness whispered something into his ear, no one else seemed to notice that the ruler pressed something into Warend's palm.

Warend looked at the king with surprise. He kissed the king's hand and approached us, Melea looked as if she wanted to ask, but he shook his head before she opened her mouth.

"I am sorry, I can't tell." Warend sat down on a chair and propped his head with his left hand, tapping the middle finger on his cheek.

"You know what you have to do?" His Majesty whispered softly, but everybody could hear his slow fading voice.

"Yes, Sire," they both answered. With his last ounce of strength, Horen pulled off the blanket and got out of the bed. Dermont and Vitorius dashed towards him putting his hands on their shoulders.

"Before I pass away, I'd like to take one last glimpse at my kingdom."

With a little help, the ruler stood up struggling slightly on his feet, every step seemed to cause him unimaginable pain and his breathing became shallow. Vitorius and Dermont held him step by step until they reached the window where Sara with Melea moved the ornamental red hangings out of the way. Warend and I opened the shutters facing the eastern forests. Fresh air flooded the room and the scent of the morning dew hit our nostrils. I felt much better; it was like a medicine.

Sara grabbed her father's hand and together they stood at the window. For the last time, Horen observed his kingdom, trying to remember its details, the birds that weave their nests at the top of the tree, the flowers growing luxuriantly on a nearby glade, dignified trees with its branches, green leaves and everything else.

His attention was focused at black locust, the first tree planted by the dying one, it was his favourite tree, with white flowers gathered in clusters on the delicate branches, surrounded by shapely, feathery bright green leaves. Horen loved to sit in a warm day under that tree, delighted with the scent of the flowers, with the sounds of the nature. The King closed his eyes holding the shutters with both hands and returned to those carefree times, when the life was not so complicated with numerous problems.

The greyish sky covered with thick clouds announced the rain; thunderbolts approached Pentelia. Horen dropped to the floor with a mysterious smile.

Sara was silent. She knelt down and grabbed her father's hand dropping only one farewell tear and placing a kiss on the forehead of the dead man.

After a while, a tiny ray of sun broke through the thick, dark cloud and fell on the king's face. Melea snuggled into my arm and I patted her hand gently. The bells in the city began to toll, carrying the news of the death of the king.

~ Chapter .17. The black letter day. ~

Horen's body was dressed in a dignified red and dark blue robe with a white ruff, under the king's hands folded on his chest, Dermont placed a lily flower and royal rapier with a big red ruby set in the golden handle. With this very sword, the ruler fought with his brother for the honour and the throne of the Land.

On the head of the dead, Vitorius placed a crown with set gemstones. The rays of the dying candles were reflected in it, creating a mysterious and glistening halo.

Together with Melea, we were standing speechless opposite the bed and staring at His Majesty. Iwar touched king's burning forehead, the blazing heat only confirmed the terrifying power of the lentra.

"I'm afraid I have to go and speak to the Council," said Dermont, giving a last look at the bed. Just after he left the room, most of the candles went out, and Horen's face took on a natural colour. Melea walked over to the princess to comfort her.

Behind the window dark clouds were accumulating and guiding the oncoming storm, which was just around the corner trying to cover the whole town with its gargantuan hands.

Thoughts were whirling in my head, everything suddenly moved so fast, from a quiet, monotonous peasant life to becoming a king's confidant. But who cared? The old man was dead and the shiny golden crown made me feel better, reminding about my epic journey full of treasures. *I want to be an adventurer; the matters of the Land don't affect me.* I could hear clearly every word spoken by the voice of reason and desire to set off for the journey.

I want to close the door as soon as possible and leave those problems behind, they don't concern me, I explained to myself. *I'm a simple, fanciful man, who just a couple days ago was a farmhand, a peasant.* At the same moment Sara and Melea both looked at me. Melea's eyes were questioning me from head to toe. I knew it would be better to stay, the treasure dream could wait, there was plenty of time.

Warend helped Iwar to clean the equipment; all the jars took their place in the basket, corked and closed properly. For the last time, Iwar looked at the purse that had contained the poison. He had done everything

168

he could to try to help His Majesty but simply failed to do so.

***

When Warend helped to push the furniture, a table hit the wall spilling the contents of a small case across the floor. Looking at those little junk treasures and trifles, he felt as though something had slammed him in the head. He had seen exactly the same things somewhere else, the dice made of nacre, a coin and a pawn chess piece made of walnut wood. Warend's hand absently went to his vest pocket, where the little bulge was still conspicuous. The last words of the king were still banging inside his head; he could not get rid of them. He had heard similar words a long time ago when he was still young.

It happened in one winter evening, when the snowstorm was raging on the streets and the breathtaking cold was almost freezing the air, thick patches of snow were regularly filling the trees and roofs of the houses. Warend's home was visited by an old man, a traveller asking for a hot meal and an overnight stay. He had ragged robes and worn-out shoes, his grey hair and beard were hiding almost all of his face, around his neck were pendants, amulets, talismans and bones of various animals. One necklace in particular had made the young boy curious; it was a silver eye-shaped medallion, two semi-circular pupils set with green emeralds.

The old man sat at the table and received a hearty soup, and barely stale bread. The boy sat on the other side of the table, not taking his eyes off the newcomer.

"What's your name?" asked the equally intrigued father, helping himself to the mulled wine. On the brown bottle there was a yellowish label with a drawing of a dragon in a crown.

"I'm Marlon, a famous soothsayer and storyteller."

These words aroused the boy. He had never met anyone like that.

"Can you really foretell the future?" Warend was fascinated, he did not allowed the guest to eat in peace, but the old man looked at him good-naturedly.

"Yes, I can."

"Oh please, bosh and tosh, I don't want to hear that," said the father and left the room.

Marlon finished his meal, took out his pipe and began to fill it up with cheap pipe weed purchased in Scarborough Fair. He lit it and inhaled strongly, thick smoke filled his lungs while his mouth tasted the scratching taste.

"How can you tell fortunes?" asked the boy, sitting next to the guest.

"Give me your hand."

Without fear, Warend stretched out his right hand in front of the soothsayer.

"The other one." He quickly swapped hands, while Marlon handed him some strange stones with runic signs. Warend took a closer look, there was no doubt that he was holding magical stones, and through his fingers he could feel that power. Marlon smiled mysteriously, and unfolded a small green shawl on the wooden table.

"Throw these stones here," said the old man. Warend cast them onto the shawl with deep interest, following the rolling stones; one of them fell on the floor. The boy smiled crookedly and was about to pick it up, when the old man stopped him. The soothsayer picked it up and examined it carefully, taking out a new portion of smoke. He looked at the boy's face, observing how curiosity was pouring from his eyes, eagerly waiting the verdict.

"You will have a long life, my boy," said Marlon at last. "This little stone represents death, thus it fell on the floor separating itself from the others. You shall live to a ripe old age." Warend looked at the shawl while the diviner muttered a few spells and after a moment he opened his eyes.

"Reveal to me." The old man's had a strange tone, his eyes were twinkling with incredible speed and the smoke released from his mouth took on strange shapes. At the beginning, it looked like a dice, a tarnished coin and a pawn chess piece. The next images revealed a whip, a strange old tree and something like a ship. Warend did not dare to blink. The ship changed into an axe that in the end formed a sword, and finally a crown.

"With these hands, you will protect your kingdom," said the old man, his mouth dripping with saliva. His feet were twitching, rhythmically hitting the floor. Scared, Warend was about to call for help, when the mysterious aura surrounding the soothsayer disappeared, and Marlon woke up, looking around anxiously.

"Please, forgive me. I lost consciousness for a moment." Warend turned around and scampered away to his room.

The next day when he woke up, the old man had disappeared. He had left some things on the table: the pebble that symbolized death, another one with a strange sign, and an old golden coin. Warend has never told anyone about that incident, not even his older brother.

***

Melea whispered something to Sara and they looked at me standing at the window. She approached after a while, with a sad expression on her face. "What are we going to do now?"

"We should stick to our plan. Let's collect our stuff from the inn and go."

Melea could not believe her ears. "We can't leave Sara like this, Besides, the prophecy..."

"We don't know anything about it. When it was revealed in the middle of the Great Room, there were a lot of people."

"Yes, but..."

"We're leaving tomorrow morning. We've settled here for too long, anyway."

Melea was staring at me in silence.

"We should have already hit the road to find some abandoned mine or rich tomb." I was trying to convince her but she did not want to leave and would not give up that easily.

"Then go alone with Warend."

For a moment, I thought everybody in the room was watching us.

"Last morning we both planned our journey, we even made preparations for it. Were it not for this wedding..."

"So what? I've known Sara longer than you, she's like a sister to me, and I'm not leaving her now, when she needs me."

"I'm truly sorry for her loss, and the burden left behind, but our plan was about something much less than the defence of her kingdom."

"Don't you care what might happen to the Land?"

"I do, but I doubt that the prophecy concerned a person like me. A few days ago I was toiling all day long with bags full of shit, yesterday they sent me into the dungeons just because some dying knight looked at me suspiciously, they tried to hang me for betraying the king, and now some people regard me as someone special. Something isn't right."

Melea bit her lip gently, trying to find the answer. "Life can be full of surprises, can't it?" She touched my hand. "I told Sara about our planned journey, and—"

"Sara is Queen of the Land now, she has to deal with issues of her kingdom."

"That's exactly what she wants, to find these elements and to hold back Serner. The Lord of the South will strike again, and this time it will

171

not be a handful of soldiers, she will have to fight off the entire army. I want to help her."

"Why we should care about some Dark Prince from the south wastelands or some stupid elements, anyway, how she is she going to find them, we don't even know what they are."

"I'm pretty sure that someone will guide us."

"I'm not going to roam all over the Land with a princess on my back!"

"You'd be surprised how she wields a sword and shoots with a bow. Aron, this is our chance for a great adventure."

"Don't you think it's too epic?"

"Not for me, I've already decided."

"What about our plans? Sara..." Melea placed a finger on my lips. "She's like us, she loves adventure." In the blink of an eye, I had felt something, after all, I have dreamed about it, the journey full of fame and glory, the epic quest, an extraordinary opportunity to become who I really wanted to be.

"I don't mind if Sara comes with us," I said finally.

"If you want to have a real adventure, you have to trust me."

"I'm going to get some rest. Let's discuss it later."

I found a free chamber one floor below, in the other wing of the palace. It was a nice cosy room with a huge fireplace and a gigantic bed on the opposite side. In less than five minutes, I was snoring like a lumberjack.

***

From behind the densely populated row of trees, the carriage emerged slowly.

"I told you, Pa, that we should take the shortcut." He spread a slice of bread with honey. The undertaker finally woke up, lying on his back on someone's carriage; his head did not hurt him as much as before.

"This time, you were lucky, you marauder. Just make sure you don't mention to anyone about that rider who nearly trampled us."

"I won't, I won't."

The father turned and noticed that Kalham had regained consciousness.

"Good morning, sir, how are you feeling?" He looked amicably at the gravedigger.

"I have to get to the palace at once. I've got terrible news for the princess."

"Oh, really? And what is it? Someone is stealing dead bodies from the graveyard?" His eyes twinkled and he stared at Kalham.

"It's about the Count who was hanged last night—"

"You mean those two hanged traitors?"

"What are you talking about? There was only one execution."

The man's face took a dangerous expression, his eyes narrowed and his eyebrows ruffled. They entered the cobbled street, passing the ornate buildings and tenements. A few lanterns were still lighted up, mixing their light with the day.

"What are you saying? I was there; I saw the execution. They hanged two traitors, one of them was my—"

"I don't give a damn who he was. I'm an undertaker and I'm well aware that only one body was transported to the graveyard. And if you really want to know, the hanged man was not actually dead."

"Undertaker or not, I know I'm right. They were both sentenced to death and they were both were executed!" shouted the carter, as a few heads looked at him.

What a stubborn mule, thought Kalham. The carriage slowly approached to the palatial walls.

"The royal palace, get out undertaker," the man said, while his son stopped the carriage in front of the main gate. Kalham jumped out of the back, thanking them for the ride.

Walking towards the gate, with a slightly wobbly pace, he was grateful for that chainmail. Two soldiers guarding the gate approached him.

"Take me to Princess Sara, at once. Important message, quickly." Kalham's words sounded serious, so the guards held him under his arms and led him to the palace.

***

Melea and the servants had returned to their bedrooms. The Council of Elders decided that everyone would be able to pay their last respects to the king.

"Princes Sara, we are ready," said one of the guards bowing his head.

"Please, go without me, I'll join you in a minute."

Warend looked at Melea, she was about to approach her friend when Dermont shook his head.

173

The procession moved slowly, step by step, down the stone steps and through the corridors and halls, everyone who passed along the way lowered their heads. Moving towards the entrance, the same three soldiers who were still standing there crossed their glaives and bowed their heads at the sight of the procession.

They entered the Great Room, where a small number of people were already standing inside waiting to see the noble dead king; no one dared to speak when the guards entered carrying the body, they stopped the procession for a moment in the place where Horen was defeated. Dermont closed his eyes imagining how terribly he must have suffered.

They laid the body on an alabaster pedestal covered with a dark blue cloth. Beautifully crafted silver-plated oil lamps were burning restlessly on both sides; the windows of the Great Room were curtained with dark hangings fluttering gently in the breeze.

"The king asked for his body to be burned. The funeral will take place tomorrow at the lake Lia Pente," announced Dermont, reading the Council Regulation.

"I'm not blind, or stupid. What's going on and when do we leave?" Warend asked Melea.

She was remembering when, a long time ago, she and Sara played happily in the palace, exploring all its nooks and crannies. They rushed to the top of the tower to see the view. Sara stood on the edge, looking down, when she lost her balance and leaned sharply, Melea quickly grabbed her and pulled back. This moment bonded their friendship.

"Soon. And Sara's coming with us," she added hastily as if afraid that he would ask too many questions. Warend did not comment; he knew exactly how things stood.

"Does Aron know?"

"I've already told him, he went to deal with it."

***

The soft mattress and downy pillows were just what I needed. I woke up feeling rested after a short nap. Stretching my hands I came across a piece of string, pleasant to touch, probably woven in wool. Curiosity made me grab it and pull it slightly. Somewhere above me mighty bells began to chime. I jumped up from the bed, waiting in suspense, for what I did not know. After a few tolls, the sound of the bell fell silent. I only heard footsteps in the hallway and some other sounds that I could not recognize. They stopped in front of my door; there was a knock.

"Yes?"

The doors opened and a young page dressed in a white shirt, navy blue livery and yellow trousers came in with a small trolley, it had a white tablecloth with three plates covered with elegant silver cloches, each of them was decorated with the royal emblem. I sat on the edge of the bed, lively with the smell of food; the aroma of the roast meat surrounded the entire chamber.

The page approached and looked as if he wanted to embrace. I raised my hands, trying to defend myself.

"The napkin, sir," said the butler calmly. He tied a triangular white scarf around my neck and put the table directly in front of me. On my right side, he put a white handkerchief folded in a triangle and a gold-plated knife and fork. All the cutlery and crockery had a royal coat of arms.

The manservant handed me a wicker basket with freshly baked goods from the palace kitchen. I took a couple of warm, crusty rolls and put them on the small plate on my left. My uncle, who himself came from a manor house, instilled good table manners in me.

The page picked up a silver cover revealing a fresh smelling fish dish, the starter. The cod was covered with pieces of onion in tartare sauce. The main course was a platter full of roast venison, the third dish was a beef stew with mushrooms and onions, every meat carefully seasoned, and tasted better with each bite.

The page put in front of me a well-crafted rummer and poured some red dry wine. I had to drink something at the end of this small feast and the bitter beverage perfectly fulfilled this task. The time had come for the dessert, a cherry cake and some strange overgrown raisins.

"What's that?" I pointed at the strange dark beans lying on the plate.

"These are the dactyls, sir. We import them from Tahalat. They have small pips inside, so please be careful."

I helped myself to one bean, curious of its taste, but after a couple seconds I spat it out; a piece of fruit landed directly under the eye of the butler.

Making a slightly frightened face, I handed him a napkin. "Oh crumbs! I'm sorry..." I choked. "The dactyls aren't my cup of tea." The butler took out a napkin and wiped his cheek carefully.

"Nothing happened," he replied clearing after my meal. "Some guests behave much more, hmm, worse."

This fact interested me, the boy had been working here for a while and was probably used to serving dignitaries of the entire Land.

"How do they behave?" I asked, cutting out small triangular piece of cake.

"Oh, I'm used to dealing with obnoxious guests. Such people complain about anything they wish. Sometimes I left their chambers with bits of food on my head." I was not hard to imagine such picture; I had seen Molten on a food rampage many times.

"The title does not make them better people, they fart, shit and die the same way as we do." The page winked and pushed the table away.

"I wish you a good day, sir."

"Thank you for everything."

Time to see Melea and Warend, we have to discuss our plans. Just as I closed the door, I heard a terrifying scream.

***

It could be clearly heard in the Great Room, where Melea looked at Warend with horror. Someone was shouting outside and a small group of people had gathered around the north-eastern tower.

"Oh God, what's she doing?"

"She's lost her mind!"

"The princess is trying to kill herself."

Everyone was watching Sara standing at the edge of the tower on a small wall, balancing dangerously on the border between life and death. It was not hard to mistake her with her white wedding dress; her voice of reason was completely suppressed, she wanted this nightmare to be over.

The princess, shedding tears one after the other, observed the gathering crowd at the foot of the tower. She did not care what would happen to the Land and its people.

Melea and Warend ran out of the room and headed through the corridor, where the guards watching over the entrance allowed them to pass. Just after they came out of the palace lightning tore the sky in half, drowning out the calls against the dark blue sky. They spotted Sara; there was no doubt about what she intended to do.

"Sara, don't do it!" Melea screamed.

"Princess, the ground won't be able to bear your weight, so please, take a couple of steps back!" shouted Warend, trying to bring some humour into the situation, Melea had to bite her tongue not to laugh.

More and more people were observing the princess, pointing at her and whispering that she had lost her mind. The death of her father had driven her to take such a drastic step, she was trying to abandon the kingdom and leave them to the mercy of Serner and his subordinates.

"Sara, things will work out, don't worry," added Warend. He was not sure if his words had reached the ears of the princess. They needed to climb the tower and speak to her, so they left the group and ran back to the palace, almost bumping into the same guards. At the entrance, Warend separated from Melea and turned left.

She looked at him with surprise. "Where are you going? The entrance to the tower is on the fourth floor."

"I know a shortcut," and he ran away, leaving Melea rushing to the palace.

***

The cries became louder and more terrified; I could imagine the whole scene. Wasting no time I ran out into the hallway and rushed down the stairs like mad, conquering two or three steps at a time. The meal I had just eaten was bouncing around in my stomach. Regardless of this, I sped up. Thanks to all that training in the forest, I was in good shape. At the bottom of the hall, I met Melea.

"Where's all this fuss coming from? I heard that Sara..."

"Wants to jump from the tower." She grabbed my hand and led me towards the stairs.

"On the fourth floor? I just ran down from there."

"A little exercise won't hurt you. You smell like a roast."

"Why we are going there? Can't we use those stairs?"

"This way will be much faster."

***

In the Great Room, there was quite a ruckus, people were frantically whispering about what was happening. Vitorius looked at us.

"Sara wants to do something stupid," said Melea. Dermont and the

177

priest joined us without saying a word. All four of us ran without stopping. Taking the same path which led to the dungeons, we turned left, ran up the stairs on the fourth floor and down the corridor to the north-east tower.

I reached the door just behind Melea; we both pushed it, but the door did not budge.

"Sara, let me in, please! It's me, can we talk?" Melea was screaming and banging her hands on the door. I made a little run-up and hit in full force, the doors only slightly twitched.

"Sara, open the door," said the priest with a loud and calm voice.

"I won't open it. Nothing makes sense anymore." We heard a quiet voice on the other side of the door.

"Together," announced Dermont and the four of us pushed the doors with all our strength, however, they were unyielding. *Storming the palace isn't an easy job*, I thought to myself.

"Nothing will work out," Sara called back in a despairing voice. "Have you seen the evil we have to fight? It's no use..." Her voice broke off suddenly.

Melea looked scared. Dermont gave Vitorius an anxious look, but the priest was sure that the princess was too strong to commit such foolishness. As the new queen she would lead her people against Serner. However, he judged her wrongly; she did not seem to have accepted the death of her father.

"Sara, remember that you're not alone," shouted Vitorius, but none of us could hear her answer.

***

Warend was racing with the incoming storm; the gusty wind had swept everything with greyness. In a nearby willow a raven squawked loudly.

Hoping it was not too late, Warend quickened his pace; he squeezed into the cranny, tapped the mechanism and opened the hidden passage. He had to crawl in the dark, there was no sign of a torch, but his eyes quickly adjusted to the darkness. It was not the first time that he had passed through a tunnel without any source of light.

"Would you be so kind as to light that torch? I'm fed up waiting for you in this gloomy tunnel," announced Rekel sitting cross-legged, with his back against a wall.

"Dammit! Stop turning up out of the blue, I almost shit my pants."

"You should put on that brown pair of yours."

"Very funny. What do you want? I have to stop the princess."

"Oh right, right. A lady in distress. So the hero on the white horse, with the shiny armour, is heading to the rescue."

"Your cynicism really amuses me. Do you think that me and—"

"Never mind." Rekel pointed at the ceiling with his blood-stained finger. "Keep going forward, you're on the right track, but watch your back while leaving the Land." Rekel pointed to a metal plate.

I'm on the right track. Warend finally reached the ladder and climbed up it as fast as his arms and legs allowed, almost crushing his head on the hatch, which he opened with a small thud.

Sara was standing at the edge of the tower, soaking in the rain. The tears on her cheeks were mingling with raindrops. She turned around immediately at the sound of the iron flap. Warend slowly lowered the hatch. The princess was holding a letter.

"I forgot to close the hatch. How did you know about it?"

"I used to work as a courier. Do something for me, Sara, please step away from the edge of the tower."

"No. You don't know what it is like to lose a father. He was brutally taken from me, and now Serner..."

"Your uncle's never had too much respect among the inhabitants of the Land." Warend took a step towards the princess. "Besides, whether you like it or not, you're now our queen, and it's your obligation to defend your kingdom, and to ensure the safety of its people. If you finish your journey here, on this very tower, you'll divest yourself of a chance to fight and believe in happy and peaceful times."

Sara hesitated for a moment, trembling with the cold. The rain was flushing the bitter tears on her face. Another flash of lightning pierced the sky, and the sound of thunder drowned out what Sara had just said.

"...through with this quest." She was sobbing and moved her hand to wipe away a tear, then realized it was a waste of time.

"You're not alone, your friends will always stand by you." Warend took another step towards the princess.

"Say it. Promise that you'll never leave me," she demanded like a small girl, swallowing the tears.

"Never, I promise." With three small steps Warend approached the princess, smiling.

Sara was about to put her leg over the wall when she overbalanced and her foot skidded at the last moment, she was caught by her sleeve and then by her hand.

"She's about to fall!" Someone shouted at the bottom of the tower.

"Hold me tight." She grabbed Warend's hand, swinging dangerously and trying to hook her feet onto something. A thunderbolt silenced the cries of lamentation and horror, when two white slippers flew down.

"I've got the shoes!" Shouted a bearded cobbler. "I wonder if I'll get a bottle of wine for them?"

"Quickly, someone bring blankets, we'll stretch them," said the tallest soldier. One of the pages brought a thick green curtain which the guards spread and stretched exactly at the spot where the princess was desperately clinging to Warend.

"Sara, you have to trust me." Warend was slowly losing his strength; the princess was slipping inch by inch.

"All right. Tell me what you're planning to do." Sara's terrified eyes were begging for help. Some inner force was motivating her to keep holding on at all costs.

"I'll pull you up a little; hang onto the edge of the wall."

"You'll what?" screamed Sara. "No way, over my dead body!"

"I won't let you die in such a stupid way. Hold on." He pulled her up sharply, so she was able to clutch the wall and hang on to it.

Warend quickly turned around to try to find some rope. The rain was heavy and cold; thunderbolts were fusing all the sounds into a loud hubbub, even the shouts coming from behind the door. He noticed the mast and the fluttering dark flag. He ran up to it and began to untie the knot, the soaked line was not making it an easy task.

"Warend, I can't hold on much longer."

"Patience is a virtue! I thought princesses knew all about the virtues."

"You can't lecture me now!"

"Can you name them for me, please?" Warend smiled.

"Can I what? It's not appropriate moment."

"I know you can, go ahead." He encouraged her and focused all his attention on the rope.

"Patience, strength, common sense, justice and..."

"The faith my queen, believe in me." Finally, he managed to untangle the knot and ran to the edge with the rope.

Sara firmly grabbed it and began to climb with hope drawn on her face. After a few moments both of her feet were safely standing on the tower. Warend took off his coat and put it round the princess's shoulders. They both slowly approached the bolted door.

***

We all stopped shouting and knocking on the door when we heard the lock. Melea quickly pulled the handle, a breath of fresh air hit us all. In the doorway stood Warend and by his side, Sara. The girls stared at each other; it was hard to tell who had a more worried expression.

"Sara, my child," began Vitorius calmly, "Do you..."

"I know and I am ashamed of that. Please excuse me, I need to rest, I'm not feeling well."

"I'll keep an eye on her." Melea and Sara went down through the hall to the main stairs.

Warend closed the door of the tower and leaned against the wall. Breathing heavily he slightly dropped his head. "I saved her life and she didn't even say, "Thank you"." Droplets of rain were running down his forehead and nose, dripping onto the carpet, soaking it almost immediately.

"I know Sara's grateful, you've saved her life," said the priest.

"Certainly, in some way, she'll thank you for that," said Dermont.

"Yes, she'll light a candle for me on my grave." he answered sarcastically. "Come on Aron, let's eat something and bring our equipment into the palace."

We passed the corridor, walked down the main stairs to the lobby, where surprisingly, we did not encounter the three familiar soldiers guarding the entrance. Sara was standing there with Melea.

At first Warend did not spot them. Melea gave me a warm smile and put a finger to her lips. I nodded and stopped suddenly.

Warend began to mutter, "Not even a "thank you"." It was loud enough for everyone to hear. "I went through fire and water! As the only one I passed through the hidden passage, came on time, convinced her and she simply walked away."

I coughed softly to give him a sign.

"Somebody would like to speak to you," said Melea.

She grabbed my hand and we went outside. It had stopped raining, but the thick clouds were still hanging over the city like some kind of curse that was to be fulfilled. Even though the king's death was a short time ago, radical changes had taken place. The town on the day of our arrival was proud of its dignity and wealth, but now everything was dimmed, the people were frightened. Their minds were plunged into sorrow and uncertainty; it was like a plague moving from one person to another, from family to family. It was a black day for Pentelia.

Melea let go of my hand just as we stood near the foot of the tower.

"Why did you drag me here? We want to go to the porterhouse for our equipment."

"There's something I need to tell you." Melea began slowly. "When I went downstairs with Sara, we stumbled across Kalham, the undertaker."

"That old one who took the body of the Count?"

"Exactly the same one. He told us something that may shock you even more."

"What's happened?" My head was spinning with thousands of ideas and I was a little nervous.

"Count De Marge is alive," she said curtly. The meaning of her words took a while to filter through to my brain.

"What?"

"Count De Marge is still alive," Melea repeated quietly.

"Melea, what are you talking about? I was standing next to him; I saw Regh perform the execution."

"Yes, I know, but..."

"I was a few steps away. It's impossible." I was trembling.

"I'm finding it hard to believe as well, but it's true. The executed man simply got up from his coffin, killed one of the pages and knocked out the undertaker; fortunately, he was wearing a mail armour. Kalham also discovered a pouch with leftovers of a strange herbs. Iwar shall examine them right away." I listened to the whole story, but I could not believe it so easily.

"It means the prophecy can also affect him, or that bloody Gildam," she added briskly.

"You mean the midget who so desperately wanted me killed?"

"Yes."

"He quarrelled with De Marge while he was next to my cell. They exchanged a few biting comments about each other. Gildam handed him a bundle making sure no one could see and he left the prisoner with an ominous laugh."

"Serner will find out about the prophecy."

After a while Warend appeared. His eyes were sparkling with a gentle glow.

"Sara went to her room, she asked you to join her." Melea looked at me and walked back to the palace.

Warend and I walked out onto the main street and headed to the Blue Roof District to collect our purchases.

"What did the princess say?" I asked.

"I'd prefer do not talk about it right now," he answered shortly and patted his shirt pocket.

While we walked in silence down the main street, I observed the nearby buildings surrounding the palace. Towering houses with their colourful roofs, cleverly constructed facades and floors. Streets were overlapping into simple angles, elegant iron lanterns carefully carved, and the worn paving stones.

We passed a market where the merchants had already set up their tents and negotiated prices with each other. It was a festival of colours, a demonstration of goods and products. The market smelled of dirt, animal and human faeces, rotten vegetables, swelling fruits, fresh fish, red meat and money. The last one smelled the most, passing from hand to hand all around.

"Trust me, this market is barely a dressing room comparing to Scarborough Fair," said Warend. "Ah, Scarborough Fair... You'll find every item you're interested in, from ordinary objects to magical artefacts and much more if you ask the right people and pay in gold."

I was listening to Warend with full my attention, when our way was blocked by a carriage. Taking a good look at this vehicle, I froze, knowing it well. So many times I'd had to drive the loose nails coming off the beam, so many hours I had scrubbed mud from its wheels. On the place of the carter was sitting none other than my uncle and Molten, Warend eyed them carefully.

My uncle threw us a quick look. "Chaps, move along, because I cannot— You!" He stopped in mid-sentence. His face was the colour of beetroot and his jaw was twitching.

"Pa, what is it?" I heard the familiar voice of my cousin. "Why aren't we going?" Then he understood. He looked at me and stared as if he had seen a ghost.

"Fatty!" said Warend and pointed at my uncle.

"Uncle?" I looked puzzled and confused.

"Ragged man!" growled Uncle and scraps of salvia shot from his mouth.

"The undead!" Molten's frightened eyes could not stop looking at me and his pointing hand was trembling with fear.

"You brat, now I'll show you what it means to run away from the farm!" Uncle grasped a small whip and jumped out from the carter's place. "Yesterday you were standing with a noose around your neck," he said through clenched teeth. "I demand you come back with us!"

"You wish, Uncle." I knew exactly how much he wanted to scold me but he was afraid of my companion. "You will be working on my farm for the rest of your life." Uncle started hitting the handle of the whip in his palm.

"Stop them!" Someone was shouting.
Warend looked round, these words were directed at us. Uncle put his thick hands on his chest, and smiled mockingly.

"There you go. I'll bind you in a minute and transport you back to the farm." After a while, the three guards ran up to us. The tallest of them stood directly in front of us.

"Many thanks. You've caught these scammers." He turned to me and Warend. Neither of us had any idea what was going on. However, I instinctively and confidently announced, "Arrest them!" The two guards grabbed my uncle and Molten by their shoulders.

"Send them for three weeks to the dungeons, they should lose a bit of flesh."

"How dare you," said my uncle, spitting at the standing officer. A wet trickle was swinging and dangling at the end of his pointed nose.

"I'm innocent," cried Molten, looking helplessly at his father.

"Shut up." Uncle scolded him.

"We've not done anything wrong, sir. But this lad has, oh yes! Arrest him, he ran away from my farm, stole all my money and—"

"Yes, the money," said the officer.

"Can we see your purse, carter?" The guard reached for my uncle's belt and tried to untie the leather strap.

Uncle quickly turned around and along with him a massive, fat belly. "Keep your hands off me," he roared. "I'm not the one to search, he is. You have to search him." He pointed at me.
Molten, held by the guard, was standing stiffly, frightened at the situation. The guard grabbed Uncle's collar and pulled him, almost knocking him off his feet.

"Give me the purse. Now," he shouted. The guard untied the leather strap, and the pouch dropped onto the stone floor. My uncle kneeled to pick it up, but his movements were too slow. The officer snatched the purse and dumped a bunch of coins in his hand, he looked at one of them and examined it in detail.

"Just as I thought. A fake one." This stunned my uncle and Molten.

"This is a misunderstanding," groaned Uncle. But it was too late. The guards bound their hands, my uncle resisted, twisting and turning.

"I'm innocent. I got this pouch of money from a—"

"Let me guess. A midget was riding on a horse, and he jumped out from the bush."

"But it's the truth. We met him on the south road close to the cemetery. A small fellow dressed in purple, he was in a hurry and didn't want to be mentioned to anybody."

Warend and I exchanged looks. However, such fairy-tales did not make any impression on the guards, they were used to the prevarication of cheats of pilferers, I found it. Somebody gave it to me. And many other excuses. A nervous uncle and a terrified cousin were escorted to palace dungeons.

"Is the dungeon food tasty? I'm hungry."

My uncle gave him a solid kick in the butt. "You and your shortcuts."

"At least we got rid of him for a while."

"No wonder you ran away from your uncle. Let's get our equipment and horses."

The bells began to toll at noon; most of the stores that we passed along the way were closed. During one day, the town had lost its charm, its sense of safety and the Land its ruler. Why did it all have to happen when I had started a new chapter in my life?

Walking in silence, we passed the road between the palace walls and the porterhouse in a quick time. Some of the people we passed were looking at me quizzically, their faces were not hostile any more, grief had struck them all. We turned into a familiar street.

"You get our purchases and weapons and I'll prepare the horses," said Warend.

"I can't do it by myself, there's too much equipment." I protested, so Warend followed me into the entrance.

The fireplace was still burning, and delicious smells were coming from the kitchen. There was no sign of the innkeeper, so we walked up the stairs, the wooden floor boards were creaking beneath our feet. Nothing had changed in the room since the day before, except maybe the window, which was open wide. Warend began to put our equipment into the knapsacks. Surprisingly they had additional slots for the weapons, so we could easily fit our swords and other things. At the bottom, there was a special buckle for a rolled sleeping bag. After a few minutes, all three backpacks were ready.

I heard a strange noise and looked behind me. I walked over to the window to reassure myself, a carriage was driving down the street loaded with apples, and people were walking down the footpath. *You're getting too sensitive.* Out of the corner of my eye, I noticed some movement on the roof on the opposite side of the street. Turning around quickly, I bumped into Warend and we both fell onto the floor.

"What the hell are you doing?" he growled.

"Look at that." I pointed to an arrow with red feathers stuck in the wall; the shaft was so sharp that it had easily made a small notch in the hard oak board.

"After him!" shouted Warend.

We both rushed out into the street to the tenement, from where we were shot. I heard footsteps on the roof tiles; someone was running in the opposite direction. Warend took the right and I took the left side of the building. The same carriage with the apples was slowly rolling down the street. The assassin hurriedly jumped behind me and landed right on a pile of apples, scattering them all over the place. The carter panicked and ducked under the seat, and passers-by stopped to look at this scene.

The assassin was too fast. He had ragged hood covering his head and leather gloves on his arms. I could not see his face. He vanished behind corners, changing now and then the directions trying to lose us. He knew the city inside out. I wanted to hunt down that man at all costs.

We ran into a long alley between two tenements, with laundry hanging on string above our heads. The owners had not managed to hide it from the storm. The man took out a small dagger from his belt and threw it into the air, cutting the thin string. A mass of bedclothes, a blanket, and a couple of shirts fell on my head. I wasted precious seconds clambering out of the trap. When I removed the sheet from my head, there was no one in sight.

No way, he couldn't have run through the entire alley, he had to have gone into a door or... I looked up and noticed the fugitive climbing the wall and reaching the roof again. I jumped on a barrel and from it onto the first-floor balcony of an old tenement. A naked woman was standing at the window. When she saw me she screamed and covered her breasts.

I climbed the wall and pulled myself up onto the roof. The assassin was a dozen or so metres from me on another building. A frantic race on the roofs began. I jumped from one building to another, all the time getting closer to the assassin. Some people on the pavement were pointing at us.

Warend was keeping us company, running all the time on the other side and trying to cut off the runner. He stopped in the middle of a small street, where the distance between one tenement and the opposite one was quite far. The assassin approached the edge, set foot on it and bounced.

The height was not an obstacle for him, and with a nimble jump, he got across, gripped the edge and with his knees, forcefully struck into the wall. The assassin pulled himself up and stood on the other side. Warend stared at the edge where the thug disappeared, and he turned to look at me. I put my right foot on the edge and bounced up, straightening my knees to cushion the impact. The thug was observing my leap; he smiled, took out a dagger from his belt, approached and attacked.

"Look out!" shouted Warend.

I had no choice; I had to let go. The blade hit the wall, chipping away a piece of brick. Landing hard on the cobblestone walkway, I had swallowed the bitter taste of defeat; the assassin disappeared. He had ambushed and attacked us with such premeditation. I would recognize that scoundrel anywhere; he left behind one important thing, an arrow with red feathers. Warend helped me to get up.

"Almost got him," he said calmly. He looked up again. You can never be too careful.

"That was close."

"Thanks for saving my ass. Let's get our things and go back to the palace. I've have enough excitement for today." We walked slowly to the porterhouse to get the horses and our equipment.

***

Melea went into Sara's room and closed the door. She took a folded card from her pocket and handed to her friend who was seated at the edge of the bed.

"It seems that you lost something while you were admiring the views from the tower," she said passing the letter to her friend. Sara had not had time to read it, she opened it gently and began to follow the text. Melea watched her intently; she already knew the contents of the letter, now she was trying to figure out what the last sentence could mean.

My dearest Sara,

If you are reading these words, I am probably dead. It is time for you to reign the Land. The authority is a gift and a curse, a burden that you have to carry till the end. Do not give up whatever happens, rule wisely and justly, a lot of people are counting on you. I will be watching your journey together with our ancestors.

Remember, you are not alone, Vitorius and Dermont are excellent advisors, I trusted them implicitly. As soon as you have any doubt do not hesitate to ask them for an opinion, or good advice. Thanks to this I accomplished so much.

You realize, of course, the danger threatening your kingdom. The great dark clouds are coming over the Land in the form of my brother and your uncle. Serner is capable of doing anything, and will use all stratagems to sit on the throne. The Grey Lord is in possession of a weapon with immense power. We also have a similar one, which is hidden in another part of the Land. This sword not only cuts but also unites; you will understand it when the time comes. Try to continue what I had started.

Fold the corners

Sara finished reading the message; her eyes followed the words written by her father, the night before his death. Word by word, line after line, she wanted to understand those riddles and mysteries.

"What could it mean, "fold the corners"?" asked the princess.

Melea took the letter and read the whole thing again, focusing on the last sentence, which clearly did not fit there, even the handwriting was different to the rest. *Fold the corners. What does it mean? The corners of what? Maybe it's a clue about that weapon.* She focused all her attention on the letter playing with the edge.

While Sara was watching her, an idea popped into her head. She took the letter from Melea. Four corners of the paper had been folded, and the princess pressed it by hand. With triumph painted on her face, she patted Melea on the shoulder. Melea smiled too. It was obvious, the lines of the corners formed one word.

"Fireplace," said Sara.

"We mustn't waste any time," said Melea.

They got up, went out into the corridor and entered Horen's bedroom.

***

The door to the shop opened wide, in spite of the „Closed" hanging plate. The thug walked into the spacious store, looking around. The seller took his wooden dentures out of his pocket and stuck them in his mouth. The old man hurriedly put on his glasses; the spectacles expanded his pupil several times.

"Blimey! Again, I broke the hinge of the prosthesis," blurted the old man, curling his lips with every word. Words paralyzed the man like a bolt from the blue. They sounded so terrible.

"We're closed, can't you see the sign, ragamuffin?" The seller approached the intruder and started tapping his chest with a long skinny finger. The thug thrust it away it with a quick movement of his hand and put the dagger to the old man's throat.

"I want to buy some clothes, old man," he said quietly. He took out four denars and tucked them brutally in the owner's mouth, pushing him into a chair facing the wall.

"I am sure you'll find something suitable over there."

The thug chose the clothes, dressed up and left without a word.

***

"Look at this." Sara pointed at the adorned casket above the fireplace. Without hesitation, she took it and opened it. There was another letter.

„The only way to stop the Grey Lord is to collect four parts of the sword, each one is hidden in the four parts of the Land. To find these parts, stand on the top tower of the palace at dawn and carefully observe the city.

The Roofs will guide you.

189

P.S. The sword can be forged only by the blacksmith Hezron. You might find him in Scarborough Fair. If he recognizes in you the true heir, he will show how to forge the blade again."

Both friends were looking at a piece of parchment following word after word. They peeped out of the window at the cathedral where the ruler had donated a great clock. The huge brass hands showed it was one o'clock.

"We wouldn't see anything today, anyway," said Melea.

"What do you think, what did my father mean when he wrote about the rooftops?"

"I've no idea."

"Let's leave it till tomorrow morning."

The friends returned to their room. So much excitement for one day was enough for anyone. Melea lay down next to Sara and quickly fell asleep, they were tired of this black day.

~ Chapter .18. At the dawn. ~

I could not sleep, the images from the previous day were muddling my mind, the night in the cell, the execution and the deadly loop tightening around my throat. The thoughts were churning in my head, swirling and confusing. I was unable to rest, standing by the window I observed the quiet town bathed in impenetrable blackness. Probably all my friends were snoring in their rooms, Warend on the right and Melea with the princess one floor above.

I went to see Vitorius and Dermont; they both were in a room on the fourth floor. I walked out into the corridor, where the pale moon was shedding its milk rays down the floor and the walls, creating white streaks. I knocked and waited in the doorway.

Dermont opened the door, he looked surprised by my presence, the priest was sitting at the table with a slightly troubled expression, the chalice standing in front of him was half full of spiced wine.

"I see that something is troubling you, Aron," said Dermont, resting his hand on the brass doorknob.

"Come in, we haven't been officially introduced to each other. Please, call me Dermont." He invited me with a hand gesture, Vitorius, sunken too deep in his thoughts, did not even realized that I was there. The shadow falling on his face was aging him; his tired gaze was fixed at the pieces of herbs poured in the gold-plated chalice.

"What brings you here at this time, dear boy?" The priest's voice only confirmed how tired he was.

"I just wish to talk..." I began shyly, entering. The room was filled with a pleasant smell of burning wood, the golden-orange flames from the fireplace, were stroking us with its warm hands. I sat next to Dermont, opposite Vitorius who eyed me carefully.

"I... I'm afraid that there was one, big terrible mistake, a coincidence." The elf and the priest waited for my explanation. "Surely, you're not taking me for someone special. The prophecy wasn't..."

"Do you remember what it was all about?" Dermont grabbed an elegantly decorated rosewood casket, and opened the lid. The box was lined with red cloth, and trimmed with gold threads, inside there were two smaller pixes, one long and the other wide. I waited for him to open them.

"Not everything, just some parts, I was more worried about myself to be honest. The ceremony interrupted by those evil men, the duel of our king, my accusation and that knight who lost his head..."

"You mean Bren, the captain of the royal guards, the one who looked at you suspiciously?" The priest smiled kindly, while Dermont opened the pix containing a hand- planed pipe and a mouthpiece made from mother of pearl. My eyes focused on the wooden casket, with the gold-plated dedication carved with decorated letters.

,,May it serve you my dear father - Melea"

He pulled out some precious pipe weed and tamped his pipe.

"My daughter made this pix for my birthday, and she bought the pipe from a merchant in Tahalat." He breathed in the smoke and exhaled heavily closing his eyes, his face turned melancholy. "Exactly one month before I threw her out of the house." I noticed how hard it was for him to admit it. Swallowing the bitter taste of despair, he nearly choked.

"So, why did you do it?" I grabbed the nearest chalice, and poured a little spicy wine.

"It used to be different, many years ago, when life was much safer, easier and cheaper. The times when weapons were rarely seen on the roads. Melea spent all her money buying a rapier and a few other weapons, she smuggled everything into the house in rolls of material, and hid it in her room. During my absence, she was practising war crafts, reading many books about the battles. One night I found her sneaking out of the house to practice in the forest with her, hmm, how shall I put it, friend... Tibbach." At the sound of that name, I almost spat out my wine. I could swear I had heard that name somewhere.

"Oh, so you've heard about...ehm, her horny friend? They trained almost every day, and when I discovered all these swords in her room, I could not restrain my anger. Weapons are disgusting, especially for a young lady, I was trying, hoping, to bring her up differently."

"Melea has never mentioned Tibbach." I do not know why, but I could barely speak that fellow's name. The priest changed the subject at once.

"Aron, may I ask you a question? Why are you still here? Your name has been cleared of all the accusations; the whole Land is waiting for you, new places, cities to visit, treasures..."

I was shocked, Vitorius certainly knew which strings to pull.

"I...am..., all right, I don't know. When the king died, I was almost ready to leave, but she held me back, she changed my mind."

"You made an oath to the king, you swore to protect the princess and..."

"Yes," I answered through clenched teeth, irritated a bit.

"There's no need to be angry, really, nobody will force you to do anything." Vitorius tried to calm me. "But the prophecy, only..."

"I'm pretty sure the prophecy doesn't say anything about me. I'm just an ordinary man from a farm, who's spent all his life carrying sacks of manure." At the very thought, I could smell the shitty stench coming out of the barn in the hot summer.

"It doesn't prove anything, you were there, right in the centre of the action, do you think it was just a coincidence?"

"There's no coincidence, only our choices and fate."

"Aha, there, you said it." I have to admit it, he caught me there.

"Chance, fortune, destiny, purpose, fate, so many terms and we still don't know what shapes our lives. Do you believe in God, Aron?"

"I do, the one and almighty."

Vitorius smiled at such answer. "That's good, we have many religions all around the Land, for instance, Dermont is an elf, his race believes in many of them. You think God has a master plan, which only He understands?"

"I... I don't know. I'm nothing special, for twenty-five years my plan was written by my uncle, I am simple redn... I mean a farmer."

"That's why we need to write the prophecy, we can only assume that some of those people will be future king of the Land.

"The prophecy certainly is talking about someone else..."

There was a loud knock, the door opened, and Melea stepped inside along with Sara and Warend at the end.

"Good morning." Melea walked slowly to the table with the folded letter in her hand. "Soon it will be dawn; we need to climb the north tower." Vitorius bowed his head to the princess. "So you know about the roofs."

"That's what we'd like to ask you about," said Warend.

"Oh, there's not much to say, you must see it for yourself. Off you go then, and enjoy the show."

I got up from the table, and followed my companions to the north wing of the palace; the entrance was situated in the attic. Sara took an old

193

rusty key out of her pocket, and opened the lock, the doors cracked terribly, at the sound a few spiders and mice fled into a dark corner.

"After you." Melea encouraged Sara and Warend so they entered first.

"Did my father ask about me?" Her sharp, piercing eyes wished to know the truth.

"Not much, we were talking mostly about me, the prophecy and... Tibbach." She looked shocked at the sound of his name and noticed that I was expecting an answer.

"So he told you about him?"

"Yes, your horny friend Tib..."

"Don't call him that!" She raised her voice slightly, clenching her fists.

"You mentioned him once, in the cottage."
Melea was trying to remember that very moment. "I don't know when you heard that name."

"You whispered it in your sleep."

"You cad! You sneaked into my room at night. What else did you hear?"

"I'm not your father. I don't care if he was your friend or lover."
Her face flushed. "None of the things that are you thinking now."

"How do you know what I'm thinking about?"

"My father had to tell you, what..."

"He only said that every night, you were slipping away from home to practise fencing in the forest with him. I really don't wish to know if you were practising something else." This dangerous conversation was interrupted by Warend.

"You two, what are you waiting for? A formal invitation? Move up, the sun will rise any minute now."

The attic was just as I was expecting, musty and neglected. Mouse holes adorned all the corners, while the ceiling was a real galaxy of cobwebs and dust, the floor was literally sprinkled with dried bat guano and owl faeces.

"This place needs a proper clean," said Sara, lifting her black dress a couple of inches more. Melea was looking around carefully. She patted her friend and pointed to some old junk: a broken wheel from a carriage, a sofa with a burned hole in the middle, and several portraits riddled with arrows, ah, the sweet smell of childhood fun and games.

We climbed the wooden ladder carefully; the view from the top was breathtaking, all heads turned towards the eastern horizon, at any moment, it would be dawn.

Melea summarized for me the contents of the two letters left by Horen, Warend rested his hands on the wooden railing and looked down, while Sara was admiring the view of her kingdom.

"What did he mean, your father, when he was writing about the roofs?" I asked the princess, snatching her from a trance.

"They will show us the place where the four elements, pieces of the sword, are hidden; it's like the sword which is now owned by my uncle." Her confident tone surprised me, yesterday it sounded like the lament of a surrendering person, and today it was reasonable and all set to work.

"Prepare yourselves!" shouted Melea, her eyes were staring intently at Achor, the distant mountain peak; it was named in honour of the king, who not so long ago had banished wild tribes who were plundering the cities of the central part of the kingdom. Many kings have sat on the throne of the Land, but none was as brave as Achor, he was betrayed by one of his soldiers and stabbed to death in his bed.

Warend looked up at the top of the mountain, where the delicate rays of the nascent sun finally reached the city. Everyone stared in disbelief when the first sunlight reflected on the roof, revealing the mirages. The view was incredible.

"Blimey, look at that!" Warend commented at the unusual sight, rubbing his eyes in amazement, the roofs were bathed in the rays and forming a fabulous picture; I could see the small details painted in the thin air.

"Green roofs, there's a shore, some water, I can't tell if it's a lake or the river, and some kind of... tree, it might be a lilac tree, there are lots of pines, and the birds above the crown, they look like robins, I think..." said Melea.

Warend focused on the red roofs, which were second in the order. At the beginning, the image was blurred; for a moment a large cathedral tower was obstructing a few smaller roofs. He looked at us for a short moment.

"Warend, hold your position, patience is a virtue."

"Look who's talking." Warend smiled and observed how the mirage became clearer when the sun shone on every roof.

The view was even better than the green roofs, in my opinion. A few metres high, there were blazing fires, sheaves shooting up with flames, and among this fiery confusion, we noticed a mountain with a truncated cone.

"I think it's a volcano."

"We'll have to study some maps and guides to look for it," said Melea.

"The only part where there are volcanoes is a desert area in Tahalat." Sara smiled at me, seeing the admiration on my face.
Then, the rays of the sun flooded the blue roofs like a stream; they painted a wonderful scene.

"Blue roofs, it's a waterfall, oh my, just look at it!" Sara squinted to find some more details and to tried not to blink.

"I think I know that one. It might be the waterfall Shiloa, but we must check it out," said Warend. For a short moment, I felt strange, like someone without any knowledge and experience, each one of them has seen so many places in their lives, especially Warend.

"Look at the rocks," said Melea.

"What about them?" asked Sara.

"The edges, they shouldn't be so sharp." Warend nodded his head in recognition. "All right, one last round."

Everyone waited impatiently for the fourth mirage, the final place, where the last piece of the sword was hidden. Sara was standing proudly with her back to the sun, facing the destination; the rays covered the entire city now, overtaking the houses of the last district arising from the mirage.

It reminded me of the interior of some grotto, perhaps a cave. However, there were no clear details to distinguish it from the many other caves. Four pairs of eyes stared at the mirage of an ordinary cave, a jagged rocky ceiling, countless numbers of stalactites grooved by nature over thousands of years, these limestone rocks were formed in an incredible way. Any cave from Tahalat to Moran, or from Southern Wasteland to Pentelia could have been formed so wonderfully.

"Look at those carefully carved walls!"

"It's not a cave! It's a..." shouted Sara with satisfaction on her face. But I was first, "It's a tomb."

"Finding the right one will take us ages," lamented Melea. "I'm afraid we don't have that much time."

We climbed down from the tower and went to the royal library, which was located on the second floor in the south wing. At the head walked Sara with Melea, followed closely by me and Warend who was still deep in thought. We turned into the corridor, which lead to an elegantly decorated oak door. One of the pages opened it wide.

We were standing in the vestibule of one of the greatest and largest libraries in Pentelia. The huge eclipse-shaped room was filled with books from floor to ceiling, all bound in leather, and carefully catalogued. At the centre of the bright and clear room was a large table with a carefully polished top and around it stood comfortable chairs with red cushions.

Sara quickly turned around, observing the reaction of her friend, who was smiling like a small girl.

"I've allowed myself to order breakfast here. My father didn't approved of eating and drinking in this room, so please be careful."

"Wonderful news, Your Highness! What's for breakfast, I'm starving?"

Melea gently snickered when Warend's stomach rumbled shortly.

"Brioche and coffee, we'll eat a more solid meal after the funeral, right before our journey."

There was an awkward silence; all three of us looked at the princess, who walked briskly to the ladder standing on the opposite side. Sara moved it to the shelves marked V, climbed almost to the top and pulled out a book bound in a maroon leather.

"Warend, catch!' shouted the princess, throwing the thin volume towards him. He was kneeling by the letter Z reading the titles, when the book hit his head.

"Oh, I'm so sorry, are you all right?" asked Sara. He was lying on the floor, with the book next to him. "What... what happened?"

"Luckily, there aren't many volcanoes in the Land. Here, *The Volcanoes of the Land*, by Haved the great traveller."

Warend sat in a comfortable armchair opposite the fireplace and leafed through the first few pages: all the volcanoes that existed in the Land were listed. Upon searching he immediately choose the appropriate sites.

Making sure that he was fine Sara climbed up to pulled out another volume.

"Melea, here goes!" She deftly caught the flying book, looked at its cover and put it on the table. It was written by the same author, however, this one was describing all the waterfalls in the Land.

"What was the name of that waterfall you mentioned before?" Warend was apparently lost in his book. "Try to find Shiloa," he said finally and began to turn over the pages.

I opened my book and found the name Shiloa on page 327. The drawing was decent, the author had marked a lot of details, but unfortunately, this waterfall was quite different from the one we had seen at the mirage. It was much smaller, the surrounding forest was leafy, not coniferous, and the rocks from the mirage had sharp edges, despite of tons of striking water, which even through the ages could had not been smoothed out.

The princess rebounded sharply from the cabinet and travelled with a wooden ladder on wheels to the gold plate engraved with the letter C, after a second she was holding a third thick volume with a description of the caves. Sara stepped off the ladder, and sat comfortably by my side.

"It's a pleasure to meet you, Aron. Now, we have some time to talk..."

"The pleasure's all mine."

"Please, forgive me. I was too hasty in sentencing you to death. I... I was under great pressure, the wedding, my father..."

"Fortunately, nothing happened, Princess."

"Please, call me Sara."

Our conversation was interrupted by a knock at the door.

"Come in!" The princess commanded imperiously. The butler walked in backward, pulling a trolley with two trays and silver cutlery. As soon as he turned around I noticed three medals – badges in the shape of a fork, knife and spoon. That was one of the highest positions in the palace service.

He quickly covered the table with a white tablecloth and set it for four people. At each place the man put a side plate and a small butter knife, in the middle of the table he placed a butter dish, a silver ewer full of freshly brewed coffee and finally a crystal platter containing four brioches.

"Thank you, Pencer, that will be all."

"Enjoy your meal." The butler bowed his head and walked away closing the door behind him.

"Breakfast is ready. Let's eat while it's warm." Warend put the book away and joined us, sitting opposite the princess.

"Bon appétit, and follow me." said Warend.

Melea was looking around now on different shelves with the letter T.

"Come on Melea, food's on the table. Are you still reading the titles of those books? I'm sure you won't find any "Tomb Guider" there."

Sara and I snorted softly and, trying to hide it, we shared a butter dish. Melea pretended nothing had happened and approached Warend. They began to talk about volcanoes.

"Sara, would you like a coffee?" I offered her the vessel.

"Not now, thank you. What do you remember from the last

mirage?"

"It wasn't a rocky cave, rather a limestone grotto which are everywhere. But the walls were carved, on the floor there was sand, it might not be a tomb either, maybe a treasury." She turned the pages and continued searching.

"I'm not sure if the king would keep such a weapon in the vault, he was a nature lover." Sara walked to the window and opened it, her attention was focused on black locust, with white flowers gathered in clusters on the delicate branches, surrounded by shapely, feathery bright green leaves.

"I've seen how he looked at his kingdom."

"My father planted that tree along with his grandfather, it was his favourite tree; he used to sit there on a warm day, delighted with the scent of the flowers, with the sounds of nature. I ordered it to be cut and prepared for today's funeral."

Melea stopped reading for a moment, taking her nose out from the book as she stared at her friend. "Why did you do that? Your father loved it so much." Sara closed her eyes. "I know, Melea, but... I made my decision." Melea nodded her head, and began to flip through the pages.

The time was passing by slowly; Warend put away his book, and poured himself another cup of coffee, while Melea agreed with Sara on some details. I could not find a single cave similar to the mirage, with each drawing it was getting worse, so many options and so little time.

"I give up, almost two hundred, and I still can't find the appropriate one."

"You're giving up even before we leave the palace? Show a little perseverance." Warend scolded me softly. Melea handed me Sara's book with the waterfalls, and reminded me of the details of the mirage.

First, I searched for categories, then quarters of the Land, all the time trying to remember how the waterfall looked and comparing it with the pictures. Every new sketch was different, making me turn the pages faster and faster, without even reading the names.

I threw the book on the table, the sound of the slapping cover filled the whole room; no one moved or spoke. Melea looked at me for a second, and immediately plunged into the next book about caves.

I opened the book at random and looked at the picture of a beautiful waterfall.

"Hey, I found it!"

They all looked at me. Sara placed her cup on the saucer, and glanced at the picture lying in front of her.

"Waterfall Riapsed, which is in Moran- western part of the Land, more precisely in the Isthmus of Doom. It was so named because of the common and strong currents and whirlpools pulling ships trying to sail that way. Even if the ship managed to break out of the deadly clutches of the vortex, it crashed into rocky cliffs. Those who dived in this area in search of pearls saw the graveyard of wrecks: masts and boards, countless numbers of bows and other deck parts."

"Well done, but we still have three more places to find," said Melea.

"No, Melea, only two. I've found four volcanoes, which are similar to our mirage." Warend came to the table and spread out a small map of the Land. "These four volcanoes are deceptively similar to each other, Toush, Tesa, Tews. The last one, Tornh is on the "Cursed Island". The first three were named after their surrounding deserts, but there isn't much about the fourth one, only something about the haunted waters, and the ghost of the volcano, I bet that Tornh is our goal. Melea, what do you think?"

"Hmm, you might be right, after all Horen had his pilgrimage in the north."

"We know the location of the waterfall, and probably the volcano, yet we still need to obtain information about the cave and that shore," said Melea.

"Are you sure it's all about the shore?"

"No, but Vitorius and Dermont will help us. They've known my father since was growing up," said Sara.

As we left the library, I turned around one more time, and looked at this truly magical place, where in spite of the imposed silence, all the books were speaking with their unique voices, and the leather covers with gold letters were shimmering in the light of the day, giving the whole room a mystical aura.

We went down to the Great Room, which was filled with flowers and wreathes; the smell of the lilies and roses gave a sweet taste, while the sun gently illuminated the walls of the hall. Vitorius was standing in the middle talking to members of the Elders, two of them were missing. Dermont immediately noticed us entering the hall, gave a signal to his friend, and together with the priest joined us.

"You came at last. Did you manage to find anything?"

"Not here, too many ears, let's go somewhere private," said Warend.

"We have to write down the prophecy as well, the guest room should be fine."

We all went to the first floor of the northern wing, through the short, well-lit corridor to the guest room. On either side were large shutters with green curtains sewn with golden threads, the solid door stood wide open.

The spacious interior of the guest room was furnished elegantly. The sun's rays were flooding through wide windows. Arrases and other splendid works of art of the greatest artists of the entire Land were hung on the light yellow walls. Extraordinarily painted landscapes, some full of realism, while the others full of surrealistic expression. I stopped for a moment at a wide picture of the forest; Warend stood beside me, the painting had attracted his attention as well, he just smiled mysteriously, and joined the rest.

We approached a huge table in the middle of the room as the page closed the door. Vitorius grabbed a few yellowed parchments lying on the desk in the corner, and Dermont handed him a quill with a small dark navy blue bottle. The priest dipped the nib gently into the ink, sat comfortably in the red leather chair and looked at us.

"Fine, we can begin." Vitorius addressed these words directly to Melea, looking straight into her eyes.

"Try to recall the words of the prophecy, it's important to understand it thoroughly, so no need to hurry."

"First, you spoke about the darkness," began Melea, closing her eyes so that nothing would distract her. Vitorius began to scrape on the parchment.

"You mentioned that in the Great Room was the one who has the power to enslave us." She tried to continue but the silence squeezed her lips, she frowned slightly. Dermont put his hands on her shoulders willing to help his daughter.

Melea calmly recited another line. "And the one who will be..."

"And the one who will be the defender of the Land, the king," Warend finished for her. Vitorius and I looked at him with admiration, while Sara and Dermont gave him an angry look.

"The traitor will tempt..."

"The traitor is obviously De Marge," he interrupted again.

"Warend!" Sara looked at him, placing her finger to her mouth.

Melea began tapping her middle finger in the top oak table and continued. "Gildam also became a traitor; we don't know which one of them the prophecy was talking about."

"I suspect De Marge because he poisoned Horen." Dermont closed his eyes slightly.

"Speaking of the devil, De Marge is still alive," I said.
Vitorius dropped his quill making a small blot, Dermont's hand twitched gently, and Warend almost choked.

"I beg your pardon?"

"What are you talking about?" Warend looked at me.

"The undertaker, Kalham, told us. The hanged corpse raised from the coffin almost killed him," explained Melea. Dermont and Vitorius exchanged glances; Warend looked at me with disbelief.

"Yes, I know. I was the closest during the execution."

Again our conversation was interrupted by a knock at the door. This time it was Iwar bringing the news about examined herbs which Kalham had found at the graveyard.

"This combination has a common name a "numb weed". The person who chews it will experience a short-term muscle paralysis. It will be aware of what is going on around, but will not be able to move. Therefore, Count De Marge so naturally pretended to be dead."

"This man is no longer a Count. He's a cunt de Marge." Warend's comment made everyone snickered and look at each other.

"I hope neither traitors can get to the south," whispered Sara.

"I'm afraid Serner will find out about the prophecy," said Dermont.

"Did you enjoy the show on the north tower?" The priest was scratching his nose with the quill.

"Oh yes, the mirages were magnificent," began Sara.

"We only know where one part of the sword is hidden," admitted Warend.

"Which one?"

"We know the waterfall in Moran, I helped Pr... I mean Sara to find it."

"And the volcano is probably on the Cursed Island. We still don't know the cave and that shore," said Melea.

"Horen never told us where he hid his sword. After the battle in Nogarat, where he realized how powerful that weapon was, he ordered it to be destroyed. Having had a dream that someday the sword might be needed, he divided it and hid the pieces. The exact places where they are can be revealed by the roofs of the four districts of Pentelia." Dermont looked for a moment at the bookshelf.

"We should set off for the four elements, the four parts of the sword," said Melea.

Vitorius noted everything, scribing not only the words of prophecy, but also our attention and comments. After a moment, he put aside the written parchment and began to write a new one.

Melea opened her eyes with a sad expression on her face, as if she had forgotten about an important detail. Something was bothering her. The priest put the quill in the ink bottle and looked at his notes. Having read everything carefully, he suddenly twitched. He covered his mouth with his left hand and stared at the picture of Horen that hung behind them.

The king looked dignified, as he stood in the background of the lake followed by a growing black locust. His crown reflected sunlight and his cape fluttered freely in the summer breeze, the royal face looked proud.

"There's something you should know," began Vitorius. "Something that's connected directly with our prophecy." We looked at the priest, petrified.

"What is it?" asked Sara.

"You think it's the right time?" Dermont looked at his friend.

"Without a doubt," replied the priest.

He stood up and slowly turned his back to us, approaching the bookcases. He stopped in the middle and sighed quietly.

"There's another prophecy, very similar to the one which we have just written." He began to read the titles of the volumes, his sharp eyes quickly found a suitable volume.

The priest grabbed *The Enigmatic Hideout by Mysterious Secret* and pulled it out. The shelves with books groaned softly, the mechanism hidden in the wall moved a cabinet and revealed a dark corridor. Dermont gave the candelabra to Vitorius, and after a while its five flames lit up the interiors of the small room. Sara and Melea looked at each other.

The room was tiny and perfectly fulfilled the role of a hidden chamber. In the middle stood a drafting table, the left corner was hiding several additional paintings, on the right was a small stool with a hammer on it. All four walls were covered with bookshelves, a couple of chests and a big box in the corner. Vitorius approached the caskets, opened the lid and took out the contents. He left the small room and walked towards us.

We all stared intently at the contents of his hand. Vitorius was holding a glass vial with a piece of parchment inside. He uncorked it and slowly began to unroll the already yellowed piece.

"Finally was born the one who will be able to save the Land. Born on the 25th day after the 9th full moon from parents who were unknown to him. In his veins flows pure red blood.

He will possess the strength, and the power to resist the evil that will be threatening to all, he will join the journey and regain the power of the four elements.

M."

Everyone listened to the words read by Vitorius. The priest put the prophecy back in its place, closed the shelf and sat in front of us.

"By whom was this prophecy revealed?"

"By M."

There was a sound of the bells; they could be heard all over the town in each of the four districts, tolling the news on the all four sides of the Land.

"No time to chat now, our king is waiting to be buried."

At noon, we went down to the Great Room. Horen"s royal guards had moved the body from the pedestal onto a golden shield – the same one on which the previous king had been buried. The procession had begun.

~ Chapter .19. The funeral. ~

Standing at the entrance to the Great Room, I could hear the wall clock's pendulum ticking; it was hanging over the oak cabinet on the left side of the massive door. All the curtains had been removed so the sun could easily flood through the remains of the stained glass windows. The body of the ruler was lying on a great golden shield, on which he would be carried like his ancestors. Sara was standing right next to it, with red eyes.

Vitorius gave the guardsmen a sign and the procession began. Four knights of the royal guard dressed in full armour raised the shield with Horen; the royal coat of arms and the symbol of Pentelia were on their golden breastplates. Right after them went the princess, holding a small bouquet of flowers. There was no one standing next to her. The only family she had was her uncle who was the cause of this funeral and the whole calamity.

Behind Sara went Vitorius with Dermont, Melea was holding a pennon with the emblem. I could swear that there was a strong bond between father and daughter, through which they could express their thoughts and feelings without actually speaking.

We went slowly out of the palace onto the Main Square, where not so long ago I had been awaiting execution. A large number of townies were holding multi-coloured floral garlands and wreaths. Most of them had lowered their heads; here and there I could see red eyes and wet cheeks.

As soon as we passed the palace walls and were out onto the street, others joined our entourage. Pentelia had changed beyond recognition, as if somebody had sucked out all the happiness, leaving the inhabitants in fear and mourning. All the bell towers in the town unceasingly rang for the funeral of the ruler.

The sky turned grey; it only intensified the feeling of fear. I tried to find a bit of blue sky, but could not. The sun hid itself behind thick clouds, and the charm of the four roofs disappeared just like all the wedding decorations; many people were eagerly ripping up the posters with the image of Count De Marge.

The procession walked slowly down the main street to the north. Purposely I slowed my pace and Warend caught up.

"What did Horen say to you on his deathbed?"

"He told me that I..." He broke suddenly. "It's not the right time for it. Anyway, it was just gibberish of a suffering old man."

I could not believe that he had treated the king's last words with such indifference.

The rest of the way was passed in silence, Vitorius folded his arms across his chest, and focused on prayer, trying to beg to God for a better life for their king. The princess sneezed once or twice, closing her eyes tightly, and wiping her nose with a white handkerchief. Behind the walls the stone road turned into a simple one; only about the width of a single carriage.

Marching over it was a lot worse, our feet were sinking into the dirt; some of the mourners had to stop now and then to get rid of the grains, which were constantly falling into their shoes. Iwar closed his eyes, and nearly tripped over a protruding root. The king's guards also had problems carrying their ruler, his body on the shield was heavy; with each step, their hands were slightly trembling, and they became so pale, as if someone or something had sucked out their blood.

We went through the worst stretch of the road, where the path was circling slightly to the left, where the escarpment was occasionally speckled with small, mundane bushes. The mere appeared before our eyes, slowly emerging from behind a turn, rocking lightly with its surface. The town, just like the central part of the Land, took its name from the lake, which was named after a fisherman Pent, who saw the beautiful Telia – a creature similar to the sirens living in the depths of the lakes.

Small waves were gently hitting the sandy shore, on which lay a few dried twigs and leaves, the cold emerald blue water seemed to me an enormous creature that now and then changed its shape. And to this creature we had to entrust the body of our Majesty. I narrowed my eyes slightly and noticed a small raft, rocking lazily, stuffed with dry twigs and red velvet.

As we approached to the shore, the residents of Pentelia stayed behind. The guards laid the body on the raft, which had insignia on both sides, along with the sword and decorative casket of personal things, at Horen's feet lay the disastrous cup, the instrument of his death.

"Wait!" Sara lifted her dress a few inches and ran to the lumberjacks standing on a hill with their axes, all eyes followed her movement; how the heels of her boots were sinking in the sand. In one moment, she reeled dangerously and almost fell. She took off her boots, and climbed onto the hill.

"Don't cut it down," she panted. The lumberjacks looked at each other and obediently put down their heavy double-edged axes. Melea smiled at the sight, happy that her friend had changed her mind.

Sara stood on tiptoe and broke off a small branch with a few leaves and a blooming flower. She returned with a slow step to the raft, holding her breath, and trying not to look at anyone, perfectly aware that all eyes were staring at her. She put a twig on her father's chest and kissed his forehead. Anointing him with the essential oils that Vitorius had given her, she poured the rest around the brushwood. Having turned to the new captain of the guards, she made a sign clenching her teeth, and tried with all her strength not to cry.

"Archers, forward!" she cried with a loud voice in the direction of the soldiers. Fifty of them withdrew from the line and stood in a row waiting to set light to the arrows and shoot.

Sara untied the raft and pushed it away from the shore, watching the oil droplets gently flowing down from the dry twigs.

"Farwell father..." she whispered and lifted up the sceptre. The captain of the guard with a torch in his hand lit an arrow of each archer. After a while, fifty burning tips were waiting for the signal. Proudly stuck at forty-five degrees they aimed at the slowly receding raft with Horen.

Time seemed to have stopped, the clouds drifting lazily across the dark sky stood still, while the surface of the lake became perfectly flat, and the wind that was combing the nearby trees with its invisible hand also sat down somewhere and watched. All eyes stared at the sceptre firmly held by Sara. Slowly I looked around and could swear that no one was breathing.

Melea closed her eyes at the same time as the princess lowered her hand. Everything was happening in slow motion, all the archers simultaneously let go of the fletching which left a dark streak, flying high in the air and digging into the raft, setting fire to brush bathed in oil. After a while, the flame shot up two metres, majestically illuminating the dark middle of the lake. Orange and yellow flames strongly contrasted against a surrounding greyness.

Of all those gathered, only the princess was not looking at the burning raft. Her hand holding the sceptre gently twitched and she almost dropped it. She could not drop it; that would mean her loss too.

Vitorius came to the centre with his bowed head and his hands clasped to his chest. All eyes were fixed on him waiting for his eulogy.

"Today we bid farewell to king Horen, our beloved ruler and great man. The man who made the wonderful things..."

The End of part I

Cezary J. Piotrowski

born in Warsaw, Poland, on the 25th September (Libran) 1986. He was educated at Wyspiański High School, for mathematical geeks. Being poor with numbers he spent most of his time playing bridge, computer games, and reading books. He went to Warsaw University to study Management and soon to find out that there are too many managers in this world.

Finding solace in imaginary worlds, stripping through thousands of pages, during one ordinary day he came up with a simple, brave idea: "I can do it myself". He started to write an epic adventures of Aron & Melea. Amazing how easy the next scenes, dialogue, names and situations flourished in his imagination, the amount of created material scribbled on rough sheets of paper encouraged and instigated him to become a next potential writer. Aftermath of which his pocket was always inhabited by a note pad and pen.

Coming from a background of multitude professions like: a credit card seller, real estate broker, banker, waiter & barista allowed him to perceive the world in a specific way.

In 2013 when he could not find a satisfying job in his hometown he decided to move to London, the capital city of the World and a land full of opportunities. Renting a box room in South- East London he started his epic journey.

Working hard and steady, day by day, he realized that he shall need a little help. Devine providence send him his first reader Kay, a good friend, an editor, companion and presently his wife who supported him as much as she could to make the work complete.

Kingdom's Quest The Journey, was finally translated and edited from Polish to English and saw its completion in 2016.

Finishing the novel was merely a half of success, now the time had come to find a book agent and grab their attention. Composing at least 6 different query letters and trying to contact agents not only based in UK but from many other countries like India, Singapore, Australia, UAE, USA & Canada the number of rejections was rapidly growing and there was no sign that the effort will be rewarded.

Without losing hope and confidently looking into the future, he did not hesitate to ask about the agents and publishers to all surrounding people. Rule "If you do not ask, you will not get it", it turned out to be the right one. One day during breakfast Cezary received an email with positive information.

Kingdom's Quest soon will be released and published.